Once a Witch

Once a Witch

_by_ CAROLYN MACCULLOUGH

CLARION BOOKS
Houghton Mifflin Harcourt
Boston   New York
2009

Clarion Books
215 Park Avenue South, New York, New York 10003
Copyright © 2009 by Carolyn MacCullough

The text was set in Horley Old Style MT Light.

Clarion Books is an imprint of
Houghton Mifflin Harcourt Publishing Company.

www.hmhbooks.com

Printed in the United States of America
Library of Congress Cataloging-in-Publication Data
MacCullough, Carolyn.
Once a witch / by Carolyn MacCullough.
p. cm.
Summary: Born into a family of witches, seventeen-year-old
Tamsin was raised believing that she alone lacked a magical
"Talent," but when her beautiful and powerful sister is taken by
an age-old rival of the family in an attempt to change the balance
of power, Tamsin discovers her true destiny.
ISBN 978-0-547-22399-5
[1. Witches—Fiction. 2. Ability—Fiction. 3. Sibling rivalry—
Fiction. 4. Identity—Fiction. 5. Time travel—Fiction. 6. Good
and evil—Fiction. 7. New York (N.Y.)—Fiction.] I. Title.

PZ7.M1389On 2009
[Fic]—dc22
2008049234

MP 10 9 8 7 6 5 4 3 2 1

For my husband, Frank Adamo,
whose love and support make all things possible

ACKNOWLEDGMENTS

My thanks to my family and friends for their encouragement throughout the writing process. My deepest gratitude to my wonderful agent, Alyssa Eisner Henkin, for her dedication and enthusiasm, and for matching me up with the wisest of editors, Jennifer Wingertzahn, who made this book the very best that it could be.

PROLOGUE

I WAS BORN on the night of Samhain, when the barrier between the worlds is whisper thin and when magic, old magic, sings its heady and sweet song to anyone who cares to hear it. All night my mother struggled, and when she finally heaved me into this world, my grandmother hovered over me, twisting her fingers in arcane shapes, murmuring in a language only she knew.

"What is it?" my mother gasped, turning her face against the lavender-scented pillow. "What's wrong?"

Finally, my grandmother answered, her voice full and triumphant. "Your daughter will be one of the most powerful we have ever seen in this family. She will be a beacon for us all."

I always wonder how my older sister, Rowena, who had been allowed into the room, reacted to that statement. No one thought to check that part of the story, but I really would have relished the one moment when I, and not Rowena, was the sun and the moon and the stars combined.

They say I never cried at birth, never made a sound, but opened my eyes immediately and regarded them all with a calm and quiet gaze. "As if she's seen so much already," my mother whispered, touching my fingers and then my face.

Well, if I had seen anything, I've long since forgotten what it was, and as for what my grandmother promised, that's been forgotten, too. Or not forgotten, but definitely scrapped.

Even now, seventeen years later, I still catch my mother's gaze lingering on me and I just know she's pondering how she managed to lose the child she'd been promised and gain me instead. I also wonder if my grandmother ever recalls the echo of her words: *one of the most powerful . . . a beacon.* Doubtful.

The story was told so many times in eager anticipation up until my eighth birthday. Then the whole family gathered and sang while my mother lit the eight golden tapers to represent the four elements and the four directions. Then they watched me, some openly, some furtively.

And what did I do?

Nothing. At. All.

Nothing that I was supposed to do, anyway. After a while, I got tired of everyone staring at me and then at one another so I went around blowing out all the candles, taking comfort in the dimness as I ate my way through two large pieces of sugar-sweet birthday cake. Eventually, everyone trickled home.

I come from a family of witches. Each and every member of my family down to my youngest cousin manifests his or her particular Talent without fail just before, and certainly no later than, the age of eight.

Except for me.

Nine years have passed since that birthday and I have nothing to show for it. Not a drop, not half a drop, not even a quarter of a half of a half drop of magic runs through my apparently very pedestrian veins.

As for what my grandmother said about me—*one of the most powerful . . . a beacon,* etc., etc., etc.—all this goes to show that contrary to popular belief, even the oldest and wisest of witches can be dead wrong.

ONE

"TWENTY MORE MINUTES, Hector," I say, "and I'm free of this hellcrater." Hector, whose tawny eyes flared open when I spoke, now only flashes his needlelike teeth at me as he yawns. He blinks once, then curls back into sleep, his tail covering his front paws.

Hellcrater is not exactly a fair description, I concede as I look around my grandmother's bookstore, making sure nothing is out of order. But *hellcrater* has become my favorite word lately. *I have to go to the hellcrater,* I like to say to my roommate, Agatha, whenever I'm summoned home for a holiday or for the weekend. Agatha always gives me a blank look in response.

"I think it must have been so awesome to have grown up in a commune," she ventured once.

I didn't bother explaining how it's not really a commune. I can kind of see how it might sound like one from the edited descriptions I've given her. A big rambling stone farmhouse in upstate New York, with a revolving door of cousins and aunts and uncles and the adjoining barn and fields and gardens, which fuel the family business, Greene's Herbal Supplies. All presided over by my mother and grandmother in their long, colorful skirts and shawls and strings of beads.

"I mean, I grew up Pine Park, Illinois, Tamsin. Come home with me sometime and you'll see a hellcrater. And by the way, that's not even a word."

"I'd love to," I answered eagerly at the time. And I meant it. I would love to see what it's like to be part of a real, normal American household. Where your mother and grandmother aren't reading tea leaves and entrails every other second. Or making strong-smelling brews from the garden herbs for dozens of village girls and women. They come after dark, rapping timidly on the back door, begging for something to slip into some man's coffee or beer when he isn't looking. The women's eyes fill with grateful tears, those same eyes that'll skitter away from meeting yours if you cross paths in town during daylight.

In a real, normal household people celebrate Thanksgiving and Christmas or Hanukkah. Halloween is for the kids to dress up in costumes. It's not a holiday when your whole family gathers in the deep woods behind your house and builds a bonfire and burns sweet herbs on the altar built to the four elements. Not a holiday when your whole family dances until the first fingernail of dawn scrapes at the hills and finally you can stumble home, bare legs scratched and bruised, hands and feet freezing, sick from Uncle Chester's homemade wine.

"Hellcrater," I say again now with feeling, as sheets of rain splatter against the oversize windows. At least there's only one more week until I can take the train back to Grand Central. I yawn, stretch my fingers to the polished tin ceiling. The bell over the door chimes three notes softly and I drop my arms midstretch, startled. I'm not the only one. Hector leaps off the counter, lands with a disgruntled meow, and disappears between two stacks of poetry books that I just remembered I was supposed to re-price and shelve in the half-off section.

But instead, I glance at the man who has just entered. He's tall, and since I'm tall myself, this is saying something. Tall and thin and muffled up in a dark overcoat that seems to overlap his frame. He politely folds his umbrella and puts it into the copper planter that serves as a stand by the door. His eyes find mine across the room. "Sorry," he says, and his voice is a nervous wisp almost blown away by the wind.

The door swings shut, sealing us in.

"For what?" I ask lightly. "You haven't even met me yet." In my mind, I can hear Agatha groan. She despairs of me and my obvious one-liners.

He indicates the area around his feet. Puddles are spreading across the hardwood floor, trickling from the wet hem of his raincoat and sleeves.

"Oh," I say. And then all my wit deserts me. "I . . . have a mop," I finish brilliantly.

He nods, shakes his coat a little, then looks abashed as more rainwater drips onto the floor. "Are you about to close?"

His accent is faint but familiar, and I try to puzzle it out. "No," I lie gamely, because after all he is a customer and I've made somewhere around twenty-two dollars in sales today.

I move behind the cash register and begin to straighten the stack of ledgers there, pretending not to watch the man as he drifts past the new fiction display. When he moves a little closer to the occult and arcane section, I feel the familiar prick of resignation. So he's one of those. An out-of-towner, definitely, who thinks that magic can be found in a book. I sigh. *Believe me,* I want to shout at him, *if magic could be found in a book, I would have found it long ago.*

I fiddle with the cash register tape, then look up again, expecting to see the man fully immersed in Starling Ravenwood's latest book, *Spells for Living a Life of Good Fortune,* our current bestseller. But he is nowhere to be seen.

I crane my neck, balance on one foot. Suddenly, he materializes from between the poetry shelves and makes his way toward me while holding up a slim bronze-colored book. Inexplicably, I find myself taking a step backward. My elbow grazes the coffeemaker that I insisted my grandmother buy if I was going to work in the store all summer.

The pot gives a hiss, its oily contents sloshing a little as I jerk my arm forward. "Ouch."

The man doesn't seem to notice. Up close, I see the glints of gold stubble on his chin and that his thick, rain-soaked hair is dark blond. His stylish black-framed glasses reflect the light back at me but don't allow me to see the color of his eyes. I put his age at about thirty. He's not convention-ally good looking, but there is something about him, some-thing that makes me look away, then look back again.

"Do you have any more like this?" he asks, and the origin of his accent niggles at me again. The clipped syllables, the perfect enunciation. English, I decide. That definitely adds to the attraction factor. Agatha, for one, goes crazy for accents.

I flip open the cover, flick through the pages. "This is one I haven't read," I say, surprised because I've read most everything in the store. At least everything worth reading. The book seems to be a photo montage of my town's ori-gins. Pencil sketches and ink drawings of early mansions give way to glossy photos of autumn foliage, the town square, the waterfalls, and the cemetery. Underneath each photo is a brief paragraph or two of text explaining the history. "Interesting," I say with a noncommittal smile, handing it back to him.

He adjusts his glasses on the bridge of his nose and says, "*Interesting* is one of the most banal words in the Eng-lish language. What does it mean, really?"

My smile freezes in place. "It means I don't have any-thing better to say so *interesting* comes in handy."

He shakes his head once. "Somehow I don't think you're the kind of person who would find herself in a situation where she has nothing better to say."

The coffeepot hisses again, and casually I rub my hand across the back of my neck to stop a chill from spreading there. Out of nowhere, Hector leaps up onto the counter again, arching his back and butting his head fiercely against the book the man is holding. The man appears startled for one second, and then suddenly lines curve around his mouth, creating these not-quite-dimples.

"Hector sees all books as rivals for people's attention."

"Bad place for him to live, then," the man comments.

"He exacts his revenge in subtle ways. Will this be all?" I ask, pointing to the book. In a flash, Hector bats at the silver bangles on my wrist and hooks a claw into my skin. "Ow!" I say, snatching my hand back. "See what I mean about revenge," I mutter, glaring at the three beads of blood that have welled up on my pale skin.

"Allow me," the man says, and swiftly, so swiftly that I don't have time to react, he pulls a blue handkerchief out of his raincoat pocket and presses it to my wrist. His tongue flickers at the corner of his mouth.

I yank my hand back, a smile wobbling across my face. "Who owns a handkerchief these days?" My voice sounds shaky—pinched, even. I examine the corner of the cloth, which is embroidered with the letters *AEK*.

He shrugs and looks embarrassed, and it disappears back into his coat pocket. "Yes, it's not a very American habit, I'm gathering."

"So you *are* English," I conclude.

He looks briefly pained. "Scottish," he says.

"Sorry," I mock-whisper. "Bad mistake. Mortal enemies and all, right?" I bring my wrist to my mouth, pressing my lips to the flaps of torn skin. He stares at me and I drop my hand, embarrassed. "On vacation here?" I ask, filling in the gap of silence.

"No. I'm at NYU."

"You're a student there?" I ask.

A fine stain of color washes over his cheeks. "I'm a *professor* there."

"You *are?*" I say, realizing belatedly how rude that sounds. "I mean . . . you are." I nod. "Sure. Sorry, you just look so young." Now *I'm* the one who's blushing. I can feel it across my cheeks and forehead. Even my nose feels hot.

"First year," he says, then adds with a slight smile, "I guess I'll grow into it."

"What do you teach?" I ask.

"Art history. Are you a college student?"

"Not yet," I say. "I go to New Hyde Prep."

He gives me a blank look.

"It's a boarding school in the city. On the Upper East Side. I'm just home in Hedgerow for the summer." I push a stack of cardboard bookmarks closer to the register, aligning their edges perfectly. "NYU is one of my top picks. So if I get in, maybe I'll end up in your class next year."

"That would be lovely," he says. Then he looks up and smiles briefly, almost wickedly, at me. "As long as you promise to not use the word *interesting* in any discussions."

"I wouldn't dare," I say. I consider letting my lashes sweep down. I've been bored all summer and in need of a little flirting practice. The small town of Hedgerow, while big on rustic charm, doesn't carry much in the way of male diversion. Even if I weren't a member of the town's most infamous family, the options are limited.

But the moment passes, so I take the book from him once more and check the flap for the price that my grandmother has penciled in with her looping scrawl. "Seven dollars," I say, taking the twenty from his outstretched fingers.

He accepts the change that I hand him, not even checking it before he puts it away in his wallet. And all the while he wears a faint look of unease. He takes off his glasses, massages the bridge of his nose, and looks up at me, and I decide that his eyes are a toss-up between blue and gray.

"There's something else I'm looking for," he blurts out suddenly. "Not a book, though." He glances at the door, as if thinking about changing his mind and escaping into the rain.

I shift on my feet, pressing Hector's ears lightly against his head the way he likes. "What is it, then?" Somehow I'm not surprised we've arrived at this. Most out-of-towners come to this part eventually.

"An old family heirloom. A clock. It was in my family for generations and then we . . . lost it." He settles his glasses back onto his face.

"Lost it?"

He waves his hand, the light catching on the steel band of his watch. Hector's eyes widen, and I put a restraining hand on the cat's neck until he settles down into a doze again. "In a card game or a wager or something to that effect in the late eighteen hundreds in New York City. Gamblers in the family, I'm afraid."

"And how can I help?" I ask and wait for him to meet my eyes, which he does with what seems like reluctance. Glacial blue, I decide finally.

"It's just that . . . well . . . I had heard that . . . that this place . . ."

"'This place'?" I repeat. As I slip the book into a bag, I trace one finger over the GREENE'S LOST AND FOUND, NEW AND USED BOOKS logo. I can't help but feel a little like Hector with a mouse caught between his paws.

He flushes again. "I had heard that this place specializes in that sort of thing. Finding things, that is. Lost things."

"Very rarely is something lost forever," I say enigmatically because that's what my grandmother always says to potential clients. Then I grow tired of this game and a little tired of myself. The poor guy traveled all the way from

New York City on a rainy night to find something, doubt-lessly something of no value except sentimental, and the last thing he needs is to be toyed with by a seventeen-year-old girl with a chip on her shoulder regarding her family's special Talents.

Since Agatha took Intro to Psychology last year, I've been prodded into becoming more self-aware.

"Okay, look . . . you've come to the right place, Professor, but—"

"Callum," he interjects. "Alistair Callum. And you're Miss Greene, of course?"

"Yes. T—"

But words are tumbling out of him now. "Frankly, I was a little doubtful that a place like . . . like this existed. I mean, how fascinating. I want to . . . I just want to say . . . what a brilliant thing this is that you do, Miss Greene."

I'm not the person you want. I know I need to tell him that. But it's so rare that anyone looks at me the way Alistair is looking at me now. With admiration and awe. I feel all at once a brightening and a dimming in my head as if someone flipped on a light switch and then just as quickly slammed it off again. Suddenly, I want to be back in my dorm room bed, skimming passages from a book propped open on my chest before giving up on my homework and ambling down to the student lounge to watch TV with any-one who happens to be there. Normal people. People who have no idea about my family's Talents. People who don't look at me sidelong with wonder or unease or fear or any combination of the three.

And yet Alistair is looking at me hopefully, his hands tightening on the counter as he leans toward me. I picture myself saying the right thing, the thing I am supposed to say should a customer ask for help beyond where to find the latest Pat Griffith mystery. *My grandmother is the one you need to talk to. She'll be in tomorrow. I'm just watching the store and I'm not the one. Not the one you need.*

Instead, I hear myself saying, "I can help you." And then I pause. *Fix it, fix it now,* a tiny voice screams at me. "This is my grandmother's store." *That's right, that's right, backpedal.* I take a breath, stomp on the voice, grind it into silence. "But I do this kind of work with her all the time." My words are steady and surprisingly assured. Hector stops purring and opens his eyes, giving me a long yellow stare.

"I heard about your family in an antique shop—"

"That answers my next question. Which one was—"

"Go see Mrs. Greene, they told me. Or her grand-daughter Rowena. Rowena Greene will be the one you want." And then he smiles again, but this time it's an odd half smile, and he adds softly, "The words I had waited so long to hear. *Rowena Greene.*"

My throat has just gone dry, a kind of wandering-in-the-desert-for-a-week-without-water dry. We have a bunch of weird names in our family. Even so, I hate mine especially. *Tamsin.* It sounds so . . . hard and unmusical. Unlike

Rowena, which ripples off the tongue, *Tamsin* falls with a splat. I asked my grandmother repeatedly when I was little why she had saddled me with such a name, but she only smiled and said it was a story best saved for another time.

Now I swallow and try to say, "Um, actually my—"

"And when I walked in the door tonight, I just had this feeling that it's you I'm supposed to talk to." He tucks the bag away into an inner pocket of his coat. "You'll likely think I'm mad. Maybe I *am* mad." He pinches the bridge of his nose briefly with two fingers.

"I don't think you're mad," I say after a moment, when it appears that he's finished speaking. It seems to be my new job to reassure him. I've seen my grandmother put nervous clients at ease in no time. "I'm flattered, really," I say truthfully and stop myself from adding, *You have no idea how flattered.* No one has ever, *ever* mistaken me for my extremely Talented older sister before.

He leans across the counter, seizes my hand, and pumps it up and down a few times. Hector utters an offended meow and edges away from our clasped, flailing hands, but Alistair doesn't seem to notice. "I'm so delighted to hear this. I just have this feeling that you really will be able to help me."

I swallow, refrain from pointing out that he's pressing on my injured wrist.

"Listen, Dr. Callum—"

"Alistair," he insists.

"Alistair," I repeat after him. "I need to tell you . . ."

"Yes?" he prompts, and when I don't answer right away, his shoulders twitch a little and his hand, suddenly limp, falls away from mine. I can't bear his disappointment.

"Um . . . I wanted to say that I can't promise anything." *Actually, I can promise you that I most likely won't be able to get the job done.*

Maybe I should have phrased it the way my grandmother does when confronted with a particularly pushy customer or an exceptionally hard case. *What wants to be found will come to light. I will not rest until I have shone this light into all corners and chased away all shadows.*

Not that she's said much of anything lately. This summer when I came home from school, I found her spending most of her time sitting quietly in the garden or in her room, a dreaming haze spreading over her face and stilling her hands. Nobody else will admit it. At least not openly. Instead, my mother told me that I'd be working in the bookstore most of the summer while Rowena stayed at home and helped with everything else. "Everything else" being the business of living as witches in a world that doesn't really know they exist.

"No, no. Of course, of course," Alistair is saying, and I focus on him again. "I completely understand. Whatever you can do." He backs up toward the door and reaches for his umbrella without taking his eyes off me, as if he's afraid I'm about to start chopping up bats' wings and muttering incantations.

"Wait. Don't you want to tell me more about it? What it is I'm supposed to be looking for?"

He stops and closes his eyes briefly, and the corners of his mouth tug upward into a small smile. "Yes, of course. But . . ." He glances at his watch. "I have a train to catch in just a few minutes. Can we make an appointment to talk in my office when the semester starts?"

"Sure," I say, struggling to keep relief from spilling into my voice. I know how it is with these people. Once he's back in his office and school starts, this night will start to seem more and more unreal as the pieces of it slip away. Soon enough he'll begin to wonder if he even had this conversation with a girl on a dark evening full of rain. Maybe it will become a story he'll tell someone someday—that he once tried to engage the services of a witch to find something that was destined to stay lost anyway. "I'll look you up. NYU, right?"

He fumbles in his coat pocket for a minute, an expression of alarm crossing his face. "I had a card in here somewhere. Just had them made." He pats his pockets with increasingly violent motions.

"Don't worry about it," I offer finally with a wide smile. "I'll find you. I mean, if I can't, you probably really don't want to hire me for the job anyway, right?"

He looks startled and then he laughs, flashing those almost-but-not-quite-dimples again. "True. And . . . well, whatever you want, whatever's your usual price?"

"My usual?" How does my grandmother handle this part? She's so effortless about everything. "Um . . . we'll discuss it when I have a better idea of the job," I say in my most official tone.

This seems to satisfy him, because he nods and finally disappears into the thick-falling rain.

I flip the CLOSED sign outward, turn the large brass key in the lock, and drift back to the cash register. I feel as if there's something I've forgotten to do, so I look around the store, my eyes skipping over the stacks of poetry books I have yet to re-price. All of a sudden, the last of the pleasure that I felt at Alistair's assumption, his assurance in me, drains away, leaving me flat. I wish I could tell Agatha this story, but somehow I don't think it would survive the heavy editing it would have to go through.

The phone jangles sharply. I give the instrument a malevolent look as it shrills and shrills and shrills. I don't need any of my family's Talent to know who it is. Finally I pick it up. "Greene's Lost and Found, New and Used Books, may I help you?" I singsong into the receiver.

"Tam," Rowena says, and her voice is all business. "We need you to pick up three gallons of vanilla ice cream at McSweeny's. The ice cream churn broke."

I roll my eyes. "Can't Uncle Chester fix it?" Uncle Chester can fix anything that's broken. Appliances, glass, china, bones.

"He tried. Now part of the handle is attached to Aunt Minna's hip." There's a short, exasperated sigh. "He's drunk," Rowena adds unnecessarily.

"Already?"

"Just close early and pick it up, would you?"

"Maybe I have customers," I say grandly. I sweep my arms out to the empty store.

"You don't have customers."

Talented as she is, my sister can see only what's in front of her, so I lie with perfect ease. "I do, actually."

"Who?" she demands. "Besides, it can't be anyone important. At least no one *you* could help," she adds.

I am silent. I touch the tip of my finger to Hector's nose. He opens his eyes and we stare at each other.

"I'll bring the ice cream," I say woodenly. "Just as soon as I close up here." *Yeah, right.*

"Tam," my sister says, and if possible she sounds even more annoyed than before. "I didn't mean—"

"You did," I say, my voice cheerful again. "Anything else?"

"Remember that Aunt Lydia and Gabriel will be here tonight."

I make a circling motion in the air with one finger. "Great." But inwardly I stifle a pang. *Gabriel.*

"Aren't you excited?" she demands. "I mean, we haven't seen them in years."

Aunt Lydia is not even our aunt, but she's part of the loose network that has formed around my family over the years, and since we call all older women "aunt" and all older men "uncle," it just slops into one big happy family. Or something like that.

Gabriel is her son. He also used to be my best friend when we were kids. Then he developed his Talent of being able to locate anything: keys, wallets, books, jewelry, any number of things that get put in one place and become lost almost instantly. People, too. At that point, Rowena and our cousin Gwyneth decreed that he could no longer play hide-and-seek with us. In protest, I stopped playing the game, too.

They moved when he was ten and I was just about to turn eight. Aunt Lydia had agreed to move across the country to California, probably to save her marriage to this Talentless guy, Uncle Phil. This caused some serious heat with my mother and grandmother because they'd like nothing better than for everyone in our family, even our "extended family," to stay in one place. Apparently, the move didn't work out. And now tonight Aunt Lydia and Gabriel are scheduled to make an appearance, where they will presumably be welcomed back into the proverbial fold.

"Great," I repeat. I rub Hector's head and he closes his eyes, arches a little into my open hand. From the other end of the line I hear someone start singing. It sounds like Uncle Chester, his rich baritone cracking and wavering in places.

"I have to go," Rowena says firmly as if I've been yammering on and on. "Don't forget the ice cream."

"The what?" I say, but she has already clicked the phone down and so my last little dig is wasted on her.

TWO

FAT RAINDROPS pelt my arms and legs all the way through town as I bike home. My feet spin the pedals, street light catching and bouncing off my reflectors. Once or twice a car swooshes past me, voices blaring over music. "Freak show," someone shouts out a window, the word slapping my face. I swallow, pedal faster, until I reach the last stretch of country road that leads to the house. Then all at once the curtain of rain lifts away and the cicadas thrum to life.

I roll my eyes. Figures Rowena couldn't have a little rain ruin her engagement party. Figures my father would have given in to her sweetly phrased demands in three seconds flat and called up clear skies and balmy breezes that whisper to the very edges of our property.

I bump and jolt over the driveway, doing my best to avoid the numerous potholes that seem to multiply each time I ride home. Lights blaze from every window of the house, bright narrow stitches against the darkness blanketing the lawn. The sweet-sharp sting of bonfire smoke drifts through the air. It seems as if the celebration has already begun. I picture my grandmother ensconced in her great chair, a queen on her throne. *Tell her, don't tell her, tell her, don't tell her. Tell her that you lied.* Even if Alistair Callum ever does come back to the store, I could always tell my family that I forgot about his request.

Because that would be so believable.

The front wheel of my bike dips into a wide divot that I swear wasn't there this morning and my back teeth clang together. I swerve wildly, try to brake, and then—*smash!*—I collide with something very solid. And human.

The next minute I'm falling and then we're both sprawled on the ground, and just in time whoever it is flings up one arm and stops my bike from crashing down on top of us.

"Oh! I am so—" I begin, just as a seriously annoyed male voice interrupts me.

"Maybe you could watch where you're going?"

The injustice of this stings, and before I can stop myself I say, "Maybe you could watch where you're *standing?*"

Belatedly, I become aware that I am still lying on top of this person and I scramble to my feet. It's so dark I can't see the full damage, but I can feel mud coating my right arm and there's a painful tingling in my left knee. I brush away a piece of gravel that's embedded itself into my skin.

Great. I can just imagine the looks I'll be getting as I walk into Rowena's party.

My front wheel is still spinning as I reach for my bike.

"Here," the guy says. "Let me—"

"No, I've got it."

Our shoulders bump together as we both struggle over the bike, and I bang the handlebar into what feels like his hip. Beside me, he lets out a sudden exhalation of breath.

At least I hope it was his hip.

"Okay, then," he says brightly, in a gritted-teeth kind of voice, and I'm suddenly glad for the darkness that's hiding my face. "I'm going to keep a few feet between us. Maybe about six."

"Sorry," I murmur as we walk toward the house. My bike is making little clicking sounds that can't be healthy. And just then it occurs to me that I've forgotten to pick up the ice cream. I try not to sigh too loudly. My only consolation is that Rowena will have expected me to have forgotten. Which isn't much of a consolation at all.

When we reach the porch, I lean my bike against the rail, turn to him, and open my mouth to say something like *I'm sorry* again, but the words evaporate in my throat.

The guy standing next to me is undeniably beautiful. He has dark shoulder-length hair, dark eyes, and a lean face. His long, supple mouth quirks up in a smile as he says, "Who knew you'd turn out to be so klutzy, Tamsin?"

I make a futile swipe at the mud crusting along my fore-arm while staring at the blue moon tattooed on the right side of his neck. *Who knew you'd turn out to be so hot?*

I swallow and say only, "Hi, Gabriel."

As soon as we enter the house, Aunt Beatrice sweeps down on us. "I've lost it," she moans and clutches at Gabriel's wrist. She examines their clasped hands for a moment and then peers up at him. "I know you," she whispers.

"This is Gabriel, Aunt Beatrice," I say loudly. In addition to her memory, which has been dicey for about ten years now, Aunt Beatrice also seems to be losing her hearing. Then again, at 101, she's the oldest member of the family. And she really is family, too, being my grandmother's sister. I never knew her husband, Uncle Roberto. He died shortly before I was born, and according to my mother that's when Aunt Beatrice really slipped her anchor.

"I know who he is," she replies, and her long nose quivers as if she is actually sniffing at me before she adds, "And I know *you*."

I nod. She's been proclaiming that she "knows" me for the past three years now. Never mind that I've seen her every day of my life with the exception of the past year when I've been away at school.

"Oh," she whimpers and releases Gabriel's hand. "I truly lost it."

"Lost what?" Gabriel asks patiently.

"Isn't it on your wrist, Aunt Beatrice?" I suggest, and when she gives me a distracted look, I motion to her bony wrist and the diamond bracelet hanging off it. Sometimes she can be fooled into thinking you really did just find whatever it is that she thinks she's lost. Then she'll be happy for a while, before her face collapses again and she starts wringing her hands.

She examines the bracelet with bright eyes for a moment, then shakes her head sadly. "No, dear," she quavers. "I've lost it." She smiles at me, a sweet smile that pulls at the millions of wrinkles on her face. Then she bestows a distracted kiss smelling of talcum powder and sherry on my cheek and I hug her with real affection. I feel some sympathy for Aunt Beatrice. Apparently, she used to be a powerful witch who could stop people from moving with just the touch of her finger. Something happened, though, long before I was born, before my mother was born, even, but no one talks about it. Now she spends most of her time wandering through her own private world searching for whatever it is she's lost.

"There you are," says Silda, my cousin, coming to stand next to us. She rolls her eyes briefly at us before saying in a bright voice, "Look what I brought you, Aunt Beatrice. Your favorite." In the cup of her palm she holds a tiny fruit tart.

Aunt Beatrice makes a small huffing noise. "I like chocolate," she says.

Silda blinks, closes her hand, and opens it again to display a large cookie bulging with chocolate chips. "Your favorite," she says again, a slight wheedle in her voice. "And there's more where that came from."

"Lost," Aunt Beatrice mutters feebly, but she allows herself to be led away.

I shake my head. "Can't you—" I begin to ask.

"She hasn't lost anything that I can find," Gabriel answers, lifting his shoulder in a little shrug. "I tried earlier. It was something about a pocket watch. But when I found a pocket watch in a drawer, it wasn't what she wanted."

I scrape at my arm. Mud flakes swirl onto the threadbare rug. Out of the corner of my eye, I see my mother standing at the far end of the room. Her head swivels my way and suddenly I'm very conscious of the holes in the knees of my jeans and my faded My Little Pony T-shirt, my favorite thrift-store score from last spring.

"I should go change," I say. "And you should go mingle. Probably not a good idea for you to spend too much time talking to the family misfit," I add lightly.

Gabriel raises his eyebrows at me. "Family misfit?"

I shrug. "You know the deal," I say, because I'm sure everyone's told him by now.

"No. And now you've got me curious." He takes a step closer to me.

The level of chatter in the room remains high, but suddenly I feel as though we're on display. "Come on, Gabriel.

You've been back all of what, forty minutes? You must have gotten the lowdown on everything that's happened since you've been gone."

He looks thoughtful for a minute and I'm expecting him to say something pseudo-consoling. But instead he says, "Maybe I would have if you had filled me in over the years."

"What?" I say, scrunching my face into confused lines. But I know what he means.

Apparently, Gabriel thinks I do too, because he echoes, "You know what I mean. What was with never writing me back? What was with the radio silence from you?" His eyes narrow in on mine as if daring me to look away. And I do.

When Aunt Lydia announced that she was leaving for California, Gabriel and I tried everything we could to convince her to leave him behind. Rational arguments, screaming fits, hunger strikes (I lasted all of five hours before I caved), and silent treatments. Nothing worked. On the day they left, I extracted a promise from a mute, white-faced Gabriel that we would write each other every week. Then they drove off, Gabriel's face turned away from the house and from all of us gathered on the lawn. Instead, he stared steadily at the back of his mother's head in the passenger seat as if hoping to bore a hole through her skull. Good thing for her that wasn't his Talent.

Two months later, he sent me a cool hand-drawn map of his new town, full of skulls and crossbones on all the places where he swore there was buried treasure, since we were crazy for buried treasure stories. But by then my infamous eighth birthday had come and gone and I was in a state of prolonged shock. A few weeks after the map, he sent me a long letter all about his new school and how it was nothing like our old one. Then he sent me a note asking only, "Why haven't you written back???" with the three question marks all in red. Then nothing after that. I still had all the letters.

But now I shrug. "Listen, Gabriel, we were just kids. Go. Mingle. Really." I step back, trying to ignore the look he is giving me, the old familiar *what are you up to* look that seems not to have changed at all. I melt into the crowd.

"Tamsin," my mother says, materializing in front of me, "have you congratulated your sister and James yet?"

"I just got here," I remind her, even though I know she knows this perfectly well.

"How was the store? Busy?"

Suddenly, Alistair's earnest face comes swimming back to me. I had forgotten all about him, what with running Gabriel over with my bike. I shake my head a little to get rid of the image. *He'll get over it after a few weeks*, I remind myself. "Not really."

She takes in a breath, puts her hand on my arm. "Will you try to be nice to your sister tonight?"

"I always try to be nice to her."

My mother shakes her head. One silvered strand springs free from the knot she's imposed on her normally wild hair. "Try harder," she says, and that persistent groove between her eyebrows deepens.

"Yes, Mom." I sigh, aware that I sound like a textbook case of the angsty teenager. If only. "Anything else? I was about to go change," I add.

My mother looks relieved. "Oh, good," she says hopefully, and I resist the urge to laugh. She smiles as I move away, but I can feel her watching me.

A few feet away, Uncle Morris blinks in and out of sight for the amusement of a baby, who shrieks and laughs in her mother's arms. She keeps reaching out to pull at Uncle Morris's little gray tuft of a goatee, and he lets her get just so close before disappearing again. I can't help smiling. I remember him playing the same game with Rowena and me when we were little.

I trudge past piles of other aunts, uncles, cousins, friends of the family. Everyone smiles and/or waves, and I smile and/or wave back but don't stop. I know the looks I must be getting behind my back—the lifted eyebrows, the overly expressive shrugs, the whispers of sympathy. *Poor Camilla—her daughter, such a waste, so unbelievable. Hasn't happened in the family since who can remember. And she was supposed to be, supposed to be, supposed to be . . .*

"Move," I say, booting a small boy out of the way as I

begin to climb the massive oak staircase. He scuffles closer to the wall but glares at me with narrowed hazel eyes. I can't remember his name, but I do remember that he's the son of one of my particularly annoying second or third cousins, Gwyneth, who can cause a rime of ice to grow on anything with one flick of her finger.

A stuffed teddy bear is floating near the vicinity of my hip, its glassy eyes whirling back in its head as a small toddler reaches desperately for it. Her fingertips just brush one paw before the bear flips lazily out of reach.

I glare at the boy with new loathing. "Just like your mother, you little brat," I snarl, snatching the animal out of midair and whacking it over the boy's head.

"Ow," he whines, reaching up to rub his forehead.

"That didn't hurt," I answer witheringly.

"We were playing a game," he mutters. This used to be one of Gwyneth's favorite defense lines whenever the adults found any of us coated in ice, our lips blue with frost.

"*You* were playing," I snap. "*She* wasn't." I present the bear to the tear-stained child, who regards me doubtfully with big brown eyes.

"You're just jealous," he mutters. "Because you can't do *anything*."

Before I can stop myself, I whip the toy back from the toddler's hesitant fingers and mash it over the boy's head a few more times.

"Ow!" he cries again.

"I was just playing," I say pointedly before holding out the bear to the little girl again. This time she snatches it away from me.

"You're welcome," I say and stomp up the rest of the stairs.

A vision of New York City in the summer—trash bags piled on the cracked sidewalks, glittering streams of traffic, and hordes of people trundling along with Century 21 shopping bags—slips through my head. A brief and lovely oasis.

I've got to get back to school.

THREE

IN THE TEMPORARY SANCTUARY of my room, I pause for a minute before the small gilt-edged mirror above my dresser to smile at a snapshot of Agatha in a pink frilly smock shirt. The words I MISS YOU. CHICAGO SUCKS! are written in black Sharpie across the bottom of the photo. I run my hands through my curly dark hair, make a brief search for my brush, give up, and jab a couple of glittery pins into the mess instead. I finger the hem of my My Little Pony T-shirt, frown, and search out my emergency pack of cigarettes that I wedged into the gap between my night table and the wall. Yanking up the window sash, I blow smoke rings through the holes in the tattered screen.

"Oh, gross, Tam," my sister's cool voice comes from behind me. My last smoke ring comes out crooked, tearing itself into jagged wisps before I turn around. "Don't you know how damaging that is to your health?"

I widen my eyes. "Really? I wish they printed warnings or something on the package. So irresponsible of them."

My sister shakes her head, somehow managing to keep every single strand of her gleaming blond hair anchored in its elegant chignon. She's wearing a knee-length sleeveless black dress, black heels, a string of pearls, and no makeup beyond a slick of pink gloss on her lips. It amazes me how Rowena, amid all the debris of chipped plates, cracked tiles, peeling wallpaper, and uneven floorboards, manages to look so *refreshing* every day. She's all polished surfaces and glimmering reflections, someone who doesn't need makeup and probably never will. In addition to all of her extraordinary Talents, she also happens to be heart-stoppingly beautiful.

I feel grubby just looking at her.

Now her large green eyes, fringed with thick lashes just a shade darker than her hair, narrow at me. "Is that what you're wearing?"

I look down, shrug. "Yeah, I just changed. Like it?" I inhale and exhale, ignoring my sister's pointed little cough. "Shouldn't you be downstairs receiving congratulations and everything?"

"I came up here to see if you were coming back down." There is just the faintest lift to her voice that I almost don't catch. But I've learned to follow every intonation of my sister's voice. Rowena is extremely Talented in the art of speech. Her voice is like pure honey mixed with cinnamon and wine. She can mesmerize when speaking, her voice looping and twining through people's heads until they would walk off cliffs into the sea if she asked. As if that's not enough, she can also give the power of speech to inanimate objects. When we were younger she used to delight me for hours by making the statues in the garden speak, their voices full of stone and dust. Then, when I turned eight and everything didn't happen the way it was supposed to happen, the usual sisterly cracks between us grew to canyon-size chasms. Any time she tried to use her power on me after that, she would catch herself, give me such a searching look that I could hardly stand it, and hurry away.

"What do you think of Gabriel?" she asks.

I know if I hesitate or blush or do anything else besides answer immediately, Rowena will latch onto it, so I say as normally as possible, "He's okay, I guess. Seems like the same old Gabriel."

"Really?" Rowena considers me as if I'm some kind of odd insect she's never seen before. "I think he's totally changed. So handsome now. I mean"—she waves one hand through the air—"if you like that look."

I can't help myself. "What look?"

She smiles. "You know. The scruffy musician look."

"He's a musician?"

"Didn't you know? He's going to Juilliard this semester. So now you'll both be in the city." She adjusts her necklace, her fingers gliding over the polished pearls. "You know," she says thoughtfully, "Uncle Chester and Aunt Rennie are going to be away for most of the fall. You could live at their house instead of in your dorm room." The way she says *dorm room* makes it sound more like *leper colony*.

"I have to live in the dorms. It's a rule." The happiest moment of my life was when I got the acceptance letter from New Hyde Prep. The second happiest moment was when I read through one of the several slick and glossy school pamphlets and learned that all students *have* to live in the dorms. "And I like the dorms."

A delicate shudder crosses my sister's face. "Why?" she says, the word infused with scorn. "Why would you want to live there among . . ."

"Among what? Among who?" I ask quietly. The cigarette bites into my fingertips and I drop it into a glass of water on my night table, watching it extinguish instantly.

"Among people who don't know what you are." My sister picks her words with care, dropping them like so many stones between us. I stare at her.

"Rowena. In school, I am not a freak. I don't stand out. I blend in. You can't imagine how wonderful that is—to blend in."

"I wouldn't want to," my sister says stiffly, straightening up.

I look at the cigarette butt bobbing in the glass of water. "Of course you wouldn't. You don't need to," I say quietly.

One of the conditions of letting me go to school in New York City was that I would live with Uncle Chester and Aunt Rennie in their century-old townhouse on Washington Square Park. But when I informed my mother that I couldn't live there because of the school rule, it set off the worst argument we've ever had. Okay, the second worst argument. The worst one was the one we had about my going away to school in the first place. We both screamed until the sky turned the color of a rotten plum and an odd combination of rain and hail began to smash into the ground. A few minutes later a fierce wind rose and rattled the windowpanes and doors as if determined to find a way in. Finally, my father entered the kitchen and explained in a serene voice that the weather would continue to worsen until we stopped arguing. Even then my mother seemed prepared to continue, until my grandmother walked into the kitchen and said simply, *Enough. Let her go.*

I remember feeling simultaneously grateful and sad. Grateful that my mother would now have to let me go and sad that my grandmother obviously didn't seem to care all that much about where I went. Then again, having me around was probably a constantly chafing reminder that she had been wrong once.

"Just because you don't have any Talent doesn't mean you're one of *them*," my sister says, and all of a sudden I'm exhausted.

"Seriously, Ro, can you go back to your party now and leave me to pollute my lungs in peace?"

My sister moves toward the door. "I know you said you just changed, but I'd reconsider if I were you. That T-shirt really isn't that flattering."

Even though Rowena doesn't have our mother's gift of moving at lightning speed, she can still move pretty fast. Especially when I've just hurled the contents of the water glass, cigarette butt and all, at her. Water splashes against the empty door frame, running in dirty rivulets down the grooves of painted wood. "Brat!" My sister's shriek, a distinctly *un*melodious sound, comes from somewhere farther down the hallway. I slam my door closed in response.

I can't help smiling.

I dawdle as long as I can but finally emerge from my room wearing my American Airlines 1960s flight attendant dress. It's a white zip-up sheath dress with red and blue piping around the hem, and there's something so cheerful about the stitched logo on the front chest pocket. Needless to say I love it, and I'm pretty sure I'll be the only one here who does. With the possible exception of Gabriel.

Pausing on the now empty landing, I catch sight of Rowena's perfectly coifed blond head studiously turned away from me. She's standing next to James, one hand lightly resting on his arm, not that he needs this anchor. James watches my sister like a child watches a night-light in a darkened room. He seems afraid that at any moment she'll flit away from him and blow out. It would drive me crazy, all that besotted staring, but Rowena seems to accept it gracefully, naturally, like everything else that falls into her lap.

At this point even some of Uncle Chester's homemade wine is starting to sound good.

But before I can find any, I see my grandmother in the corner of the room seated in the massive blue velvet chair. This is where she prefers to sit during any of the family gatherings. Relatives ebb and flow past her, paying their respects. At ninety-three she is the official head of the family.

I make my way toward her, waiting until Aunt Linnie has kissed her papery cheek and fluttered away, sparks of light dancing from the tips of her fingers as they do whenever she gets excited.

"Tamsin," my grandmother says. Her deep, rich voice issuing from her narrow body never fails to surprise me. At any given moment, she would have to raise it only a half degree to command the attention of the room.

"Grandmother," I say, bending to kiss her. She smells like the tinctures and poultices she's forever making, a mix of something sharp and sweet, like the first breath of spring. Tonight she's dressed all in white, diamond clips skewering the silvery bundle of hair piled atop her head. But despite the obvious effort, I can't help but notice that her skin has the yellowing sheen of old satin and her eyes seem to have sunk deeper into the hollows of her face.

"Sit beside me," she bids, and I sink to my knees. Surreptitiously, I touch the fringed hem of my dress, focusing only on the feel of the suede between my fingers, emptying my mind of everything else.

My grandmother can walk through people's minds like the smallest and lightest of spiders on their skin. They will almost never feel the impact. The last time she did it to me was when I was six.

My cousin Jerom had recently discovered his Talent of slowing down or speeding up his motions, so I'd convinced him we should try to "fly" (or actually fall really slowly) off the roof. I think my added weight on Jerom's back messed up his calculations, because one broken ankle later, I found myself blabbering that this wasn't my idea to my grandmother and mother, who had come running at the sound of Jerom's wails. My mother was hovering over Jerom, calling for Uncle Chester, and I was watching her, when suddenly there was the lightest touch inside me, like the first drops of rain. A rush tumbled over me, and my vision darkened and then suddenly sharpened again. My grandmother shook her head at me, and I felt as if I had swallowed mouthfuls of dirt. Anyway, I don't think that she's done it to me since then, but just in case she tries, I am always on guard.

My eyes skip over the room, coming to rest on Gabriel, who is talking to Rowena. She's smiling that cool half smile that makes her look as though she knows a delicious secret, and her face is inclined down, only half turned to his. This is one of Rowena's favorite poses, doubtlessly because it allows people to drink in the beauty of her flawless profile. I bite my lip. I can't watch this, so I look down at my hands.

"You've met Gabriel again, I see," my grandmother says, and I start.

"Yeah. I kind of . . . ran over him. With my bike."

My grandmother looks at me, then closes her right eye briefly. It's unnerving the way she can close one eye completely while the other remains wide open, unblinking. "Why ever would you do that?"

"Not on purpose," I protest before I realize she's laughing.

"How was the bookshop? Any customers?"

"A few," I answer, briefly considering Alistair Callum. *Tell her, tell her now!* Then I let my mind go blank. "I didn't get to re-price those poetry books for you."

One eyebrow twitches upward, sending a ripple effect of wrinkles across her forehead.

"I'll do it tomorrow," I add hastily.

The eyebrow slowly relaxes. "You work hard," she says at last, her voice gruff.

"Yeah. I . . . thanks."

A shattering sound makes me look up. Uncle Chester has opened the china cabinet and is hurling plates to the floor and then grinding the shards underneath his shoes for good measure. I watch him do this until the cabinet is empty.

Then he runs his hands over the shards and hands whole plates back to his audience of rapt children. From his elaborate hand gestures, I can only surmise that he's encouraging them to smash the plates so the fun can start all over again.

Suddenly, my mother catapults into view, snatching plates left and right out of the children's hands. Her face has this tight look on it and I'm expecting her to start breaking plates over Uncle Chester's head any second now. But just then the front door opens. My father has arrived, straight from the greenhouse from the looks of him. Still cradling plates, my mother vanishes from Uncle Chester's side to rematerialize next to my father. She leans toward him, her lips moving rapidly. No doubt she's furious that he's late and covered in dirt.

Later we all troop out to the backyard where the stone altar resides. There is no hint of the rain that slashed down earlier in the evening or the humidity that's been lingering all summer. Instead the sky is clear and the stars bright, and a soft breeze scented by night-blooming jasmine is blowing across the yard, catching lightly at skirts and shirts and hair alike. But I'm unable to enjoy my father's best efforts at weather-induced good cheer. I'm too aware of Gabriel and how he hasn't looked at me beyond a quick glance as we all filed through the back doors. Okay, so yes, I pushed him away before, but that doesn't mean that he has to *stay* away. I'm sure Agatha would have a ball analyzing this one.

Before I can even think about smiling at him, Rowena and Gwyneth link arms with him and swing him away. So instead, I walk next to Aunt Beatrice, who keeps stopping to stare at the tips of her gold shoes as if she can't understand how these apparatus have found their way onto her feet.

And even when we form a great circle around the stone altar, still, *still* I keep hoping that Gabriel will look my way, wink at me, something. To distract myself, I study the massive block of the altar, the blue-gray veins running through the dark stone, the thickly strewn summer flower petals, and the eight unlit candles made from the creamy beeswax of my father's hives.

"Greetings," my mother says, and on cue the breeze vanishes and her voice rings out in the clear and beautiful silence. "Well met tonight as on all nights."

"Well met," everyone choruses back. Except for me. I'm not in the mood.

"Tonight is special," my mother continues, diverging slightly from the usual opening *blah blah blah* of these ceremonies during which I always tune right out. "Tonight we celebrate the union of two beloved people, Rowena and James." My mother pauses and beams in their general direction, as does everyone else. My eyes skip over faces in a distracted blur. "We also give thanks that two members of our family have finally returned home: Lydia and Gabriel. To honor them tonight, I ask them to light the eight candles."

A soft murmur breaks through the air. I blink. This *is* an honor. I've never seen anyone besides my mother and grandmother light the tapers unless it's an Initiation Rite. Fascinated, I study Rowena and the slight flush rising in her cheeks. Then there's a general shuffle as everyone joins hands.

Aunt Beatrice's hand finds its way into my own and I hold it lightly, afraid that too much pressure will crush her tiny bird bones. On my other side, my cousin Jerom envelops my hand with his much larger and unfortunately sweaty one. "Ow, not so tight," I hiss, wishing I could pull my hand free and wipe it down the side of my dress.

Of course I get the quelling glance from my mother, who holds my grandmother's hand on one side and my father's on the other. As Gabriel and his mother step into the circle and approach the altar to the four elements, my grandmother begins the ritual prayer, her voice rich and full despite her wizened appearance. "Earth my Body, Water my Blood."

I wonder if I'm the only one to note the hitch in her breathing.

Everyone echoes her, Rowena's voice rising clear and true above the murmured responses. Gracefully, Lydia takes the first taper and lights West and South, then turns and hands the flame to Gabriel. I study his face closely, but he looks calm, relaxed, as if this is the most natural occasion, and with a sudden jolt I realize that for him it is. He's truly home now, in a way that I'll never be. I rest my eyes on a lone dandelion head that's been crushed in the grass next to my left foot. The sparkles on Aunt Beatrice's shoes blur as my eyes fill.

"Fire my Soul and Air my Spirit," my grandmother says as Gabriel lights East and North.

My lips move automatically in the shape of the words, but no sound can force its way past the block in my throat.

"And now Rowena," my mother says. My sister steps forward as Gabriel and Lydia melt back into the circle. Rowena comes to stand before the altar, then pauses. The circle around me fills with a frisson of yearning. She opens her pretty bow-shaped mouth and begins to sing the words of thanks to the stars and heavens above us. With seemingly no effort, her voice lifts and carries, circling and spreading throughout the yard, the notes pure and sweet, the way a harp made of clouds and moonlight must sound.

Everyone else's eyes are closed, but I stare at my sister's face as she sings on and on and *on*. And all the while her earlier words keep biting into my skin. *Just because you don't have any Talent . . . just because you don't have any Talent . . . just because you don't have any Talent . . .*

And then, like a balm coating over the rough edges of those words, I remember Alistair's voice and the way he looked at me tonight. *I just have this feeling that you really will be able to help me.*

And in that moment I don't care what it takes—I vow that I will find Alistair Callum's clock.

"THREE, FOUR, FIVE, *six*," Agatha counts rapidly as we walk down Ninety-third Street. "There he is—that's your future husband."

I look at the short, round man bobbing toward us. His briefcase swings out from his left side in a way that seems destined to clock someone in the shins, and his blue checked tie is flapping in the breeze as if trying to take flight. He wears a panicked expression as he fumbles through his pockets. If Gabriel were here he could tell this guy exactly where he left his BlackBerry. Even I can guess that's what he's searching for. Then I shake my head a little. There's no need to think about Gabriel.

Nope. No need at all to think about him. Or the fact that we haven't spoken since Rowena and James's engagement party last week. He must have really decided to take my advice on steering clear of the family misfit.

"Okay, my turn," Agatha says, taking a sip of her raspberry smoothie. "Nineteen," she says.

I raise an eyebrow at her. "Shooting high?" Then I start counting as quickly as I can. "Fifteen, sixteen—ooh, too bad that one's seventeen," I say as a guy roller-skates right by us, his left arm brushing up against my shopping bag. Turning, I follow his progress, checking out the tight cords of muscle in his calves and arms. "Eighteen, nineteen. Hmm." This one is very clean-cut, with a square jaw and wearing a dark suit and sunglasses. Normally I don't like a man in a suit. But somehow this one seems to fit.

"He looks like a banker," Agatha complains. She's more into the tall, skinny hipsters who wear thick-framed glasses and Ramones T-shirts.

"You never know. You could have it all. The house with the white picket fence, the SUV, and two point four blond, blue-eyed children."

Agatha makes a face at me. "That sounds perfectly hideous."

I smile at her. Since her British literature class last semester, a lot of words like *perfectly* and *perhaps* have permeated her language.

"What's your idea of the perfect life, anyway?" She weaves her way around a doublewide stroller and then falls back in next to me.

I sip some of my strawberry banana smoothie, crunching the crushed ice between my teeth. "Now," I say.

"Now? What do you mean?" Agatha is staring at me bemusedly.

I wave my hands around me to encompass the bright air, the sidewalk cafés, the chatter and clatter and bustle of everything. "Now. This. This is perfect."

She's squinting at me, a little the way she does at a particularly hard problem in her math book.

"I mean, walking around, drinking smoothies, buying all these books, thinking about my classes this fall, and I don't know . . . just being here, and this is all that's expected, this is all I can be."

Okay, now I'm starting to sound like an army slogan.

"My turn," I add brightly. "I pick number . . ." I say a little loudly, hoping Agatha will stop giving me that look. "Seven."

"Seven it is," Agatha says. "One, two, three, four," she begins, and then, "Yum," she says as a guy wearing a bandanna and a dark blue T-shirt wanders by. "Too bad he's only number five." She puts her hand out and stops me from crossing the street. Agatha takes the traffic laws *very* seriously. Two bikers hurtle past us as we wait for the light to change. "Six, seven. Mmm," she says and smacks her lips in appreciation. With a not-so-subtle hand movement, she points out my next future husband.

I nearly choke on my straw. Alistair Callum is crossing the street toward us, clutching a dry cleaner's bag and a sheaf of papers under one arm. I blink and then blink again, but no, he's really solidly here and not just a figment of my overactive imagination. A taxi cruises past and it seems as though he's about to hail it when all of a sudden he looks up and our eyes lock. I raise my hand and make a flapping motion that I hope he takes for a wave.

"Omigod!" Agatha murmurs. "Your future husband is coming right at us. Look cute!" she instructs, swiping at my hair.

"Um, listen, yeah, thanks," I say, batting away her hand. "I know him. And by the way, he thinks my name is Rowena. Don't say anything!"

"What—" And then thankfully she swallows the rest of her words as Alistair arrives.

"Rowena," he says, shifting his papers from one arm to the other. "What a pleasant surprise."

"Hi, Alistair," I say brightly, smiling up at him. A bus swooshes past and we all step back onto the curb. The gold-flecked stubble is gone, revealing a firm chin divided by a slight cleft. "Funny, running into you on the Upper East Side. You're a long way from NYU."

"Yes, well, occasionally I do escape to other parts of the city," he says, nodding politely at Agatha. "Was my office too difficult to find, then?" A quick smile blooms on his face and I realize he's trying to make a joke.

"What? Oh, no, no, not at all!" Great. Now he thinks I don't want to help him after all. "No, I just got back yesterday and today was our first day of classes and then I had to buy all these books," I say, hefting my bag into the air as proof. "I swear I was coming to see you this week," I add, all too aware of Agatha's fascinated scrutiny in my peripheral vision. "By the way, this is my roommate, Agatha. Agatha, this is Alistair Callum."

"Charmed," Agatha says, and I try not to roll my eyes. She must be giddy that he's British.

Alistair smiles at her. "A pleasure, Agatha." Then he turns back to me. "You still will?" The note of hope in his voice is too much to handle.

"Of course. I have back-to-back free periods Wednesday. Are you—"

"Perfect. I have office hours on Wednesday from ten to twelve. I'm in Lerner Hall. 245 Waverly Street. Do you know where that is?"

"No. I mean, yes, I can find it." I pinch the end of my straw between two fingers. "Wednesday," I repeat, because he's looking worried again. "245 Waverly Street. Trust me, I'll be there."

"Wonderful," Alistair says, bestowing a smile on me and another on Agatha. "Back to the office for me now. No rest for the weary and all that," he says, and turning, he plunges back into the whirl of people. I watch as he navigates his way, his dry cleaning flung over one shoulder, the plastic sleeves now curling up in what seems like a jaunty manner.

"Just out of mild curiosity," Agatha begins.

Okay, here it comes.

"Why, pray tell . . ."

More Briticisms. Will they never end?

". . . did your future husband call you Rowena?"

"Um . . ." I put my straw to my lips and drink half the smoothie in one gulp. A few feet away, a tiny old man stoops over a trash can on the street corner and begins rummaging through it. He fishes out a soda can, shakes it fiercely, then tucks it away in the pocket of his tattered black sweatpants.

When I turn back to Agatha, she's still waiting for my reply. Her eyes behind her green cat-framed glasses are narrowed, possibly against the sun, more likely against me. "He's this professor at NYU and he . . . came into the bookstore over the summer and he thought I was Rowena."

"Ooh," Agatha coos excitedly. "A professor at NYU. He looks so young to be a professor. But I *knew* he was one of those intellectual types." Then she gives me a pointed look. "Wait a minute. Back up here. He thought you were *Rowena* and you didn't tell him otherwise because . . . ?"

Because he thinks I'm a witch who can help him recover a lost family heirloom using my Talent and the Talents particular to my family.

"Just because," I say miserably, ducking my head a little. Agatha reaches over and scrubs my head affectionately with her knuckles.

"You've got issues. Your sister is not all that, okay? And what does he want with you anyway?"

I shrug. "I mentioned my interest in medieval art and

he wants to lend me some books." The lies leave an oily taste on my tongue and I gulp down the rest of my smoothie.

Agatha nods. "I bet that's not all he wants to lend you," she says with an exaggerated wink. I sputter, just managing to keep from spraying my smoothie everywhere. Agatha bats her lashes at me before continuing in her normal voice. "Maybe he could write you a recommendation letter. Don't you want to go to NYU?"

I want to go anywhere as long as it's not back to Hedgerow.

Two days later, I exit the overly air-conditioned subway car and enter into the din of the station. I climb countless stairs blackened with old chewing gum and finally emerge on the corner of Bleeker and Lafayette. After wandering through a tangle of streets while peering hopefully at any building that displays the purple NYU flag outside its door, I finally make my way into Lerner Hall.

My eyes skip across the hall and a little thrill shoots through me. I could be a student here next year. I assess this skinny guy who is propped up against the wall outside a closed classroom door. He's wearing cutoff jeans and flip-flops. Several dragon tattoos spiral up and down his arms, all in various shades of gold and green. On a roll, I decide he could be my boyfriend next year.

He sees me looking, returns the once-over, and then makes a motion to unhook the earphones of his iPod. I give him a regretful smile as if to convey that I really am pressed for time and move away, my heart beating a little too fast. I'm always good at the initial part. I'm not so good at the closing. But like most things, I figure it's just a matter of practice.

I wander down the hallway, past offices with their doors mostly open. Inside, professors sit looking professor-like, examining pieces of paper with grave attention or making furious notes in the margins of a book or talking emphatically on the telephone. In one office, a girl is sitting with her back to me, her posture needle straight, her voice ragged as she says, "But if I don't take this class this semester, the whole sequencing for my major will be thrown off. You *have* to understand that!"

At the end of the hallway, I come to a partially open door bearing the nameplate ALISTAIR CALLUM. I raise my hand to knock but pause instead, and study the name again. Something about the letters catches at my memory, then flickers away before I can grasp it. I shake my head and knock firmly before pushing the door open.

"Come in—oh, hi! Hello! Yes, welcome," he says, scrambling to his feet. "How—how are you?" He runs one hand along his face as if checking to see if he shaved that morning. Judging from the faint *scritch*ing noise that follows, he didn't.

The small square of his office is taken up mainly by a massive desk and a large green leather chair, the arms of which are embossed with tarnished brass rivets. His desk is full of papers and books, some opened to marked passages. Several framed photos and sketches line the walls of his office, and as I move farther into the room, I step onto a worn antique rug. I smile to myself. It's as if someone looked up the term *professor's office* in the dictionary and then decorated according to the definition found there.

"Tea?"

I shake my head. "I'm fine." We observe a small moment of deeply uncomfortable silence, and then, as if prompted, Alistair says abruptly, "Sit down, sit down," and points me to a smaller black chair before settling back into his green one. "I'm so glad you came," he says simply.

I have to tell him, I have to, have to, have to. How is another matter entirely.

He steeples his fingers in the classic professor's pose. It makes me wonder if they teach that little gesture before you're allowed to get a PhD.

"I have to . . . tell you something."

"You can't help me?" Alistair says, the dismay in his voice so vibrant that I stare down at my hands, twisting the chunky silver ring on my left thumb over and over. I can't do it. I can't tell him. Not just yet. *Later,* I promise myself. When I find the clock for him. Then he won't care that I lied.

"I . . . yes. I just wanted to ask you if you know anything about how we . . . find things?"

He shifts in his chair, one long finger circling a brass rivet. "I didn't want to . . . appear . . . unseemly," he says at last. "It's magic. Something like that."

I smile. "Something like that," I agree. "Although we don't call it magic in our family. We call it Talent. As in, we all have certain Talents." I swallow. Now it's my turn to look uncomfortable, and my chair has no brass rivets to fiddle with. I settle for twisting my hands in my lap. "I can help you, but it may take a while. I'm not—"

"Are you sure you won't have tea? I know I'd like a cup." He's looking seriously nervous again.

"Sure."

He springs to his feet, clatters through a drawer, and pulls out two dusty-looking mugs. "Back in a sec—there's hot water in the faculty lounge," he explains and practically runs out of the office. I lean back in my chair, and from this vantage point I can see pockmarks of blistered paint on the wall next to the radiator.

This is exhausting. Granted, the subject of Talent makes all normal people feel odd if they even believe you at all and don't give you the *there are places for people like you to get help* look. Although I've never really tried explaining my family to anyone ever since third grade, when Denise Winters told the whole class that my house was actually a mental asylum and that they let me out only to go to school. Not that I blamed her. I've had a similar impression over the years.

"Here we are," Alistair says, coming back in with two steaming mugs and a dish of lemon wedges. "English Breakfast is acceptable?" he asks, and I nod. With his back to me, he busies himself adding tea to the cups and stirring. "Sugar, lemon?"

"Sugar, please."

He turns around, hands me a mug, and adds lemon to his own. "I have sugar here. I'm afraid I'm not a fan of white sugar," he says in a confidential manner, his eyes sliding away apologetically across his desk, as if presenting this small piece of information about himself is almost too shameful. From another desk drawer he produces an open box of sugar and hands it to me with a plastic teaspoon.

"Thanks." I take some and add it to my cup, watching as the raw crystals swirl and sink slowly into the tea as I stir. "So," I begin again after a moment, "this clock that you want me to find. Can you tell me a little more about it?"

Alistair sets down his cup of tea, pushing it slightly away from him. "It's been in my family for three hundred years. It was quite a handsome piece. A wall clock, inlaid with mother-of-pearl and with rubies for the hours."

I raise my eyebrows and nod. "Sounds nice."

"*Nice* is not quite the word," he says, and his voice has taken on a professorial tone.

"No better than *interesting*, I guess?"

He smiles briefly, then continues. "Apparently it was

given to us by some king or other for some service. Who knows with these old stories. At any rate, it got lost more than a hundred years ago in a card game between some members of my family and . . . another family. This happened in New York City in 1887. And as you can imagine, the trail goes cold after that."

"So that's where I come in," I add, because he seems to have stopped talking.

"Yes." He's staring at me now. "That's where you come in." He breaks the gaze first, reaches down, and sets a small black case on his desk. The sound of the locks snapping back seems to startle him momentarily, and I notice that his fingers are trembling a little.

I blow on my tea to cool it, watching the stray tea leaves coalesce into a vague question mark shape before dissipating. Wouldn't it be nice if that were my Talent—to read the future so I could see exactly how to proceed out of this situation?

"Here we are," Alistair says and passes a piece of paper across the desk to me. I lean forward to take it and study it in silence. It's a reproduction of a painting—an old one by the texture of the paper, worn and frayed in the corners. It looks as if it was framed at one point; I can see faint yellow outlines around the borders of the page. A clock, simple and straightforward, is set in the middle of the page. The face is inscribed with jewel-colored roman numerals and the hands are gold. Some fancy scrollwork design runs along the edges of the clock; I run one finger along the bottom of the page. Something is familiar about the clock, but I can't say exactly what.

Apparently, my face must have given this away, because I can feel Alistair lean closer to me. "What is it?" he asks, and his accent is suddenly more resonant and intense. I look up and meet his eyes, and for one inexplicable second I feel as though I am looking at someone else. Or rather, as if another person is looking out from behind his eyes, watching me eagerly. Hungrily.

I jerk sideways uncontrollably, my hand knocking my tea and spilling the cup onto the floor. It lands with a sharp cracking sound. "I'm so sorry," I cry, down on my knees in an instant, turning the mug upright. The handle has snapped off cleanly. "I broke the cup, but I think the tea missed the rug at least. I'm—"

"It's no trouble, really. Let me see, napkins somewhere—ah, yes, here." And he joins me on the floor with a wad of napkins in each hand. I take some and we begin dabbing at the liquid seeping into the cracks between the floorboards.

"Oh!" says a female voice from somewhere above our heads, and we both look up instantly. Suddenly, my face is blazing, and it doesn't help that Alistair is already stammering.

"Oh, y-yes, Ms. Barnes, wh-what can I do to you? *For* you?"

I choke and busy myself with recovering the mug handle, which has flown under the desk.

"Your copies," Ms. Barnes says, and her voice sounds iced over.

"Yes, right, thank you. Excellent. Excellent," Alistair says a few more times, and thankfully when I surface from under the desk, Ms. Barnes is gone with a swish of her starched skirt.

"Well," I say in my most normal voice, even though I'm sure my face is still red, "this has been eventful."

"Hasn't it, though?" Alistair says and straightens up, holding out his hand for me. Awkwardly I take it, then nearly pull back. His palm feels hot and dry, as if there's a fire burning right underneath the skin. To cover my confusion, I clamber to my feet and brush my jeans free of imaginary lint.

"Can I have this?" I point to the painting.

"Of course, of course. That's yours."

I nod. "I'll see what I can do. I'll be in touch," I say, because that sounds professional enough, even though I'm not exactly sure why I'm worrying about being professional at this point, since I've been lying from the moment I met this man.

He nods back at me, his eyes suddenly two hard and glittering bits of polished stone. "I look forward to it."

I nod some more. "Okay," I say finally. I need to stop

nodding now. We smile briefly at each other and I turn to go. At the door I stop and turn back. "Just out of curiosity . . ."

"Yes?" Alistair says, and I watch how his body goes still. It's something about the way he draws his elbows into his sides, like a hawk about to plunge.

"I know you mentioned that you heard of us through an antique shop. Which one was it, again?"

"Oh." He smiles. "Pinkerton, I believe, was his name."

I nod thoughtfully. Angus Pinkerton flashes into my head. He looks sort of like a rabbit with his red-rimmed eyes and pinched, twitchy nose. I remember a visit to his shop years ago with my grandmother. He kept one eye on me the whole time he was talking to her and seemed on the point of bursting into tears when I ran one finger over a dusty blue glass globe. Still, my grandmother has "found" a number of things for him over the years, and in return he's sent her plenty of business.

"He mentioned that if I was looking for something that couldn't be found, well, I could try your grandmother's shop. It seems your family has quite a reputation."

I smile. "You have no idea."

FIVE

"STOP MOVING SO MUCH."

"I'm not moving at all!"

"Your face is moving."

"It's called breathing, Agatha!" I glare at my roommate. She frowns back at me, then looks down at her sketchbook and makes three decisive strokes across the page.

I have a feeling that she just crossed out my face.

"This isn't working. Your face just isn't working."

"Thanks," I mutter. "Can I move now?"

"Yes." She sighs, waving her pencil like a conductor. "Take a break." Then she jabs the pencil at me, blue eyes intent under dark eyebrows. "But we are trying this again in ten minutes. This is due tomorrow and I'm not searching for another subject now." She opens the mini fridge. "Did you drink my Coke?"

"Um . . . no."

"Pig," Agatha says briefly before scooping up a stack of shiny quarters on my desk that I was saving for laundry.

"Want one?" she so generously asks, and I nod, watching her swing out of the room.

I hop up from the beanbag that we have wedged into the corner under the window in our version of a window seat. It's my favorite place to read, listening to the noise of traffic eleven floors below. I wander over to my desk, stretch, and look down at the painting of the clock that I have half hidden under some textbooks. I'm still puzzling over where I've seen it before.

"OH MY GOD!!!" a female voice exclaims angrily from somewhere down the hallway. New Hyde Prep is an all girls' school, and it seems as if someone is shrieking about something every other minute. I wait, listening for more, but when nothing happens, I go back to studying the painting.

Agatha had pronounced it "pretty" earlier but was completely unfamiliar with it. Therefore, I deducted with my superior sleuthing skills that it's not something I saw in my Intro to Art History class last year, since she took the class with me. I spent two hours at the library yesterday combing through a selection of art history textbooks, trying without any success to find its match. Then I came home and stared at the wall for a while, trying my hardest to remember where I've seen this clock before. Something is circling in the back of my mind, but it's too—

A brisk knock on the door snatches me out of my reverie. I flip some folders over the picture, then turn. The door, which was half ajar to begin with, now swings all the way open. I look up to find Gabriel standing just outside the room. Both of his hands are anchored over his eyes. "Is it safe?" he asks.

Gabriel. Here. In my dorm room!

I have only enough time to really regret that I'm wearing my least favorite jeans, grubby flip-flops, and a plain blue T-shirt that shows absolutely nothing. "Is what safe?" I ask.

Gabriel widens his fingers, peers through the gaps. "Did you hear that screaming down the hall?"

"Yeah," I say, drawing out the word. "Are you telling me you had something to do with that?"

"Apparently, I knocked on the wrong door and walked in on a girl who wasn't wearing . . . much. She was jumping up and down on the bed, singing 'Respect.' More like howling it, really."

"Mary," I say instantly. "She's been blasting that all week since she broke up with her boyfriend."

"Yeah, I didn't stop for introductions. She was looking for something to throw at me."

I can't help myself—I laugh. "How'd you get past Hags, anyway?"

"Hags?"

"Downstairs at the front desk? Large woman." I spread my hands wide. "With a wart on her chin? All visitors are supposed to be announced. Especially gentleman callers," I finish airily.

"Maybe I was such a gentleman that she let me up here on good faith."

I snort. "To what do I owe this honor? Is this part of the family outreach program?"

Gabriel smiles pleasantly at me. "Actually, brat, I came by to tell you about this show I'm playing down at Silver Tree next weekend. You should come." He pulls a fluorescent yellow flyer from his backpack.

"Cool, thanks." I hesitate, then turn back to my desk. Oh, screw it. I'm lost anyway. "I'm glad you came by . . . I was wondering if you could . . . help me with something."

"What is it?"

"It's not something I can't handle for myself, you know. Just because I'm asking you doesn't mean anything," I say in a rush. "Okay? I just need to get that straight."

Gabriel studies me. "This is really starting to sound like fun," he says, his voice completely bland.

"Sorry," I mutter. Before I can change my mind, I snatch the painting out from under the folders and shove it at him. "Does this look familiar?"

He takes it, gives it a brief glance, then looks back at me, raising both eyebrows at once. "Somehow, this was not what I was hoping you'd ask me."

"What were you hoping . . . oh, God, never mind. Give me that back." I make a swipe for the paper.

But he holds it out of my reach, fluttering it just above

my head. I switch tactics and try to barrel into him instead, but with his free arm he fends me off easily enough.

"Why did I ever forget how annoying you are?" I say through clenched teeth.

"Oh, I don't know. Maybe because you forgot to write me and therefore remind yourself," he says cheerfully, taking another look at the painting. "What do you want to know about this?"

"Can you find it?"

"As in *find* find it?"

"*Yes.*"

He lowers his arm abruptly. "First tell me why."

"Er . . . homework assignment?"

Gabriel gives me a pained look. "That's weak, Tam. Try again."

Damn. "I . . . can't."

"Okay, tell me why you can't."

"I *can't* tell you why I can't." I sigh. I don't know what I was expecting. If the old Gabriel would never have let me get away with being so close lipped, I shouldn't have hoped that the new Gabriel would either.

"Why don't you trust me, Tam?"

"I do."

"You don't. You've been really weird ever since I came back. Fine, you didn't want to keep in touch. But we're not kids anymore, and what's with—"

"You've seen the way everyone looks at me. Everyone in my family. You know what happened to me."

"I know what *didn't* happen to you, yeah, but—"

"I'm not like you."

"True. I'm a guy, you're a girl—"

"You're obtuse," I inform him and whisk the paper out of his hand. "And never mind about this—"

But he snatches it right back. "Oh, I can assure you that now I am finding it for you. Then you're going to *have* to tell me what's going on." He grins at me.

"Don't hold your breath," I say, but I can't help smiling back. "You know, the funny thing is, I swear I've seen it before."

"I can't say that, but there is . . . something about it." He tucks the paper away in his backpack, then props his foot up on Agatha's desk chair to tie his shoelace, which has loosened. The muscles in his arms stretch, jump briefly, and I have the craziest desire to run one finger down the length of his back. I open my mouth to say something undoubtedly stupid and am saved by Agatha, who walks back into the room carrying two cans of soda. She stops, looks from Gabriel to me, then back to Gabriel.

"*Hel*-lo," she says. "I love a man who feels free to put his filthy feet all over my furniture." But she's using her pudding voice, warm and sweet and familiar. Agatha can say anything in that tone and no one would take offense.

Compared to Rowena, she's an amateur, but then again it's hardly fair to compare *anyone* to Rowena, and I've seen the Agatha Effect in action.

And Gabriel is no exception. He dusts off her chair with wide sweeping motions while saying, "Wow, sorry—this looks like a family heirloom."

"Maybe it is," Agatha says, handing me my Coke before cracking hers open. Then she gives him her lightning-fast smile and holds up her can. "Want some? I'll find a cup for you since I don't want your germs all over the place. I mean, maybe if I knew you better—"

I obey my cue. "Gabriel, this is Agatha. Agatha, this is Gabriel."

They shake hands, the movement of their arms long and ropy. I press the edge of the soda tab into my palm until the metal pinches my skin.

"So how do you know Tam?" Agatha asks him.

"Tam and I go way back." His eyes meet mine briefly. My face feels warm and I drink some Coke quickly.

"Oh?" Agatha says.

"Family friends," I say. "Gabriel and his mom just moved back here."

"Cool," Agatha says. "So, do you think I captured her essence?" she asks and, to my horror, holds out her sketchpad to Gabriel. "That's my assignment. 'Capture the essence of your subject.'"

"Um . . . he doesn't need to see that," I say, moving forward to snag the sketchpad out of Agatha's hand. But she sidesteps me and I'm too late anyway—Gabriel is already examining her drawing with interest.

"Not so good, right?" she prompts as they both study the page and then me so intently that I want to sink through the floor.

"Not your fault," Gabriel says at last. "Take it from me, Tam's pretty hard to pin down on *paper*."

"You're right," Agatha says as if that's the most profound thing she's heard all day. Just in time I remind myself it's probably not all that attractive to snort.

Her gaze snags on the yellow flyer, now on my desk. "What's this?"

"That's my show. You should come."

Agatha nods enthusiastically. Like me, she loves checking out bands on the weekends. "Where?"

"Silver Tree."

"Awesome. Our fake IDs work there." She drinks more of her Coke, sets the can on her desk, and rummages around for a few minutes. "Where did I put my freaking charcoals?"

"They're probably in your closet. On the top shelf," Gabriel says helpfully.

Agatha gives him a dubious look but walks over to her closet anyway, reaching for the top shelf. Then she whirls around, charcoal set in hand, her eyes wide and wondering. "How did you know that?"

Gabriel shrugs. "Uh . . . it's where I like to keep all my important stuff. In the closet."

"Thanks for stopping by," I say brightly, pinning the flyer to the cluttered square of corkboard over my desk.

"So you're coming next weekend?"

I nod. I really wish that I could come up with something witty right about now, but he doesn't give me time. "Great to meet you," he tells Agatha before winking at me and walking out the door.

"Does that mean he's gay?" Agatha muses after we hear the hallway door close. I choke on my soda. "That closet comment he made," she prompts when I stare at her.

"I don't think so," I gasp, my nose tingling sharply.

Agatha whacks me on the back.

"Good, because he is hot. Hot with three *t*'s."

I settle back down onto the beanbag, arranging my legs in a more comfortable position. "You think so?" I say neutrally after a minute. The soda tab snaps off the top of the Coke can. The metal is now warm from my hand.

"Don't you?"

"He's okay," I say.

Agatha gives me a wry look over the top of her sketchpad. "And he's totally in love with you."

"What?" I sit upright.

"Be still," Agatha says, lifting her pencil. She's smiling.

"But you don't—"

She rolls her eyes, tapping her pencil on the page. "It's obvious, stupid."

I lean back, trying to digest this information, trying to figure out how I feel. Then I shake my head. "He's a friend of the family."

Agatha frowns at me. "So what?"

How can I explain to Agatha that for me that's something to be avoided at all costs? That falling for Gabriel would really torch any hope of escaping from the seriously suffocating arms of my family. I roll the soda tab between my fingers. "Not my type."

"Hmm," Agatha says, studying my face a little too long. "Try not to move so much this time."

I sigh inwardly, relieved that she's off the topic of Gabriel.

But then she adds, "And stop blushing, too."

SIX

BY THE TIME Gabriel's show comes around a week later, I feel ready for a break from school. Agatha and I have been quizzing each other relentlessly on SAT vocab words every night before bed. Consequently, I dream of opening up a test booklet full of words that I've never seen before. And every day more and more college catalogs arrive at the downstairs front desk for us to look at. Agatha keeps mentioning Reed and Stanford and the University of San Diego. I don't have the heart to tell her that my parents will never let me leave the state, let alone go across the country.

We spend our usual amount of time getting ready. Me: ten minutes. Agatha: going on an hour as she tries on and discards every shirt in her closet before moving over to mine. "That looks great," I say for the fourth time, my head bent over my copy of *The Tempest*.

"Am I getting fat?" Agatha moans, standing before the full-length mirror that we glued to the back of the door. Who knows how we're getting it off at the end of the year.

"No," I say automatically, then snap my book shut. I wander over to my makeup kit, pick up my green glitter eye shadow, and decide to apply another coat to my eyelids. I'm relatively happy with my outfit, a denim overalls mini dress with my green and gold tube top underneath.

"Okay, how's this?" Agatha has paired my My Little Pony T-shirt with a white miniskirt.

"Great! Ready?"

She looks at me, horrified. "I *have* to do my makeup!"

When we reach the bar, it's standing room only and the show has already started. Gabriel is on stage, wearing jeans and a black T-shirt with the sleeves cut off. His acoustic guitar is cradled in his arms, his face illuminated by a narrow spotlight overhead. A girl wearing a pink and black slip over incredibly skinny jeans is singing in a whispery, almost breathless way into the mike, her hips twisting and turning slowly with the music. The guitar chords wrap just under her silvery voice as she sings something about the sea and a shadow she can't ever forget. I listen to the words and try to ignore the thought that she's probably Gabriel's girlfriend.

"Beer?" Agatha says in my ear, and I nod, my eyes still fixed to the stage.

Gabriel plays on and the girl sings another song, sometimes picking up a flute to accompany him on the guitar. The bar is crowded, people flickering in and out of the dim light, sometimes jostling into me. Agatha comes back after a while and presses a cold glass into my hand, then waves away my offer of money.

"They're pretty good," she says finally, and I'm grateful that she doesn't say *she's* pretty good. I nod and sip my beer, and just then the girl announces in a totally normal voice that they will take a set break. Then her voice dips a little again and she reminds the crowd that CDs on the back table are an *amazing* bargain at ten dollars each. She gives this hint of a smile and a wiggle of her body as she says this, and all around me people clap and a few guys wolf whistle. The lights brighten slightly and a crush of people moves to the bar on the other side of the room.

"Bathroom," Agatha announces. "Hold this?"

I take her beer and stand in the crowd, letting it break around me until Gabriel appears in front of me.

"You made it," he says simply, then lifts one of the glasses from my hand.

"Keep drinking that and you owe Agatha a beer," I say after he takes a swallow. He grins but hands the glass back to me, and I spend a few seconds studying the open hollow of his throat and the way his tattoo seems to shine against his faintly damp skin.

"So—" he begins.

At the same moment I rush in with, "You're great. Great up there. Looking good." *Shut up, shut up*, I tell myself.

"Thanks." He studies me for a minute and then says

abruptly, "That clock you want me to find. Are you sure that's really what you want me to find?"

I gape at him. "What? Yeah, I'm sure. Why?"

He shrugs. "I don't know. It's like . . . it doesn't exist."

"It has to," I say doggedly. Why would Alistair ask me to find something that doesn't exist? An image of Alistair's face when he didn't look like Alistair flashes into my head.

"What?" Gabriel says intently, staring at me.

"Nothing." I drain my glass and start drinking Agatha's beer absent-mindedly.

"Anyway, I found something—" he begins.

"What?" I say, nearly choking on the beer. "Why didn't you say so right away?" I jump on the balls of my feet until beer sloshes over my wrist.

"Because I didn't find the actual clock," Gabriel says, and my happy fantasies abruptly end. "I was going to say I found something that you might want to see, but it's complicated. It's not what you asked me to find."

"Well, that's helpful," I mutter, dabbing ineffectually at my wrist.

He pins my gaze with his own, then says, "Maybe if you would tell me the truth about—"

The girl who he was singing with appears at his side. "We're up, baby," she coos into his ear. She gives me a fleeting smile, a lip spasm, really, before winding her long white arms around Gabriel's neck as if preparing to drag him back to the stage.

"Tomorrow?"

I nod. "Where?"

"Chester and Rennie's house."

I frown. "Why there? It's . . . oh, are you staying there? I thought you were staying in the dorms at Juilliard?" *I thought you were like me.*

"I am. Sometimes I practice there with the band. Anyway, tomorrow. Eight o'clock?"

"Sure," I call as he follows the girl back to the stage, their hands entwined.

SEVEN

FAINT STREET NOISE penetrates the thick walls of Uncle Chester and Aunt Rennie's townhouse: the occasional honk of a horn, a burst of song from someone passing by the windows. But inside, the house is silent, waiting.

Gabriel stares at the painting on the wall for so long that I think he's gone into a trance. It's a drawing room scene, very similar to the upstairs drawing room. Rich yellow drapes with fancy-looking gold tiebacks frame the large picture windows and the room is scattered with sofas and chairs. A fire is blazing in the fireplace, the flames looking as though they're about to leap beyond the fire screen. However, the three people standing in the picture don't seem to be paying attention. Two of them are men, dressed in long black frock coats. Their backs are turned to the viewer while the third figure, a woman, is caught in profile. My eyes wander over her slim painted features and then over her dress, a brilliant red, which is a perfect echo of the tiny points of red, maybe rubies, on the face of the clock hanging directly above her head.

The clock that looks *exactly* like the one that Alistair wants me to find.

"That's not the same clock," Gabriel says at last.

I've been holding my breath without realizing it, and now it all escapes me in a rush that sounds like a cross between a *what* and a *huh*. "Whua!"

Smiling for the first time since we entered the house, he says, "'Whua'? Well—"

But I'm not in the mood. "Look!" I snap Alistair's painting at him, the paper making a crackling noise as I wave it in front of Gabriel's face. "It's exactly the same. And that explains why it was so familiar to me," I add, rattling Alistair's paper some more. "Obviously, I've seen Uncle Chester and Aunt Rennie's painting before."

Gabriel looks at the print I'm holding and then at the painting on the wall. "Yeah, I know," he says with what I feel is exaggerated patience. "Let me explain again. That object"—and here he points to the clock in the painting—"is not what you *told* me you want to find."

"What do you even mean?" I ask, trying not to sound sulky.

Gabriel walks over to the massive staircase and folds his long frame onto the second step. There's a rip in his jeans and his right knee pokes through briefly as he arranges his legs in a sprawl. I follow, sit beside him. After a minute, he sways his knee into mine and says gently, "It's not calling to me the way that it normally does. It doesn't feel real. Maybe it never really existed."

"But it might have," I say softly. "Right?"

Gabriel shrugs. "Possibly."

"Okay, okay," I say, more to myself than to him, as the glimmerings of an idea are taking shape in my head. "The clock in the painting and the clock on this piece of paper are one and the same. I'm sure of it. But you can't find this clock." I fan him with the edge of the paper.

"It's not—"

"Shhh!" I knock the back of my hand against his arm. "I'm processing." Another term I learned from Agatha. "That's an old painting there," I say slowly. "I checked the date. 1899. And he said the clock was lost in 1887. So maybe you can't find it now because it doesn't exist anymore. But it does in that painting." I try to keep my voice level. "Gabriel, don't you think that's it? That it existed once but it doesn't currently?"

Gabriel inclines his head slightly toward me. "Who said the clock was lost in 1887?"

I open my mouth, close it again.

"Tam, tell me what's going on," he says. When I don't answer, he hooks his fingers under my chin and turns my face up to his. "Please," he adds simply.

"Okay, okay," I say at last and lean back a little because his fingers are too warm on my skin. "This guy came into the bookshop over the summer, this professor at NYU—the night you came home, actually. Anyway, he had heard of the bookstore—you know, the finder's agency part—and he asked if I could help him find something, a family heirloom that was lost more than a hundred years ago. And I agreed to do it." I pause, giving him a hopeful look.

Gabriel waits me out.

"Um . . . I didn't tell him that I don't have . . . any Talent. Oh, but I did tell him that I was Rowena." But it comes out more like *ohbutIdidtellhimthatIwasRowena.*

"*What?*"

"Yeah, okay, it was stupid, I know. But he thought I was Rowena and then I just sort of . . ."

"Went along with it?"

"Exactly."

"But you told him later, right?"

I'm not sure if he means the no Talent part or the not being Rowena part, but I decide to tackle both. "No," I whisper, staring at my toes in their neon green sandals. "I should have, but then maybe he wouldn't want me on the case anymore. He'd just go back and ask for Ro. And I . . . wanted to prove to my family that . . . oh, forget it, it's stupid."

"Why would you pretend to be Rowena?" Gabriel asks. "You're way prettier."

Now it's my turn to stare at him. "*What?*"

But he's moved on. "So that answers why I couldn't find this," he says and raps the paper with his thumb. "It doesn't exist anymore. Even if it is the same clock as the one in that painting, it's still not what your professor wants. At least not currently."

"Explain to me how it works."

"How what—you mean how I find things?" And now for some reason he looks worried.

"I want to know," I say simply. And for once I really do.

Gabriel doesn't answer right away. But at last he says, "Okay. It's like, when someone wants to find something, I can hear the object."

"You don't see it?"

He gives a quick shake of his head. "No. And *hear* is the closest word I can think of, but it's more like feeling an echo. I feel this echo of whatever the thing or person or place that's lost is, and then I . . . follow it."

"Even through time?" I whisper.

Gabriel's face goes completely blank. "Why would you ask that?"

"I don't know. No reason, really. I just thought it was . . ." I break off, staring at him, and even though his face hasn't changed at all, not even by one twitch, somehow I know. "You can, can't you?"

A siren wails past the front windows, blaring its warning into the dark.

"I've never told anyone that I could do that. I didn't know at first. It took me a couple of years before I figured out that yes, I could follow something through time. But . . ."

"But what?"

"We're not supposed to," he says simply. And all of a sudden I feel the gulf in that *we*.

"Why not?"

"This has never been explained to you?"

I look at him.

"Apparently, they do this at the Initiation Rites," he adds.

When a person turns twelve in my family, he or she has been Talented for four years. Four years is the general time that it takes for a person's power to fully strengthen. So on Samhain, the entire family gathers and celebrates the new Initiates. The year I turned twelve, two of my cousins did, too, so of course a big celebration rite was planned. The night of Samhain, I locked myself in my room. For once my mother didn't pop into view to confront me and Rowena didn't try to convince me with sugar-syrup words and my grandmother didn't order me downstairs. Alone in the suddenly silent house, I watched everyone troop out to the woods before opening my science textbook and trying to study for the quiz we were having that week on ecosystems. Later, I tried not to strain my eyes for the telltale ladders of smoke that would signal the bonfire had started. Instead, I colored the photos of arid deserts in my textbook a vile shade of green, not caring that I was defacing a school text-book, and tried to block the sounds of chanting from my ears, even as my lips moved reflexively in the four prayers. In my mind's eye, I can still see the stain of color spreading from the tip of my marker across the porous page. I'd have to say that ranks as my second worst birthday, only just behind the year I turned eight.

"I never went through those," I point out, even though he knows this.

"Neither did I," Gabriel answers, and I blink in surprise.

"You didn't? Why not?"

"Oh yeah, my dad would have loved that shit." His voice is mocking. "Those were the years when my mom was pretending that we were actually normal people. The all-American family. We did normal Halloween things. My mom dressed up every year as a pumpkin or something equally stupid."

I try not to smile. "Not a witch?"

Gabriel shakes his head. "Hell, no. Never that. That would be a little too close to home for my dad. No, I trick-or-treated until, like, thirteen, and then I went out with my friends and did the usual stuff—"

"I've read about that," I say wistfully. "Toilet-papering houses and shaving cream."

"Stealing candy from little kids is more like it. That and lighting dog shit on fire."

"Oh." I think about this for a few seconds. "That's lame. And disgusting."

Gabriel shrugs. "What can I say? I was thirteen."

"So your mom never told you about—"

"She was weird about being Talented." He pauses, rubs one hand across the back of his neck. "She had this mini altar that she took down every day right before my dad came home. Dirt from the backyard, flower petals. A dish of water. You know the drill."

I nod.

"Anyway, she still believed in everything, but it's like it went into hiding whenever my dad was there. This whole other person came out. And I could never figure out why."

"Why what?"

"Why would she ever want to be with someone if she could only be a quarter of who she truly was in front of him? And I could never figure out why my dad accepted that—required that—from her. It's like being with someone and their arms or their legs are missing and you don't even notice. It was crazy." Gabriel shakes his head, then looks at me and grins. "Okay, that's probably more than you needed to hear."

"No, I . . ." I adjust the strap of my sandal where it's pressing into the arch of my foot. "I like talking to you about this. It's . . . nice," I finish lamely. "I never talk to anyone about their . . . Talent."

"Why not?"

"I . . ." My fingers press into the worn spot on my skin until pain pricks across my nerve endings. "It hurts too much," I say finally. I can't look at him as I continue. "I feel like my family tolerates me but that I'm a constant failure to them."

And instead of saying things like "You're not a failure" or "That's not true," Gabriel says nothing at all but rests one hand on my arm.

Heat pours through my skin.

"Things . . . weren't supposed to be like this," I add. We're quiet for a while, listening to the house creak around us.

"I'm sorry we moved away," Gabriel says. And then his hand tightens on my arm until I look at him. "Why didn't you write me back?" he asks.

"I . . . felt weird." *Like you wouldn't like me anymore.*

"Even with *me*?"

I shrug. "Even with you."

Our faces are close enough for me to observe that his eyes are not as dark as they first seem. Instead, there are tiny flecks of green radiating from his irises.

And then the grandfather clock in the hall strikes the half hour and I'm jolted back to what I need to be jolted back to.

"Okay, what if I want to find that object there?" I say and point toward the painting on the wall. "Forget about this piece of paper. What if I want to find the clock in the painting?"

"Somehow, I knew you were going to say that." Gabriel sighs and leans back away from me.

"And what if I want to go with you?" And now I'm holding my breath, too afraid of what he'll answer.

"Whoa! Who said that I would even go in the first place?"

"Please." I wedge my feet on the bottom stairs. "I know we're not supposed to tamper with time or whatever the rule is, but—"

Gabriel's brows twist. "It's not just that," he says in a way that makes me think he cares little about breaking rules. "It's dangerous. I've read enough about time to know that it's not a good idea to mess with it on the whole."

"What if we were really, really careful? And we did it just this once. And no one has to know, right?" Inwardly, I imagine the looks on my mother's and grandmother's and Rowena's faces when I bring home the payment that Alistair will give me after finding his clock. I could drop the money onto the table. *What's this? Oh, just a little something that a customer gave me after I—*

The stairway creaks a little as if weighing in and I jump. Thankfully Gabriel doesn't seem to notice. He's too busy staring off at the painting.

"You know," Gabriel says thoughtfully, "my mom never really explained that rule to me anyway. It was one of those conversations that we had to have on the down low, and my dad came home in the middle of it and we never picked it up again."

"And no one's ever explained it to me, either. I mean, why would they bother?" I say, making my face as innocent as possible.

Gabriel puts one finger to his chin in an overly thoughtful pose. "So no one's actually forbidden us to do this or explained why it would be a particularly bad idea?"

"Nope." I shake my head sorrowfully. "No one."

We grin at each other, and suddenly he stands up and pulls me to my feet. Off balance, I rock close to him for a minute. Close enough to learn that he smells like clean laundry. His hands linger on my arms a second and I try to step back, but he tightens his grip. "Do you really want to do this?" His voice is low and all traces of his grin are gone.

I nod.

"Do you promise me that if we do this, you won't touch anything? That you will follow my lead at all times?"

I would salute but he's pinning my arms to my side, so I settle for nodding again.

But Gabriel looks unconvinced, so finally I say, "Yes, I promise."

"Okay." He releases me and steps back to study the painting again. Surreptitiously, I rub my arms. I can't help but stare at him. He looks so intense, so determined and otherworldly, that I'm having a hard time remembering that this is the person who used to play sock puppets with me when he was six and I was four.

Then he turns, holds out his hand. I give him mine, feeling the strong close of his fingers. "You ready?"

No! I want to say suddenly. *And by the way, will it hurt?* I want to ask. As if I've spoken out loud, Gabriel gives my hand a little shake.

"We don't have to do this, you know."

"I want to," I answer. "I really want to."

He nods, looking back at the painting. He closes his eyes, so I close mine, too. All of a sudden I have that feeling you get on a roller coaster, just at the moment when the car has inched all the way up to the highest peak of the track and is poised, waiting to plummet and hurl down, down, down. Then everything shifts and swirls past me and I feel as if I'm standing in the ocean, the sand beneath my feet disappearing under my heels, leaving me balanced on air.

My eyes snap open. *Focus,* I think desperately, clinging to Gabriel, the bones of his hand solid and real. I concentrate on watching the shadows skim across the hardwood floors to pool in the corners of the foyer. A breeze is coming in from somewhere. There must be a window open and now it's making the candlelight flicker and sway.

Candlelight?

I turn my head. Branches and branches of candles line the wainscoted walls, their lights dancing and bobbing. Somewhere above our heads music is playing, violins and maybe a piano. "You did it!" I say, and Gabriel grins. "Is it always like that?"

Gabriel raises one eyebrow at me. "Did the earth move for you, too?"

"Oh, shut up!" I snap. Then I take a second look around. "Gabriel, this is Aunt Rennie and Uncle Chester's house." I gaze up at the familiar ceiling covered in polished tin that rains pieces of light all along the white walls. The windows are large and arched with wooden shutters pressed closed across the bottom halves, and the floors, polished to a gleaming mahogany, are interrupted here and there with the same Persian rugs that look decidedly newer in this century than in ours. And the life-size metal knight that's usually on the second floor now stands like a sentinel at the foot of the stairs. "Alistair said his family lost the clock in a card game to another family. It must have been ours and—"

"Really, Miranda," comes a voice from somewhere to our left. "I think you're being quite ridiculous. He's only the most eligible bachelor in town. It's natural that I danced with him."

"Yes, but you danced three times with him and you know that's not allowed by Mama's dance rules and—"

"Quick," Gabriel hisses in my ear, and we dart toward a closet. Just in time we press together into the small dark space that smells overwhelmingly of mothballs. Leaving the door slightly open, I try not to breathe in too much.

Two girls sweep into view and I can't help but wish

that Agatha could be here to see their dresses—she would die. I feel a quick pinch of sadness that I'll never be able to tell her about this.

They're both wearing long white trailing gowns made of some silky material. One has her dark hair sculpted in elaborate swirls, and a large white feather curls over the left side of her face. She is the taller of the two, definitely more beautiful, and from the look of things the other girl seems to know this. Her gown is just as elaborate, but it doesn't seem to fit her body, which is shorter and stubbier. In a wheedling tone, the shorter girl says, "Yes, but *I* wanted to dance the waltz with him. You know the waltz shows me off perfectly, and you deliberately took that dance."

The first girl gives a light laugh that snaps off abruptly, like breaking icicles. "I did nothing of the sort. Did I fling my dance card at him? No, he approached and asked for that dance. What would you have me do? Tell him"—and here she puts on a sweet falsetto—"'No, my little sister would care to have that dance with you, and I must condemn you to that experience of missed steps, bruised toes, and insipid conversation'?"

"Oh!" The younger girl balls her hands into fists, and then quick as a flash she reaches up, snatches the feather from her sister's hair, and shreds it.

"You little wretch," the older girl exclaims. Suddenly, the pieces of feather in the younger girl's hand burst into flame and she drops them with a little cry. She sucks on her fingers, regarding her sister through narrow eyes. But before she can retaliate, an older woman enters the foyer. I can see her assessing the scene rapidly before the feather scraps disappear in a puff of smoke. She advances slowly on the two girls, the skirts of her blue taffeta dress rustling with every step.

"Mama," the younger girl wails, "Lavina did it again."

"She started it," the older girl murmurs. She passes one long hand over her hair as if to make sure it's all still there.

"Girls, what have I said about using Talents against each other?" Their mother's voice is low but forceful, and even I feel like taking a step back in the closet. "There's been enough division and strife as it is between us all and you have to turn against each other like that? Has our history taught you nothing?"

The two girls look down at the mahogany floor, the picture of guilt, and eventually their mother's face softens. "Now, they're about to serve dinner. Lavina, Mr. Collins is waiting to escort you in." A blaze of triumph spasms across the older girl's face before she quickly composes her features into a bland mask. Her sister is not so skilled, because she looks up, her mouth open in a mute wail. "Come along, Miranda," her mother says hurriedly. "Your brother will escort you." Miranda shuts her mouth, but she reaches over and gives her sister's waist a pinch as her mother turns to lead them out of the hall. Finally, they're gone and the hall is empty once more.

"Wow," I whisper as we step out of the closet.

"And you thought Rowena was bad," Gabriel murmurs. He rubs his hip. "Something was poking me in that closet."

"Gabriel," I say. "What did their mother mean about the strife 'between us all'?"

Gabriel shrugs. "I don't know."

"They were witches, weren't they?" I frown, trying to consider the implications as I think back over our history. I mean, I know the Puritans weren't the only ones who came over with the *Mayflower*. Uncle Morris has traced our family roots to the 1600s, but records are sketchy.

But Gabriel is already on to something else. "Okay, it seems everyone's going to be at dinner, so we've got a little time to check this out."

Suddenly, I look around. "Why didn't we land in the drawing room of the painting?"

Gabriel looks slightly abashed. "Um, sometimes I can get close, but it's not an exact science."

I nod, then say sweetly encouraging, "Don't worry. It happens to a lot of guys."

Grinning, he takes a step closer to me. "When we get out of here—"

But I'm already moving ahead of him. "Upstairs."

We cross the hall, duck past several open doorways, and steal up the stairs after I rub the knight's helmet for good luck. "Here," I whisper, and Gabriel, who is a few steps ahead of me, turns and comes back. We enter the room I'm pointing out. Thankfully it's empty of people. We navigate among the velvet couches and the settees, all the little knobs on the ornate furniture. "Wow, we could make a killing in the antiques market if we could carry this back. Can you—"

"Don't touch anything," Gabriel warns.

"Just this end table. We could sell it at the Chelsea Fair and—"

Gabriel gives me a warning look.

"Oh, fine. Be that way."

But he doesn't respond because he's staring at the clock. "Tam," he whispers. "That's it."

"I know that's it. I told you—"

"No," he says, giving my arm a squeeze to shut me up. "That's the clock. *That's* what he wants. Why, why?" he says, turning the word over as if looking for a way in. "Why here in this time, but not in ours?"

I don't have an answer as I study the clock. Up close it's even more beautiful than in either painting. It's small, about two feet long and a foot and a half wide. The wood is burnished to a deep cherry glow and the ruby chips on the face sparkle brilliantly. "Can we take it down?" I whisper to Gabriel. "I mean, we did come for it."

He looks doubtful, then moves forward, reaching out one arm to touch it.

"Stop this instant!" a voice rings out from behind us.

EIGHT

WE BOTH WHIRL to find a tall man dressed in a black frock coat and glowing white shirt standing in the doorway. Even though his hair and his curled mustache are iron gray, his face is unlined, giving the unsettling impression that he could be any age at all. Moving toward us, he seems to be taking in our appearance with a mixture of shock and stern resolution.

"Who are you and what are you doing here?" he demands, stopping a few feet away from us. His gaze settles on my sandals and he opens his mouth as if to speak again but then checks himself and stares at us, his eyes the color of ice on a river.

"We . . . I . . . just wanted to take a closer look at it," I squeak. "Someone I know is looking for it."

"*Who? Who sent you?*"

"A professor," I say inanely, as if that esteemed profession is going to ease all of this man's doubts.

He shakes his head, studying us in silence. Faint

laughter from downstairs drifts through the room. "You're children," he says finally, and the sadness in his voice makes me uneasy. Gabriel and I exchange glances. "And I gather"—here his gaze lingers on Gabriel's torn jeans and my sandals again—"you've Traveled quite a long way. Still, what must be must be," he says, and then his thin lips harden into a flat line and he lifts one palm. The flames in the fireplace leap and heighten as if in response and then my eyes are drawn back to the man's hand, where a spark suddenly flares into existence.

"Tam," Gabriel says in a low voice and wraps his arm around my waist just as the man shoots his hand out as if throwing a fastball. Fire blooms in the air and slams toward us like a tiny comet just as a wave of dizziness sweeps over me. Swaying against Gabriel's side, I raise one arm reflexively to shield my face, expecting any second to feel flames charring my skin.

And then the fire disappears in midair without ever reaching us.

The air is shimmering with a weird intensity. It's so clear that it's ringing in my ears, and with a start I realize that the same clear intensity is echoing inside me.

"How . . . impossible," the man hisses and raises his other hand. This time the fireball flies at us with twice the speed of the first one. But nothing touches me. Again the fire vanishes.

Gabriel's arm slips from my waist and I look at him.

His eyes seem huge in his face. "What the hell just happened?" he whispers fiercely to me.

"He tried to—"

"*No!* I just tried to take us back. And . . . I couldn't."

Before I can digest this, the man raises his hand again and fire erupts from his palm.

Only to evaporate a second later.

I blink, then take one staggering step closer to the clock, my eye drawn to the scrollwork across the bottom half. Out of the corner of my eye, I see the man shake his fingers as if burned by his own fire. He sways backward, his lips shaped into a perfect O of surprise.

Seizing the moment, I move toward the clock, my eyes drawn to the hour hand, which looks sharp enough to cut flesh. It's pointing toward the roman numeral XII.

"Tam, don't," Gabriel mutters, and I look sideways at him, amazed to see the fear on his face.

"What?"

"I don't think you should."

"Why?" I am all too aware of the man a few feet away, listening to us.

Gabriel shakes his head. "Something about this . . . let me." He looks at me. "Please, Tam. You don't have . . ."

I swallow, say nothing. *Of course. I really can get only so far.*

Frowning, Gabriel moves closer to the clock and reaches out one hand to touch it. *"No,"* the man says, and I glance back to see him standing upright again, determination etching deep lines on his forehead. Just before Gabriel's fingers brush the scrolled edge, the man raises his hand again.

There's a hissing sound as Gabriel's hand fades right into the mahogany surface of the clock. From where I'm standing, it looks as if his arm ends at his wrist. At the same time he cries out, a single short breath of pain. "It's stuck. My arm. Burning off. Get it off!" His shoulder convulses, but he can't seem to pull his arm back. "Tam." His skin is draining of all color.

Furious, I turn back to the man. "Let him go, you bastard. *Let him go!*"

The man shakes his head, a stern expression on his face. "I did warn you. No one can touch that clock without consequences."

I turn back to Gabriel. Two thin streams of blood are trickling from his nose. "Run," he whispers.

Instead, I seize his arm and pull hard. Suddenly, we stumble backward onto a small couch. Moaning, Gabriel cradles his hand, but he lets me take it between my own. I examine his fingers. They appear to be whole and unbent. "It's okay, it's okay," I whisper as he trembles beside me.

"Impossible," I hear the man whisper again, and I lift my head, glaring at him. He looks even more shaken than before.

"Decided to take pity on us?" I snap.

A frown unfurls across his face. "I did nothing of the kind."

I stare at him. Something whispers in the back of my mind and settles into place with a soft click. I leap up from the couch, flinging myself forward toward the clock.

"Tam, no," Gabriel calls. There's a small thud as if a chair has tipped backward and I feel a rush of movement behind me as if something or someone is reaching for me.

But I put out both hands and lift the clock off the wall, as easily as pulling a pin from my hair.

NINE

"NOW WHAT?" I say defiantly to the man in the frock coat. "Now what do you have to say?" But my words sound weird, as if there is a sudden echo in the room. It takes me three seconds to figure out what's wrong. There's no sound outside of my voice. The fire has stopped cracking and popping behind me. Even Gabriel's breathing, ragged and hoarse just a few seconds ago, is cut off. It's as though a door has swung shut and all sound has vanished. I look at Gabriel. His eyes are glazed over, his mouth set in a straight line, his long fingers still, the way they never are in life. Suddenly, I am more afraid than ever. "Gabriel?" I whisper, stepping toward him.

What have I done?

I whirl to look at the man in the long frock coat. I stare intently at him, waiting, waiting, until finally he blinks. "You're awake!" I accuse. "What happened to Gabriel?"

If possible, the man looks even more shaken than I feel. "I assumed you knew what you were doing."

"Does it look like I know what I'm doing?" I snap. I look down at the clock in my hands, then squint and shake my head. Faint letters have begun scrolling across the bottom of the face, but every time I try to focus on them, they shimmer and rearrange themselves to spell out gibberish.

He hesitates, then says slowly, "You don't . . . no idea . . ." He runs a hand over his mouth, stares at me. Finally, he pieces together a full sentence. "You really don't know what you've done, do you?" he asks, and there is a darker, more desperate note in his voice now. He steeples his long fingers, presses them to his lips, and eyes me doubtfully, as if waiting for something.

I stare at him.

Finally, he steps back and sighs. "The minute is up. The power has passed. I suppose the damage could be worse." But it sounds as though he doesn't even believe himself.

"What are you talking about?" I wrap my arms more tightly around the clock and he gives me a half smile, as if too weary to complete the effort.

"Oh no, young lady. You are mistaken. I don't want that clock anymore."

"You did just a minute ago. You seemed ready to kill us over it!"

"Yes," the man agrees. "But that was a minute ago. That is now . . . merely a clock." He tilts his head to one side, adding, "I think your professor will be disappointed.

And now"—he straightens up, smoothes the front of his coat—"I must be going. And so should you."

And with that he's gone. No puff of smoke, no dazzle of lights. Just a sudden and complete winking out of existence.

"Tam?" A weak voice from the couch pulls my attention away from the now empty corner of the room. Gabriel is blinking up at me. "What happened?"

"You're alive," I say, and to my intense embarrassment my voice wavers and cracks.

I set the clock down on a spindly-legged table next to me and then walk over to the couch, sinking down beside Gabriel. His head has fallen back and his eyes are closed. At least his nose has stopped bleeding. "Are you okay?" I ask. At this he opens his eyes, looks at me.

"Once I did this bar crawl on St. Patrick's Day. Ever do one of those?"

I shake my head.

"Right. Well, I threw up beer for hours. Hours. Green beer."

I wince.

"At the time I thought the only thing worse than throwing up beer was throwing up green beer in the back of a cab." He glances at the clock again. "But that was nothing compared to what I just felt." He straightens up and puts his good hand on my knee for a second. "Let's get out of here. I've had enough of 1899."

I nod, then stand and pick up the clock again. A soft rhythmic ticking is coming from it.

"You're taking that?" Gabriel looks at me from the couch.

"Why not? It's just a clock now. You heard him."

Gabriel approaches warily but finally takes my hand and closes his eyes again.

This time I keep my eyes open.

Colors and light blur past me in a dizzy kaleidoscope. *Why can't I, Mama?* I hear a petulant voice say, but I never do hear the response because a man is laughing. *You will burn as a witch for all eternity,* someone else says in a cold, precise voice, and then cutting across anything else that voice might have said is the long and lonely sound of a train whistle. All sound speeds up and I have to close my eyes because I can't close my ears, and then suddenly I feel cool wood pressing against my skin and I open my eyes again. I am lying on the floor, sprawled in Gabriel's arms. Obviously, he's still not feeling that well, because the expected innuendoes are not forthcoming. Instead, his eyes remain closed and his skin has taken on a faint gray tinge. From this vantage point, I can see that Aunt Rennie and Uncle Chester aren't too into mopping the floor.

Aunt Rennie and Uncle Chester! I untangle myself from Gabriel, leap up from the floor, and rush to the window. Dusk seems to have fallen and with it a light rain. The streetlamps of Washington Square Park are blazing, and yellow taxis, some with their off-duty lights blinking, swish past. Here and there people shake open black umbrellas while others just run past, wet shoes slapping against the pavement, books or newspapers covering their heads.

I turn and look at Gabriel and find that he is sitting up, looking at me. Looking at me differently.

As if he's afraid of me.

"Why did that happen?" I ask finally, my voice unnaturally loud in the stillness. "Why was I able to touch the clock and you weren't?"

"I don't know, Tam," he says at last, and his voice is heavy.

"Yes, you do," I insist. "There's something you're not telling me. Something you're hiding."

He holds up both hands and spreads his shaking fingers wide. "I don't *know*, Tam. I don't know why you felt nothing when you touched it. I don't even know what that thing is." His eyes travel to the clock still cradled in my arms.

I shake my head. "It's nothing now. You heard the man. The power has passed, whatever that means."

"Wait, what? What are you talking about?"

"You know," I insist and then stop, frowning. "Did you . . . what do you remember?"

"My hand. Burning off. And then you touched the clock and then nothing after that."

I think back to the quiet of the room after I lifted the

clock from the wall. "You froze," I say wonderingly. So I try to repeat the conversation, if it passes for that, as best I can for Gabriel, finishing with "And then he said the power has passed and he disappeared."

Throughout my monologue, Gabriel keeps his eyes on the clock. When I finish speaking, he nods slowly, then says, "Maybe that explains why once again I can tell you that that is just a clock. It's not what your professor wants. Anymore."

We stare at each other and then both of us shift our gaze to the painting above our heads. I frown. Only two people are depicted in the room now, one man and one woman. They are still standing in the same places, but the woman is wearing a deep blue dress the exact shade of a twilight sky and her face is turned away from the wall—which is now empty. "Gabriel," I gasp. "It's gone."

There is a small and heavy silence and then we both head to the kitchen without a word. After some searching, I dig out a copper skillet and examine the contents of the ancient-looking refrigerator. Since Aunt Rennie and Uncle Chester left only five days ago, I decide the enameled white bowl of eggs that I find in the fridge must be reasonably safe. And the block of cheese on the top shelf has only a few sprouts of grayish-blue mold, which I manage to sliver off with a knife before proceeding. While Gabriel wedges bread into the toaster that looks as if it hasn't been cleaned in three years, I grate the remaining cheese and beat the eggs into a yellow froth. Soon enough I'm sliding thick wedges of omelet onto Aunt Rennie's eggshell china plates.

"So," I say, spreading butter on the toast, "what do I do with this clock?"

Gabriel shovels some eggs into his mouth and chews for a long time, long enough so that I think he's avoiding my question. "Who is this guy?" he demands finally.

"A professor at NYU. His name is Alistair Callum. I told you this already."

"Tell me again," Gabriel says, leaning across the table until I'm forced to meet his eyes.

I blow on the tea I made since I couldn't find any coffee and taste it. It's still scalding hot. "Okay." I hold up one hand, begin ticking off facts. "He came into the store. He bought a book on the local history of the area. Everything seemed fine. Then he asked me if I could find something for him as he had heard that we often found things for people and—"

"How did he know about that?"

I shrug. "Remember Angus Pinkerton? He has that antiques store—you know, the guy we used to think looked like a damp rabbit?"

"Sweaty guy? Never wanted us to touch anything. Anal Pinkerton?"

I had forgotten about that nickname. "He always did like Rowena, though," I muse.

"Who doesn't?" Gabriel says, and I give him a glare.

He tucks his face lower into his plate but not before I can see him smiling.

"You're such a typical guy. Falling for a pretty face and—"

"All right, all right," Gabriel says mildly. "I know Rowena's a harpy."

I am moderately gratified until he adds, "You've told me about two hundred times. But back to the point. This professor of yours, what exactly did he say about the clock?"

"He said that it was a family heirloom—lost in a card game back in 1887." I turn my empty plate in circles on the table. "But why . . ." and here my voice trails off. I don't know which *why* to start with.

Gabriel taps his fork lightly against the rim of his plate, then harder until without thinking I reach over and take it from him. "I think you need to talk to your grandmother about all this," he says.

I groan, push my plate aside, and let my head rest on the wide wooden table. *Why, why, why did I ever think helping Alistair was a good idea?*

"Man, I feel like I could sleep for a week," Gabriel says as he stands and scoops up our plates from the table. "You did find what he asked for. It's not your fault that it isn't what he really wants." He comes around the table and I notice that he gives the clock a wide berth as he heads into the kitchen.

Pausing in the doorway, he looks at me and says, "So," and his tone has changed completely, putting me on alert. "Maybe we should go out sometime. You know? Like dinner, a movie? Something kind of normal."

Feeling positive that my ears are a bright burning pink, I study a particularly fascinating knothole in the table. "I thought you had a girlfriend. You know, that girl from the club. The one you—"

"Callie? We're just friends. She's cool and all. Not my type, though."

I consider this, remembering all the wolf whistles in the bar that night, the way she sang. She seemed pretty perfect to me.

"So," Gabriel continues, "dinner?"

"I don't know. I mean, you just took me back, like, a hundred years. Dinner would probably be so . . . anticlimactic now." There is a small silence and finally I dare to look up at him.

One eyebrow jabs upward. "If you and I went out on a date, the last thing it would be is anticlimactic."

My stomach gives a little leap that has nothing to do with the most likely expired eggs that I just consumed. And then, all unbidden, the image of Gabriel in the circle, standing in the place of honor at my grandmother's side as he lit the tapers, comes rushing back to me. The way he walked so easily into my family's house that night, so sure of the welcome he'd receive. "My family would love that," I say at last.

Now both of his eyebrows scrunch down. "Tam. Can we leave your family out of it for one minute?"

I look at him despairingly. *How?* I want to ask. *Tell me how.* The silence stretches and pulls between us like a rubber band. Then it snaps. "No big deal," he says with a shrug in his voice, although his shoulders are stiff. He turns away.

Over the scrape and clink of dishes being washed, I stare at the clock. I picture Alistair's face when I present it to him and wonder if that other Alistair will flash out behind his eyes. I put one finger out, touch the ruby numeral twelve. Somehow I know this is not the last of it.

Monday night, after I find myself reading page 143 of my *Art After 1945* textbook for a solid fifteen minutes, I slam the book shut. Then I look over at Agatha's side of the room. Her bed is a jumbled sprawl of clothes, books, and notebooks, and in the middle of all this mess she's curled up on one side asleep, her right hand covering her forehead as if in an exclamation of distress.

I open my book, slam it shut again. No luck. She doesn't even twitch. Sighing loudly, I reach for my cell phone and pick it up, and then for extra protection, even though I feel like an idiot, I tuck myself into our closet. After kicking aside some shoes, I wedge myself into a corner and close the door, then nearly jump out of my skin when something whispers against my arm. But it's only this gauzy dress that I bought last year and still haven't worn. Agatha and I were browsing in the East Village when we came across a tiny store. Most of the stuff was junk, and I don't use that word lightly, but in the back we found a rolling rack of dresses from the 1920s and '30s. Somehow I left that day carrying this rose-colored dress circa 1935 that was perfect for me, not counting the fact that it had a small stain on the hem and that it smelled entirely of mothballs. Oh yeah, and that it cost way more than I could afford.

In the dimness my cell phone keypad glimmers and I dial the numbers. The phone rings once, twice. "Hello?" my mother's voice on the phone is hesitant, as if she isn't really sure she means what she's saying.

"Hi, Mom," I say.

"Tamsin." Now her voice is full of surprise. I brush aside a pair of leggings, which have draped themselves over my head. "This isn't your usual—"

"Hello?" a voice says at the same time—slow, melodic. I grit my teeth.

"On the phone, Rowena," I say brightly.

"Well, well," Rowena drawls. "What's the occasion? Are you in jail?"

I'm sure she can hear the grinding noise I'm making with my back molars.

"Tamsin, what's going on?" my mother interjects. Undoubtedly, the word *jail* has thrown her into a tizzy.

"Nothing. I just wanted to—"

"Tam," Rowena says over me, "I'm glad you called, actually. I'm coming to the city in a few days and—"

"What? Here?"

"Yes. To. New. York. City." Rowena enunciates each word slowly and carefully. "Where you live, right? Right," she agrees with herself. I pull the phone away from my ear and check the signal bars hopefully. Damn. A solid three. No chance of a dropped call. "Anyway," Rowena continues, "I've made a few appointments with some bridal salons and I'd like you to come along."

"Bridal salons," I repeat.

"Yes." Rowena is back to using her super-slow voice again. "Remember? James and I? Getting married. Dum, dum da da dum, dum . . ."

"Don't call me dumb," I say feebly. It's the best I can do.

She sighs, and at the same time my mother begins with "Now, girls . . ."

"Even though you and I have *wildly* different tastes in clothes, I think you should come along. Besides, since you'll be a bridesmaid—"

"Wait, nobody told me that," I say, startled. "Aren't you supposed to ask? And do witches even have bridesmaids?"

"Well, not—" my mother begins again.

"Yes, Mother! They do," Rowena interjects, and

suddenly I feel as if I'm eavesdropping. The truth is, my family doesn't really have weddings. At least not like the ones on TV. There's a hand fasting ceremony, but that quickly turns into the same party we have for most any occasion. Dancing, singing, invoking the four elements, burning flowers on a bonfire in the woods. Drinking Uncle Chester's disgusting brew.

"Are you having a *wedding*?" I ask, fascinated in spite of myself. Who knew that Rowena would ever even think to break with tradition?

"It's still under discussion. In any case she needs a lovely dress and so do you," my mother replies hastily. Then she draws in a breath. "You know, Aunt Linnie is very good with a sewing machine and—"

"I'll call you in the morning, Tam," Rowena says shortly, and then she's gone.

"So," my mother begins yet again, and then she makes an attempt at normalcy. "How are your classes going?"

"Fine," I say.

"And what are you taking this semester?"

"Art history, English, pre-calc—you know."

"Pre-calc?" my mother says doubtfully, as though it's some sort of disease.

"Math."

"Oh, well, good. That all sounds very . . . interesting," she says at last. My stomach clenches on that word.

"Actually, I was wondering if I could talk to Grandmother. Is she around?"

"Well, she's not out playing bingo," my mother says, and I blink, then start to laugh. The image of my grandmother in nylons and pumps, clutching a purse to her chest and squinting at a score sheet, flashes through my head. It feels almost sacrilegious and I quiet down.

"But . . ." My mother hesitates and I try to fill in the blank. *She won't necessarily want to talk to you right now. Or she's busy in the stillroom brewing up some love spell for any number of idiotic women in the town who—*

"She may be sleeping. She's not been . . . well lately."

Suddenly, I am all too aware of my own heartbeat. "What do you mean she's not well? How is—"

"She's old, Tam," my mother says, as if this is somehow new information. "It will be her time soon. She knows this."

"Mom—this is a lot of mumbo jumbo, okay? What about a doctor?"

"Your grandmother is a doctor."

"Oh, really? Excuse me, but I don't exactly recall where she got her MD?"

My mother blows out a sigh, short and gusty, and it crackles down the phone wires into the hollows of my ear. "You know your grandmother is skilled in healing." And before I can retort, my mother adds abruptly, "Hang on, let me see if she's awake," and puts the phone down with a *clunk.*

I shift and push away a few more shoes before cracking open the door and peeking into the room. A gentle snore coming from Agatha's bed reassures me.

There is a soft rustling noise on the other end of the line and a rush of breathing before "Hello?" My grandmother's deep voice floods my ear. Instantly, I concentrate on clothes. Thrift-store T-shirts and fishnet stockings, preferably purple, my favorite color.

"Hi," I say through all this. "Sorry to bother you."

My grandmother is silent.

"But I have something I need to . . ." *Confess? No, too guilty-sounding already.* "I have something I need to tell you."

More silence.

I take a breath. The cell phone is growing hot against my head, but I lost my earpiece more than a week ago. "In the store the night of Rowena's engagement party, I met someone. A man came in looking for something."

"Ah," my grandmother says. It's one of her favorite words. Depending on the inflection, it means a whole bunch of different things. It could mean *I was wondering when you would get around to telling me this.* Or *you continue to amuse me with your oh-so-predictable troubles.* Or *I see the solution to your problem even if you cannot.*

Right now I'm hoping it means a little of all three.

"Anyway . . ." There is a large thumping going on above my head and I finish in a rush. "I didn't tell him that I couldn't. I said I would help him find what he wanted to find."

"And did you?"

"I did," I say, and pride creeps into my voice. *I didn't need your help or Rowena's.* Okay, so I needed Gabriel's, but I'll get to that in a minute.

But before I can continue, my grandmother says, "Congratulations. So what's the problem, then?"

Um . . . how to answer that one? Let's see. I pretended to be Rowena, lied about being able to "find" something for a stranger, found it in 1899, and nearly got killed in the process. Finally, I whisper, "I think what I found for him is not what he wanted. And I don't think I should have found it anyway."

"Ah," she says again, and I wait for what feels like an hour until she speaks again. "It seems that you've just stumbled onto one of life's greatest lessons, then. Things are rarely what they first appear to be."

Somehow this conversation is not going the way I thought it would go.

But before I can say anything else, she sighs and suddenly I have a vision of her, the phone pressed to her ear, her face lined with an undeniable weariness. "Tamsin, regardless of what you should have done, you've started down this path. Now, I believe the only thing you can do is see it through. You *have* to see it through. If you don't, I can't see any other way for you. Or for all of us, for that matter." And somehow her voice holds a mixture of sadness and resignation.

I blow out a breath, then say in what I think is a pretty calm tone, "What are you talking about?" Is it possible she doesn't understand? "I'm . . ."

I'm not a witch, I want to howl.

But apparently that's all I'm going to get because she says in an entirely different tone, "Now, if you'll excuse me, *Jeopardy!* is about to begin."

And with a soft click my grandmother is gone.

TEN

"WHAT ABOUT this one?" Rowena asks, pirouetting before me. Her reflection catches in the three-way mirror, a dizzying spin of ivory silk and lace.

"It's great," I say. "Very bridal."

Rowena stops twirling, her skirts settling slowly. She stares at me, eyes narrow. "You said that about the last one and the one before that and the one before that."

I raise my hands in mock defense. "You look great in all of them." What can I say? Rowena, with her ripples of blond hair, her pale skin, and her green eyes, was born to waltz around in long white trailing dresses. "Why isn't Mom here for this? Isn't this something she should be tearing up over?"

Rowena snorts. "She hates the city. You know that."

It's true. Last year Rowena drove me to New Hyde Prep. I wouldn't have minded taking the train, but my mother insisted that we drive. She sat in the passenger seat, her hand pressed to the window, her eyes fixed on the diminishing

squares of sky between the tall buildings. When my resi-
dent adviser handed me a subway map, my mother looked
startled and fearful and advised me not to take the subway
after nine o'clock. Rowena and I had exchanged rare but
entirely complicit eye rolls. After my sister had packed our
mother back into the car, Rowena pressed her cool cheek
against my hot and sweaty face for an instant. Then they
drove off. They had stayed exactly forty-two minutes.

"And there's nothing up around Hedgerow. Unless I
want to find my dress in a consignment shop." She gives
a delicate shudder, as if imagining the horror of donning
dusty lace.

"I've found some of my best pieces in consignment
shops. Like this necklace. I just bought it last week for
twenty dollars." I hold up the round locket that is dangling
from its silver chain around my neck. "And look—it opens
and it's a watch inside." I study the tiny watch face inside
the locket. The slender hands are permanently fixed on
twelve o'clock. "It doesn't work, but it's still pretty. I call it
my clocket. Get it? A clock crossed with a locket?"

My sister meets my eyes in the mirror. "Charming,"
she says briefly and then fingers a creamy ruffle edging the
bodice of her dress. "What do you think if I took this off
and—"

Thankfully, I don't have to weigh in, because just then
the saleslady comes bustling into the back and coos and
oohs until Rowena is glowing and I can sneak glimpses at

my copy of *Macbeth* that I am supposed to write a five-page paper on for this Monday. In my opinion, the three witches are overrated. Maybe that'll be my thesis.

When we leave the shop, a persistent wind is eddying random flyers, crumpled napkins, and a few stained coffee cup lids along the sidewalk. A waft of incense, burning so strongly that I can almost taste it in the back of my throat, lingers in the air. Glancing around, I pinpoint the source: a corner table where a man dressed in a bright multi-colored robe is waving narrow purple and yellow packets and calling out prices to anyone who walks by. *"Twodollarstwodollarstwodollars."*

I look upward at the clock tower on the Jefferson branch of the New York Public Library. With its red-brick turret it always looks like a castle to me, but apparently it was once a women's prison before it became a library branch. Close to six o'clock. The sun is already setting and I am all for edging my way back to the dorm, where I promised Agatha we'd go to the campus movie tonight. But then Rowena says, "Let's get a cappuccino. You can never get a good one at home."

"Um . . . I can't. I have to be somewhere."

"You really do?" Rowena says, then adds almost wistfully, "I never see you anymore, Tam."

I blink. "I'm home, like, every other weekend."

"Yeah, but . . ." She frees a strand of blond hair that's caught underneath the shoulder strap of her purse and gives me a wry smile. "Only because you have to be."

I consider lying and telling her I have to sign in at the dorm by six. And then I wonder if Rowena is possibly ever lonely up in Hedgerow now that I'm gone. In the next instant I'm scoffing at this. She has James, and she has Gwyneth (although who would want Gwyneth, really?). True, she doesn't have her own version of Agatha (Gwyneth does *not* count), but she has . . . pretty much everything else.

But right now she looks so eager to sit down and have a coffee with me that I don't have the heart to lie. "Okay. Le Petit Café is down the block," I say, hoping to myself it's up to Rowena's standards.

"Great," she says with a smile that catches at me no matter how hard I try not to let it. "My treat," she adds, swinging me around with her and starting off in the direction I've indicated.

Le Petit Café is predictably crowded at this hour. I find seats at last by the window, dust the crumbs from the table's scarred surface, and wait for my sister to return. When she does, she's balancing our drinks and a cookie plate somehow very gracefully.

"The guy at the counter gave me these cookies for free. He said they were just baked." My eyes skip to the front of the room. Figures. It's the cute blond guy who I thought I had been flirting with successfully all last year. I hadn't seen him yet this term and I had come to the sad conclusion that he had gotten fired or quit. But no, here he is. Showering Rowena with desserts. I crunch into the biscotti my sister held out to me, pressing a sharp edge of the cookie against my tongue.

"So, Tam," Rowena begins slowly after she has settled herself. "Have you given any thought about what you're going to do after you graduate from high school?"

I take a sip of my iced mocha, tear the corner off a packet of raw sugar, and pour it into my glass.

"I mean, will you come live at home or . . ."

"No," I say, more vehemently than I should.

Rowena's slender brows pull together. "Why not? Mom would love it."

"And do what? I'm not like you, Rowena. I don't . . . fit. Besides, I want to go to college."

It's no secret that my mother and grandmother are grooming Rowena to take over the family one day. She'll be the one who everyone turns to when a decision needs to be made; she'll be the one to lead the rituals and rites every spring and harvest season; and she'll be the one to diagnose the town's men and women when they come after dark, tripping up to the back door in search of help. It's a good future, an assured and self-sustaining one.

"Tam," she says gently now. "It's your home. You'll always have a place. James and I will always—"

I stiffen. Already it's *James and I this* and *James and I that. James and I want to build a website for Greene's Herbals instead of using those old-fashioned mail-order catalogs.* "Rowena," I break in. "Don't you ever want more out of life than . . ." I circle my hands high in the air. "Than our family and the house and . . ."

"And what?" she asks, her voice perplexed.

Everything, I want to say, but of course I can't. Who would want more than to be Talented the way she is, the way everyone is except for me. "Nothing," I mutter. I glance around the crowded café, desperately hoping to change the subject, and that's when I see Alistair Callum reading what looks like student papers, a white mug at his elbow.

He raises his head, turns slowly, and smiles at me.

Oh, nooooooooooo!

ELEVEN

INSTANTLY, I DUCK behind my tall skinny iced mocha, some part of me knowing that it's futile to hide, and not just because a tall and skinny glass does not provide much cover.

"Tam," my sister is saying, and I get the feeling that she's been saying this for a while. Alistair is pushing back his chair now, gathering up papers and stacking them neatly in his briefcase.

"I . . . know that professor." I stand so suddenly that I knock my chair into the table behind me, where a young mother is cooing into a red bullet of a baby stroller. She glares up at me.

"Sorry," I whisper, straightening the chair. Turning, I angle my body outward with the half-formed idea of reaching Alistair before he arrives at our table.

But I am too late.

"Rowena," Alistair says to me, and even though he is

tall already, I get the sudden impression that he could touch the ceiling if he stretched out his arms.

Out of the corner of my eye, I see Rowena swivel her head from Alistair to me, then back to Alistair, her lips parted in surprise.

"Have we—" she says.

"Professor Callum," I cut in, striving for the formal. "I always seem to be running into you. I didn't realize you came here," I add, realizing too late how inane this sounds.

"Yes, well, sometimes being in my office gets too . . . quiet."

I can't really see how that's funny at all, but of course my sister laughs, her famous one-look-at-me-and-you'll-lose-your-heart-forever laugh, and right on cue Alistair does look at her.

"And this is my sister, Rowena," I say, focusing on the pattern of Alistair's tie, red diamonds on a black background, until it makes me slightly nauseated. "Rowena, Professor Callum." Alistair shifts his briefcase from one hand to the other, looks at me through the prism of his glasses, then angles his head toward my sister. All the hum and chatter of the café seem to have fallen away at this moment, leaving a hollow ringing in my ears.

"How lovely to meet you, *Rowena*," Alistair says at last. Her name curls, falls slowly off his tongue, the three syllables so sharply distinguished that I lift my eyes to stare at him.

Rowena makes a motion to rise, and of course Alistair makes the reciprocal motion to indicate *no, don't get up*, so she doesn't. She extends her slim hand. "How nice to finally meet one of Tam's professors," Rowena says, as if I have been deliberately squirreling all my teachers away from her.

"He's not my—"

But Rowena is already saying, "Please, sit," to Alistair.

"Oh, no, Professor Callum, we don't want to keep you," I interject, but he has already pulled back a chair.

"So formal," he chides me gently. "And here I was sure that we were on a first-name basis, *Miss Greene*." And he bares his teeth in what could pass for a smile.

Swallowing, I pull my chair out, careful not to bump into anyone this time. I sit, studying the flecks of cinnamon in my iced mocha.

"Are you also a student at"—here Alistair pauses and looks at me for confirmation—"New Hyde Prep, was it?"

Rowena laughs merrily and I see two guys at a neighboring table look over at her. I trace my spoon through the muddy dregs at the bottom of my glass. "Oh, no. I'm older than Tamsin," she says, leaning forward a little as if revealing a secret.

"Indeed?" Alistair says politely. "I couldn't tell who was older."

"Thanks," I say.

Alistair looks amused at my tone. "You're far too young to be worried about looking old, Miss Gr—oh, yes, *Tamsin*." He and Rowena smile at each other and all at once I want to kick his chair.

"I just happened to be in the city and Tamsin was helping me shop for my wedding dress," she informs him as if they're old confidants. I give the ice cubes in my drink a stir with my straw, hard enough so that they rattle audibly.

"Oh, yes? When is the happy event?"

As Rowena chatters on about details and Alistair makes the appropriate noises here and there, I study him covertly. He looks tired, and his fingers are trembling slightly as they grip and flex around his mug of tea, like mine do when I've had too much caffeine.

"But I'm afraid we're boring Tam," Rowena's voice cuts into my thoughts. "She doesn't find wedding dresses all that fascinating. Or dresses in particular." I stare at her. So much for the sisterly camaraderie she's been foisting on me for the past two hours.

Alistair smiles politely and turns to me. "So," he says, "have you had any luck with the . . . project?"

My fingers tighten on my straw. "Yes, but why don't I come by your office tomorrow and—"

"Oh, but if you found it, then why not—"

"What's this?" Rowena breaks in, leaning across the

table. "Is this a homework assignment?" she asks and gives another one of her delicate laughs.

"I just told you he's not my professor," I say. Underneath the table, I try to mash my foot down on hers but end up kicking the table leg instead.

"You haven't told your sister?" Alistair says to me now, and I give up all hope of getting out of this situation alive.

"Alistair asked me to find something," I burst out.

"To find . . . oh!" Rowena gives a little gasp as if she just got burned. "But . . . Tam . . ." I stare at her, wishing that one of her gifts is telepathy so I can scream silently at her to *shut up*. "How would you even manage . . ." She trails off, and now I feel like reaching across the table and slapping the look of confusion off her perfect face.

"I found it," I hiss at her. Her jaw doesn't exactly drop, but her eyes go wide, and I try to memorize the moment since it's probably all the satisfaction I'm ever going to get.

Alistair pins his gaze on me. "You have?" he asks quietly. His fingers are trembling again and he pushes the mug away from him.

I nod, suddenly reluctant to speak.

"What is it?" Rowena asks and then, toying with the sugar packets on the table, adds, "Of course, if you'd rather not . . ."

"No, no, that's fine. After all, you are sisters," Alistair says, and there is something in the way that he draws on the word *sisters*, similar to the way he said Rowena's name, that makes me suddenly sit up straighter. "I mean, it's the family business and all, right?"

"I'll bring it to you tomorrow. Do you have office hours?"

I watch as the features in his face shift to accommodate this. "Yes, but—"

"Why not now?" Rowena interjects. This time I do connect the blunt edge of my sneaker with her shin, but she barely reacts. "Your dorm's close by, isn't it?"

"No. And it isn't at the dorm," I say through clenched teeth.

"Where is it, then?" Alistair asks, leaning forward a little.

"Yes, where is it, Tam?" Rowena echoes. Then she puts it together. "Oh, at Uncle Chester's house."

"Your uncle's house?" Alistair prompts with the perfect amount of confusion in his voice, and of course Rowena supplies the answer.

"Yes, our aunt and uncle live in the city. On Washington Square Park. In this wonderful old townhouse that's more than one hundred years old. I always think it should be a museum in its own right."

"Really?" Alistair leans back in his chair, his eyes on Rowena's face. "Perhaps you know that I am a professor of art history. Medieval objects are my specialty, but I do love art and artifacts from the Victorian era as well."

"Wonderful," Rowena says. "Medieval art is so fascinating!"

I stare at her. I can't help myself. "You don't even know how to spell the word *medieval*."

There is a little silence and then Rowena smiles graciously, leans forward, and puts her hand on Alistair's arm. "Forgive my sister. Our parents did raise her correctly, but sometimes it doesn't show." She extends one wrist and checks her gold watch. "I've missed my train, of course," she says serenely. "And now I'll have to wait for the next one, which is more than an hour away. Perhaps we could show Dr. Callum the house and retrieve his object for him. I'm sure you've kept him waiting long enough, Tam." My sister gives me what I like to think of as her poison-apple smile.

How did we get here? I had planned to bring the clock to Alistair tomorrow in his office. And to ask him a few questions. I don't know what I expected to accomplish, or why Alistair would be able to shed any light on the mystery of why I was able to touch the clock and not Gabriel. But with Rowena along for the ride, there would be no light shedding tonight.

TWELVE

"AND HERE IS AUNT RENNIE'S collection of ink-wells. She has a fascination with them that no one really understands."

I trail after Rowena and Alistair as she leads him through the house room by room, pointing out each treasure. She's at her best, her most charming. Her voice has flexed and stretched into that honey smoothness. She could be discussing the ingredients in Wite-Out and anyone would be absorbing her every word as if it were a drop of gold.

And yet not Alistair. He's making all the right motions—nodding here, smiling there—and I have no doubt that Rowena is completely convinced he finds her irresistible. But there is a stillness to him that's deceiving, an ice-thin stillness that might shatter at any minute.

As we troop back into the foyer, I deliberately keep my eyes turned away from the painting that once held the clock. "I'm sure you want to see what Tam has found for you," Rowena says at last. *As do I*, I can almost hear her add.

"Well," Alistair says a little dazedly, as if this thought did just cross his mind. "This has been fascinating. What a wonderful old house. How lucky you two are to have it." Then he turns to me expectantly.

"Okay," I say, trying to keep my voice steady. "It's in here." I lead the way toward the kitchen. The clock is sitting on the table where I left it last Saturday.

There is a sudden breathless pause from Alistair as he moves forward and takes the clock in his trembling hands. "Wonderful," he says, and he touches the tip of the hour hand with one finger. "Simply marvelous." His eyes skip over the clock and then his voice takes on a heavy heartiness as he says again, "Yes, marvelous."

"This is it?" Rowena asks, and I smile to myself. I can almost hear her thinking, *What is so special about this?*

"Where did . . . how did you find it?" Alistair turns to me, eyes blazing strangely, and my urge to smile slides away.

"Oh, well, I can't reveal my sources," I say, striving to make my voice light. A brief spasm twists across his face and he looks entirely different. But it happens so quickly that I almost doubt myself. And then Alistair looks like Alistair again. But this time I am not fooled.

Who are you? And what do you truly want? It's obviously not the clock, no matter how pleased you pretend to be. I don't know how long we might have kept the staring contest up, but Rowena breaks in with a delicate laugh. "Well, I have to say it's certainly a beautiful piece. I'm so glad that

Tam was able to find it for you. And so glad that you were able to find us. Not everyone knows the right way to ask."

"Yes," Alistair says slowly. "I realize how lucky I was." He turns to her, smiles, and then checks his watch. "I believe your train will leave without you unless you hurry."

"Yes, of course. And my fiancé will be wondering where I am."

I roll my eyes. Rowena has a love affair with that word. She even affects a slight French accent when uttering it.

"Shall we share a cab, then? You're headed to Grand Central, yes? Unless you were planning to take the tube?"

"The tube?" Three curved lines appear on Rowena's forehead and then vanish like words written on water. "Oh, you mean the subway! Oh, no! I'm not too proud to admit that I've never ridden the subway before." She wrinkles her nose impishly. "The unwashed masses," she mock-whispers to Alistair.

"You should try it sometime," I say loudly. "We don't smell that bad."

Rowena hardly spares me a glance. "Of course we can share a cab," she says graciously and then, "Tam, can we drop you anywhere?"

"No, I'll walk," I say shortly. We bustle out of the house into the light rain that has begun to fall.

"Oh, dear," Alistair says. "I'm without my umbrella."

"Some Englishman you are," Rowena teases and reaches into her oversize black bag.

"He's not English," I mutter. "He's—"

"Here it is," Rowena says triumphantly. She has produced a small black umbrella and is now attempting to loosen the catch as the rain begins to patter more swiftly. "Of course, it's stuck. I can't—"

"Allow me," Alistair says eagerly, as if he's been waiting all his life to be at her service. He puts his long fingers over hers and they both struggle with the umbrella for a second before it suddenly bursts open.

"Oh!" Rowena gives a small cry of distress, which clangs in my ear like a bell. It's the first genuine sound she's made since Alistair sat down at our table. She shakes her hand in an oddly graceless gesture, then stops to examine it. From where I'm standing, I can see a thin scratch of blood blooming on her skin.

"Oh, I *am* sorry," Alistair says, his voice smooth.

A chill travels across my skin that has nothing to do with the rain.

A flash of blue appears in his hand and then he's pressing his handkerchief against Rowena's hand, the same handkerchief that he pressed against my wrist in the bookstore. "It's my fault entirely."

"Thank you," she murmurs as he dabs at her hand, then tucks the handkerchief away. "It's better now."

"Rowena," I say, my voice raw and full of warning. But when she turns to me, the words strangle in my throat.

The unease in my mind is building, but I can't articulate anything right here and now. "I . . . nothing."

"Look, there's a cab now," Alistair says. He flings up one arm and the cab sheers through a curbside puddle and slides to a halt beside him. Scattered drops of water spark against my ankles. "Tamsin, thank you for *every*thing." He opens the door and indicates that my sister should climb in first.

Rowena kisses me on each cheek, then draws back and gives me a look. "Mom will be calling you," she murmurs. "She'll be particularly interested in hearing *all* about this clock and how you found it. As will I." Handing me the umbrella, she steps off the curb, poised again, and tucks herself into the cab.

Alistair puts one foot in the cab and is about to slide in after her. "I'll come by to discuss my price," I say boldly to his shoulder. He turns, and his teeth gleam in a smile.

"Oh, I look forward to that. I think we have a few things to discuss." The door slams shut and the cab slicks away, and I'm left contemplating all the puddles on the sidewalk that hold small, blurry streetlight moons.

THIRTEEN

"YOUR MOM CALLED," Agatha says as I nudge open our door, my arms full of books. She is sitting at her desk appearing hard at work, a notebook spread open before her and a thick yellow highlighter in her hand. Except the room smells like nail polish remover and I notice that Agatha's toenails, which used to be fluorescent pink, are now bright blue.

"Umph," I reply as I toss the books across my unmade bed. Most of them make it, but two slide to the floor. "What else is new?" I've been avoiding Mom's calls for a week.

"Paper?" Agatha asks, eyeing the sprawl.

"Three," I answer, sinking down in the beanbag chair. I look over at our half-size fridge and give a little jump. My eyes are staring back at me. "Agatha!" I cry and leap up to snatch her sketch off the fridge door.

"Oh, that," she says, waving her highlighter at me. "Like it?"

I hold the sketch at arm's length. "You made my nose crooked."

Agatha looks at me, then examines the sketch. "Oh, yeah. What about that one?" she asks, pointing toward the closet door, which is uncharacteristically closed. I hate to think about all the clothes, shoes, belts, and purses massed up against it, waiting to tumble out the next time we open it. I study the second sketch of me taped to the door. "My eyes are too close together in that one. Yuck—is that how you see me?"

"Okay, *picky*, how about that one?"

"What one?"

"The one on the mirror. Gabriel liked that one the best."

"What? Where? He came here?" I whirl as if he might step out from behind the dresser at any moment. "Why didn't he just find me?" I ask my reflection in the mirror. Then I notice that Agatha is staring at me.

"I think that was the point of him coming by?"

"Oh, yeah . . . I mean . . . why didn't he just call my cell phone?"

"He said that he did. It was off."

I fumble for my phone and look at its blank face. "Oh, yeah. I turned it off when I went to the library." I flick it back on and watch the screen light up. Three missed calls. Gabriel. HELLCRATER. And another one from

HELLCRATER. "So, um . . . what did Gabriel want?" It's probably too late to sound casual, but I try.

There's a crinkling sound as Agatha rips open a bag of Twizzlers with her teeth. "You," she answers through a mouthful of plastic.

"*What?*"

She's grinning as she pokes through the bag of candy. "Kidding. He said he was in the neighborhood. That kind of thing. Wanted to see how you were." Chewing thoughtfully, she adds, "He's really cute. If you're not going to go for him, can I?"

"What?"

"I thought you'd say that. Twizzler?" she asks, holding the open bag toward me.

"Thanks, but I'm not that into red plastic."

Waving a thin red rope at me, she says, "Puritan."

After Agatha heads out to her pre-calc study group, I straighten every single magazine in the room, aligning the edges perfectly. Then I pull out Agatha's Swiffer wipes and dust our desks, our night tables, and the dresser we share. I untangle all the necklaces in my jewelry box, stack my rings and bracelets and anklets in neat shining piles, and then begin to whip through my stack of SAT flash cards.

When the words begin to blur in my brain, I finally pick up the phone and dial home, taking about a minute between each digit.

My mother answers before the first ring has even gone halfway through. "Hello!" she commands, and I nearly drop the phone.

Then I take a breath, probably my last one, and say, "Mom, hey—Agatha said you called? And I know you've been calling my cell. I've just been so crazy busy here with papers and tests and SAT stuff and, well, I just sort of forgot to tell you that—"

"Oh, Tamsin," she murmurs.

I wrap the phone cord around my finger tighter and tighter until all the blood drains from the tip. "I can explain," I say numbly. "I'm not sure what Rowena said, but—"

"How was the wedding dress shopping?"

The cord springs free from my hand. "Um . . . it was okay. You know, Rowena tried on a bunch of dresses and looked bridelike and then . . ." Suddenly, I wonder if this is even about Alistair at all. Hoping my mother is distracted by the wedding drama, I add hastily, "You know, maybe she isn't sold on the white-dress thing after all. I mean, she didn't buy anything."

"She's insisting on going into the *city* again this week. On Friday." My mother says *city* but really it sounds more like *den of iniquity*.

"Oh, well . . ." Idly I begin counting the books in a pile on my desk. I'm up to nine when a horrifying thought occurs to me. "Do I have to go shopping with her? Again?"

There is a damp and heavy silence on the other end.

I stare at Agatha's side of the room, at the pile of clean laundry that I just folded and left on her bed. "Mom? What's going on?"

"Your sister seems . . . off lately."

"Well . . . popular wisdom has it that people go a little crazy before getting married."

"Yes, I know. But . . . for the past few days she's been . . . different."

"Different how?"

My mother sniffles a little and I frown at the phone. "Mom, are you—"

"Just . . . just keep an eye on her in the city, will you?"

"Sure, fine, no problem." We hang up, but I have the distinct feeling that my mother is not reassured.

And neither am I.

Why didn't Rowena tell my mother what I had done?

"As you will see from this next slide, Pollock's essential form and structure remained. But the size of his canvas—this slide doesn't actually do it justice, but the size—"

My phone buzzes against my hip and I jolt awake. Although I'm pretty sure the vibration can't be heard all the way at the front of the room, Mr. McDobbins pauses for a moment of throat clearing. He usually does this whenever students walk in late, they whisper too loudly, or someone's cell phone goes off in the dead quiet that he requires for his lectures. It's easier to bore us all to tears that way.

Glancing down, I see the word HELLCRATER light up the screen. I frown, click my phone off, and try to pay attention.

"Pollock's career as an artist didn't really take off until—"

I just spoke to my mother yesterday. If she's calling again that means something dire has happened. My grandmother! I push back my chair and of course it screeches across the linoleum floor.

Light spills from the slide projector, giving McDobbins's face a lurid glow. "Ahem," he says finally after an agonizing pause while I try to gather my books and papers. A pen clatters to the floor, as loud as an exploding bomb in the now tomblike silence. I watch it disappear under this oblivious girl's chair. Damn. It was my favorite, even though I know it's stupid to have favorite pens.

Somehow, I manage to shuffle toward the door, and thankfully, when my hand is on the tarnished knob, McDobbins resumes speaking. The door closes off whatever other fascinating information he was about to impart on Pollock— no doubt taken straight from page 188 of the textbook under "Biographical Information on Jackson Pollock." I had been skimming that section last night while Agatha drank a shot of vodka for courage and then began cutting her hair. When the piercing yowls of distress from her side of the room became too much, I had to pry the scissors from her hand, and I pretty much gave up on my reading after that.

Now I half crouch, finish stuffing all my books into my bag, and stop just before exiting the building. A soft and steady rain is pattering down. As usual I have no umbrella. Leaning in the doorway, I watch as three girls dash by and come to a halt at the crosswalk, which is now submerged in slick gray water. Their squeals travel through the thin-paned glass door and one girl, her face pulled into an expression of acute distress, holds up her foot, revealing red sequined flip-flops.

A flicker of movement catches my eye. Across the street, a man and a woman have paused in a doorway to a building, taking shelter under the arched stone awning. I watch the girl's bright head incline upward toward her companion. He bends over her and seems to whisper something in her ear. For three seconds they are frozen in this tableau and I can't help but study them like a painting: the girl's golden hair, her pale face, her whole body turned into his, while he, wrapped in a dark raincoat, stands like a slash of poisonous ink against the white marble archway. Then he turns his head, the sheen of his glasses winking briefly at me just as he moves out into the rain, striding briskly away. The girl stares after him, then slumps suddenly against the door frame, one hand drifting to her throat. She seems about to faint.

Bursting through the door of my building, I scream out, "Rowena!"

FOURTEEN

PUDDLES HAVE SWAMPED the sidewalk, but I plunge straight through them. The rain is slashing down now, and I temporarily lose sight of my sister as a city bus roars past, tossing up a slap of water that instantly soaks my jeans. In those few frantic seconds, my mind is churning. *Rowena and Alistair? Rowena and Alistair? How? Why?* When I reach the other side of the street, miraculously she is still there. "Rowena," I say again, and at last her head turns and she stares at me.

"Oh," she says vaguely.

"*Oh*"?

She is wearing the same black dress that she wore the night of her engagement party and heels, which I can't imagine are very useful for navigating puddles. She is paler than usual but her eyes are shining, and I have to admit that whatever the circumstances, my sister looks beautiful.

"What are you doing here?" I blurt out, trying to wedge myself into the shallow protection of the doorway while rain falls against the right side of my face. "What's going on? And why were you with Alistair? That was Professor Callum I saw you with, right?" I take a deep breath and try to slow down, try to ignore the fact that my sister is looking at me as though she's never seen me before. "Mom said you were coming here to go dress shopping again. But she said Friday. It's only Wednesday, Rowena. *Wednesday*," I insist, as if somehow my naming the day of the week will make my sister snap to.

"Wednesday?" she repeats in a faint voice so unlike her usual warm honey tones. My hands and feet are tingling suddenly and I turn, but the sidewalk is now empty except for rivulets of rain running into the cracked concrete. Turning back, I notice that my sister is also craning her neck, as if looking for someone. A shiver seems to pass over her and she huddles in the doorway, a crumpled heap of a girl. "What's he really like, Tam?" she says, her eyes imploring, her fingers scrabbling at the sleeve of my coat. I'm about to ask if she is talking about Alistair when my eyes are drawn to something on her exposed wrist. Without asking, I grab her arm, push her coat sleeve back. Three dark lines, barely scabbed over, mar the otherwise clean surface of her skin. What's even worse is that she doesn't resist, doesn't seem to notice that my fingers have tightened into what must be a painful clench around her hand.

"What is this?" I say roughly, shaking her hand a little, staring at the crusts of blood. My mouth feels dry, as if I've just swallowed sand, as I add, "You need . . . you . . . you shouldn't be here."

Her fingers under mine spasm briefly and finally she tugs herself free. "I want to be here. I *need* to be here. With him. You wouldn't understand."

I step back until the stone lintel edges against my shoulders. I don't ask who she means. It feels as though my heart has briefly stopped beating.

Rain is running down my neck and soaking into the collar of my jacket, but I don't care. I cup my hand over my cell phone, listening to the ringing on the other end of the line. *Please, please, ple—*

"Hello?"

"I need you."

"I *like* it," Gabriel exclaims, his whole voice filling my head. But I can't even smile. "You know, I was wondering how long it would take—"

"You have your car in the city, right?" A man bundled tightly in a dark raincoat brushes past me and I bite back a scream, but he doesn't even look at me. *Not Alistair, not Alistair, not Alistair.*

"Um . . . yeah. You need me to take you to IKEA or something?"

I wish. "I need you to take me home. Me and Rowena."

"Wait a sec—what's—"

"I don't have time to explain," I whisper into the phone,

and then my voice chips into pieces. "There's something *wrong* with her."

"Tell me where you are."

Because of the rain it takes us more than an hour to get out of the city.

It feels more like three.

"Tamsin," Rowena says from the back seat. "Where are we going?" This is the third time she's asked.

"We're going home, Ro," I tell her again. "Remember? Big house, fields, garden, goats." Gabriel looks at me sideways but makes no comment. I shift in the passenger seat and an empty Coke can spins away from my foot.

"I don't want to go home," she says predictably, and I sigh, digging my nails deeper into my thighs.

"Yes, I know. It's only for a little while. Then we're coming back. Okay, Rowena?"

I crane my neck, try to smile at my sister. But she won't return my smile, won't even look at me. Instead her face and hands are pressed to the rain-smeared window and I have a sudden absurd flash of what she must look like to other drivers and passengers on the highway. Her fingers twitch restlessly on the glass, her nails tapping out a Morse code message of distress.

"He doesn't want me to go," she whispers so softly that it's like a thread of sound, practically lost over the rush of wheels and rain. "He needs me." At last she turns a fretful face to me and says, "I need to go back. I know it. I know it here," and she thumps her chest so hard that I almost feel the vibration in my own body. She shifts in the back seat but then immediately lurches forward again, her mouth stretched into a narrow slash.

"Listen, Rowena," I beg, barely clear on what I'm saying. "We just need to go home for a little while. Just a little, little while. And then we're going back. I promise." In the same breath I mutter to Gabriel, "Can't you go any faster?"

Gabriel looks sideways at me again and answers in the same muttering tone. "I'm pushing eighty-five. That's about all this piece-of-crap car can do."

"He wants me back!" Rowena shrieks suddenly, slamming her hands into the back of Gabriel's headrest.

"Shit!" he exclaims, and we lurch around a car in our lane, just scraping past.

"Rowena," I say, reaching out to grab her hands. She twists away as the pale point of her tongue darts across her upper lip. Her eyes, which seem all pupils right now, grow darker. "We're going to go back. But it's good this way. Really," I babble. "It's good to play hard to get. Guys get more intrigued this way. Right, Gabriel? *Gabriel?*"

He looks in the rearview mirror, regarding my sister like she's a rabid animal. "Um . . . oh, yeah. We . . . love that stuff. Gets us really hot."

I nod maniacally as my sister's eyes flicker to me. For one brief instant her face is blank and then she shakes her head. "What do you know, Tam? What do you know about love?"

Swallowing hard, I silently acknowledge that the words, at least, are pure Rowena, even if the tone—blank, emotionless—is all wrong. "I know this isn't love," I say, all pretense of remaining calm gone. "This is something, but it sure as shit isn't love." I wrap my hands around my knees—otherwise I'm afraid I will reach out and attempt to slap my sister back to sense.

"Easy, Tam," Gabriel murmurs, reaching out one hand, and I take it, feeling the comforting squeeze of his warm fingers. But Rowena's next words drive all that from my head.

"He told me you would say that. That you wouldn't understand. None of you."

"Oh, really?" I say, my voice dripping with scorn. "And what did he—"

"We need to turn back," Rowena says again, and now her voice has smoothed, stretched into its familiar sweetness. "He wants me to come back. To him." I stare at her, helpless. "Gabriel," my sister singsongs, ignoring me now. "Turn the car around. At the next exit you are going to turn around and head back to New York City."

"Tam," Gabriel says slowly, dreamily, "maybe we should go back."

"What? No! Are you crazy? Don't listen to her!"

"Yes, listen to me," my sister adds, her voice supple and beseeching. "This is what you have to do. Turn the car around."

"Okay, okay," Gabriel agrees, his voice brightening as if he is only too happy to oblige my sister. I punch him. Hard. "Ow! What the hell?" He shakes his head briefly, his fingers tightening on the wheel, and then he gives me a look. "Tam, what do I . . . I feel—"

Rowena leans back against the seat. "That's it, Gabriel," she purrs, her voice looping and twirling through the car like warm butterscotch taffy. "You're doing the right thing," she encourages as Gabriel flicks on his blinker and heads into the right lane. A truck's horn blares at us, its headlights slashing through the car.

"Don't kill us in the process," I snap.

"Don't listen to her," Rowena says. "She doesn't understand. Anything."

Ignoring her, I reach across Gabriel's lap and crank down the window. Rain splatters through, soaking us both. "Shake it off," I tell him.

"I can't . . . she needs me to do this," he murmurs. His fingers tighten even more on the wheel, but we're heading for the exit too fast. *Tick, tick, tick.* The sound of the blinker seems unnaturally loud.

"Calm down, Tamsin," my sister says. "Stop trying to tell Gabriel what to do." Her voice is butter rich, starting to reverberate warmly inside me, like ripples spreading outward across the surface of a lake. She hasn't used her Talent on me in years, but I remember that this is what it feels like.

And then I get the weirdest sensation. It's as if the widening rings of Rowena's voice hit a stone wall inside me and shatter on impact. Just like that they go silent.

Without pausing to think, I lean forward and tap Gabriel on the shoulder. "Stop listening to her. Stop." I stare at my sister, who is staring back at me. "Enough," I say quietly.

Gabriel blinks and twitches as if he's received an electric shock. "What was that?" he whispers. In the next instant he flips off the blinker and we glide past the exit.

"Nooooooooo!" Rowena screams, pounding the seat next to her in fury.

I think I've never heard anything so sweet.

An hour and a half later we grind to a halt. "Home sweet home," I say, and for once I mean it. Rowena seems to be asleep in the back seat, although every once in a while a spasm crosses her face and she moans as if in pain. Gabriel switches off the ignition, leans forward a little, and rests his head on the wheel. With one hand he rubs at his neck, his fingers circling the blue moon tattoo. "Aren't you glad you came back?" I ask after a few seconds. He gives me a look, one side of his mouth hooking upward in what I hope is a smile, but he doesn't answer. And I don't have time to thank him because the door crashes open and my mother is flying down the driveway, her hair struggling free of whatever she's managed to stick in it. In the next second she disappears and then flickers into view in the back seat of the car.

"Hi, Mom," I say, my voice somewhat muffled as she has me enveloped in as much of a hug as she can from the back seat. My head is smashed into her shoulder and my neck is starting to develop a serious kink. Her skin smells of lavender and sage, its heady perfume thickening all around me.

"Um . . . Mom, can you—"

"Oh, Tamsin," she says, her arms releasing me suddenly. I gulp in air. "You found her. Thank the earth and stars above." Her face is so sharply drawn and so blotchy from crying that I feel a terrible pang that I didn't think to call her from my cell sooner than I did. Then again I was dealing with a maniac.

"About that, Mom," I say, pulling back a little. "I've just made a couple of interesting discoveries."

But my mother's gaze is pinned to Rowena as my sister stirs and opens her eyes. She peers at all of us, blinking several times as if we are apparitions from the wrong dream. "Where is he?" she murmurs. Her hands comb through her hair as though she's searching for answers there, and I have to turn away. Movement flickers at the edge of my vision and I look out the window to see my father and Uncle Morris heading down the driveway.

"Where's James, you mean? He's coming. He'll be here right away." My mother speaks in a loud, extra-careful voice, the kind people seem to reserve for non-native speakers and children.

"Uh, Mom," I begin. "She doesn't—"

"He wants me back," Rowena frets.

"He certainly does," my mother agrees too quickly. "We all do, sweetheart. You haven't been yourself these past few days. You . . ." The little rush of my mother's words tumbles to a halt. She has found the marks on Rowena's wrist, and now she smoothes her fingers over and over them, her mouth working with the weight of what she can't or won't say.

Rowena stumbles out of the car and my mother almost trips in her haste to follow. Gabriel and I look at each other.

"What did it feel like?" I ask him finally.

He wraps his fingers around the keys still dangling in the ignition and pulls them out but says nothing.

"Back on the highway, when—"

"I know when," he says abruptly. "It felt like I had to do this. Like I had to turn the car around or I would . . . I would die or something." He snorts, but I notice that he's clutching the keys. "I just knew I had to do this. That it was the right thing to do. And then . . ."

"And then what?" I whisper.

"Then it stopped. When you touched me. When you told her to stop." He is staring at me now. "What exactly did you do?"

"I don't know."

"You don't *know*?"

I gulp under his fiercely incredulous look. "I swear I don't. I felt something, too, and then . . . it stopped. I wanted it to stop and so it did." I stare out the window. Rowena is staggering down the driveway, her arms outstretched as if reaching for someone, while my mother bobs beside her. As I watch, my mother reaches out to grab my sister's shoulder, but she shakes her off with an impatient movement. My father, holding an uprooted plant aloft, is trailing behind them. And Uncle Morris simply stands in the driveway shaking his head. "Why don't they *do* something?" I whisper.

"I don't know. I don't think they can." Then his voice sharpens with excitement. "But maybe you can, Tam."

I shake my head and say automatically, "I can't stop Rowena." In the quiet of the car my words spin like a coin and slowly come to rest. I stare at Gabriel. "She's . . . I *did* stop her. From persuading you. You really didn't do anything?"

"I couldn't," he says simply. Then he taps the keys on my knee as if to get my attention. "Tam, don't you get it? You stopped Rowena. She wanted me to turn the car around and I would have—"

"She can do that," I murmur in a daze. "She can make anyone do anything she tells them to—"

"Apparently not," Gabriel interrupted, slapping at my knee again. "And what's more, you stopped that man from killing us in 1899."

"I did?"

"Yes, you idiot! Don't you see? He was going to kill us. With the clock—"

"I remember," I say. "And stop shouting. I'm right here." But something is unfurling deep inside me and I feel as if I too might start shouting at any moment. Something like, *Take that, everyone who said that it was really such a shame about me.* In my mind I can see the proverbial rooftop and me climbing up there to make the announcement to all the stunned faces below.

"And you touched the clock. And nothing happened to you. Twice is too much of a coincidence, Tam," Gabriel is saying, and I look at him dazedly. "You have a Talent."

"But why? Why now? Why didn't I know any of this before? Why didn't my mother or my grandmother or anyone know this?" I break off to look at Gabriel, who is suddenly *not* looking at me. Instead, he reaches forward, picks up a loose CD, and slips it back into a cracked purple case. "What? What is it?"

But before he can answer, a navy blue Saab roars up the driveway with no care for the potholes. It comes to a stop in a spray of muddy gravel that echoes against the side of Gabriel's Volvo. A second later James is tumbling out of the car. "This is about to get ugly," I murmur and exit the car, aware that Gabriel has done the same. The rain has softened to a drizzle as I stand next to James.

I've always thought of my sister's fiancé as my sister's fiancé. Everyone knew they would be a match someday. Personally, I think it's because they're both arrogant and opinionated. Even when we were kids, he never seemed like one. I think it's because of his Talent—he's able to absorb words and store them like a cactus stores water. He can read a book once and years later recite it page for page. I think all those words line the walls of his brain and smother any desire to speak with us lesser mortals. Or maybe we smothered that out of him long ago when we refused to listen to his vast stores of knowledge for more than two seconds before running off or stuffing him headfirst into one of the barrels outside the barn that collected rainwater. In my defense I never did that. I just served as lookout whenever anyone else did.

Who knows what he talks about with Rowena or if he ever gets a chance to talk when he's with her. But he does burn with this kind of cool fire, an intensity that seems to serve as an eloquent foil for my sister's beauty and brightness.

Now, however, his face has a pinched white cast to it, like a man who is standing in a blizzard. "Hi, Tam," he says dully, staring down the driveway. My mother is holding Rowena by the shoulders, and my father has come to stand next to them as if blocking Rowena's escape. My sister twitches under my mother's hands like a dishcloth pinned to the line. I wonder suddenly when Rowena last slept. Or ate.

"How long has she been like this?" I ask.

"A week," James answers in a hollow voice. "I was hoping that when your mother called . . . when she said you were bringing her back . . . that Ro would be . . . better." The last word breaks and I lower my eyes, staring at a thicket of bristlebright weeds blooming in a particularly deep pothole.

Gabriel whistles between his teeth. "What do they think?"

"That she's under some kind of"—a pained look crosses James's face—"spell. A love spell." He turns to me so suddenly that I take a step back. "Who *is* this man?"

I swallow. I don't know if now is the time to tell James that I introduced Alistair, however unwillingly, into Rowena's life. Into all our lives. But just then Rowena breaks free from my mother and runs toward us, her arms spread, her hair flying. James steps forward as if to catch her, but she pulls herself up short, seeming to barely register his presence except to say, "I need the keys."

"Ro," he says softly. "Wait a minute. Do you even—"

"The keys," she repeats, making an impatient motion

with her left hand toward the Saab. Her eyes are like two holes burned into her face.

"No," James says. His voice splinters, and I wonder if this is the first time he has ever uttered that word to her.

"James," Rowena says, and her voice becomes custard-soft and sweet. "Give me your keys now. I need them and you want to help me." Swaying forward, she puts one hand on his arm.

"Rowena." He says her name in a long rush of sound and there is compliance and love and utmost despair all mixed up into it. And at the same time he is reaching into his pocket and I hear the faint clink of metal.

I don't even need Gabriel's fiercely whispered "Tam" in my ear before I'm moving forward.

"Stop listening to her," I say to James, and because I still can't get a sense of this, I jerk Rowena's arm and say brutally, "Stop telling him to give you the keys."

Beside me, I feel James give a little jolt and then he pulls his hand from his pocket as if burned. When she sees that his hand is empty, my sister howls. Then she turns and slaps me. Hard.

"Whoa!" Gabriel shouts, and then he's moving past me, pinning Rowena's arms to her sides. She screams, strands of her blond hair falling across her face and clinging to her wide-open mouth. Out of the corner of my eye I see my parents start toward us. In midstep my mother winks out and then she's standing next to me, breathing hard as if she really did just sprint up the driveway.

"What happened?" she gasps. She throws the question out to all of us, eyeing my sister, who is still struggling in Gabriel's grasp. I touch my stinging cheek, my fingers brushing across what feels like a scratch from my sister's ring.

"Tamsin stopped her. From compelling me," James says in a wondering voice. "One minute I knew that I needed to give her the keys and then . . . the next second I knew I *didn't* have to. The feeling was gone."

"She did that for me, too. In the car ride up here," Gabriel adds. "Otherwise, we wouldn't be here right now." Just then my sister's head jerks up and slams into Gabriel's chin. "Ow—dammit." There is blood on his lip as he adds under his breath, "And that might be nice," but I think I'm the only one who hears him.

James steps forward and puts out his hands to my sister, who's breathing hard now. "Traitor," she spits, turning her head away. She goes very still and maybe Gabriel relaxes, because all of a sudden she jerks forward and frees herself in one sharp movement. She stumbles a little away from us, nearly crashing into my father, and regards us all balefully. Then she flings herself at the Saab, her fingers scrabbling at the door. I don't know if my sister plans to hot-wire the car somehow—I doubt she knows, either— but my mother gives a little mewl of despair, then turns and makes a beckoning motion toward the house, where a small knot of people have gathered on the porch.

Gabriel's mother, Lydia, detaches herself from the group and comes forward slowly, almost reluctantly. There are circles under her eyes as she puts a hand on my mother's shoulder, squeezing it briefly. She nods at my father, who looks distinctly troubled, and then moves toward my sister.

"Oh, no way," Gabriel mutters, and I shoot a look at him. But he is eyeing his mother with trepidation.

"I need you to distract her," Lydia murmurs to James, and he takes a step toward the wild woman that is my sister, hunching his shoulders and lowering his head. Somehow, he reminds me of nothing more than a weary bull resigned to charging the matador once again.

"Rowena," he says softly. "I'll drive you back to the city," he offers, and she turns, staring blankly at him as if trying to remember his name. "I'll drive you back to . . . him." His voice chokes a little, but he rushes on. "Let's leave now, okay?"

She takes a step toward him hesitantly. "You'll drive me?" she repeats in a ragged voice, and he nods. She moves closer to him. "Thank you," she whispers.

Quicker than thought, Lydia's hands slip through the air, like white blurring birds, and clamp firmly on either side of my sister's temples. Rowena's face contorts for one slash of a second and then she sways into James's waiting arms.

Lydia shrugs, rubs one hand across her face. "She'll sleep for a while, Camilla," she says to my mother. "Call me when you need me again," she adds and picks her way back to the porch, her hands wrapped around her elbows.

James bundles Rowena more tightly into his arms and touches his face to hers for just an instant, like a man gulping air. Then he straightens up and begins carrying my sister to the house. The spikes of her high heels are scuffed with mud from the driveway and her right arm flops bonelessly in the air with every jouncing step. I don't think I've ever seen my sister this graceless.

I look over at my mother, who is leaning against my father's shoulder, tears gilding her face.

FIFTEEN

I AM SITTING on the top step of the staircase, my arms looped through the wooden railings, when Gabriel finds me. He walks up the stairs, balancing a full plate and a cup, and as he lifts his gaze to me, a flash of silver slides off the plate and falls through the air clattering onto the steps below me.

"Shit—sorry," Gabriel whispers with a glance toward the closed door of the library at the bottom of the staircase.

"No big deal," I say. "They know I'm out here." My parents have been sequestered in the library for more than an hour now.

"Who's in *there*?" Gabriel asks, motioning with his chin since I still haven't taken the plate from him. I follow the movement, glancing the opposite way down the hallway to the also tightly closed door that leads to Rowena's room.

"Your mom."

Gabriel nods, sits next to me, and holds out the plate. The smell of slightly burned bread wafts upward. He has made me a grilled cheese sandwich, the filling oozing out in a white gooey mess. Somewhere he also found a handful of carrots that have been chopped into thick coin-shaped pieces. I'm trying to figure out why he thought I might need a fork and knife, but I decide it would sound ungrateful if I ask.

"It's not sushi or fish tacos or pizza, but I did the best I could," he offers, and I take the plate into my hands, finding its warmth comforting.

I look sideways at him. "How do you know I like sushi and fish tacos and pizza?"

"My sources are excellent."

"Agatha." I think about my roommate for a minute. I didn't even tell her I was leaving the city. There wasn't any time, but still, I know she'll be worried by now. "I should call her," I say, but somehow I can't find the energy to get up and do it.

"You should eat first," Gabriel says, and bumps the plate toward me. I pick up a triangle of sandwich, watch as more cheese filling drips out, and put it down again.

"So your mom's been pretty useful these past few days," I say, chasing a carrot around the plate before bringing it to my mouth.

"Apparently," Gabriel murmurs. "She used to do that to me when I wouldn't go to bed."

"When did she stop?"

"When I was seventeen," he says, plucking a carrot

coin from the plate and making it vanish in his fingers. "Joking," he adds and pulls out the carrot from behind my ear.

I knock his hand away. "Cut it out," I say. "Or is this more of your Talent?"

He shakes his head. "Nah. Just stuff I learned. Card tricks, coin tricks, stuff like that. Begging for money on the street is much easier if you can entertain people first."

I nibble a corner of my sandwich. "You begged for money?"

He shrugs. "My dad kicked me out for a while." He says this lightly, easily, but still I feel a tremor under the words.

I chew, swallow, wait. When nothing is forthcoming, I ask, "Why?"

Gabriel studies his hands, turning the leather cords on his wrist over and over. "Because I kept finding things for him. That he didn't want me to find. Or my mother to find."

"Oh," I say through another mouthful. I think better of asking, then do it anyway. "What things?"

A grin travels across his face. "Oh, phone numbers, condoms, jewelry that wasn't for my mother. That last one really caused a scene."

"What happened?" I ask through a shower of crumbs. Somehow the first half of my sandwich has disappeared and I start in on the second, trying to eat more gracefully.

Gabriel scratches the back of his neck thoughtfully. "Well, he took a swing at me. Which I could have handled. In fact, it was a relief after everything else. I mean, he had already kicked me out, but I came back to see my mom for a while and he came home, and anyway, my mom got in the way."

My eyes widen and I put my sandwich down. "Did he hit her?"

Gabriel shakes his head. "No, she got in the way as in she put him to sleep. For a while. That was it, I guess. We packed while he was passed out on the floor. I think she knew it was over then. But I don't think she's ever forgiven herself." He takes a breath, picks up my sandwich half, and bites into it. "Or me," he says, or at least I think he says that, but just then, as if on cue, the door to Rowena's room opens and Lydia steps out.

She eyes Gabriel and me on the steps and moves toward us, her filmy skirt swaying gently with the motion. "I need—"

"A break," I say hastily and jump up. Carrot coins tumble down the steps and I see Gabriel snatch one out of midair. I hope she hasn't overheard anything.

"I'll sit with her," I say, nodding toward my sister's door. Lydia hesitates, looks at Gabriel, then at me, and then at the closed library door at the foot of the stairs. She nods briefly. I start to move past her, but she catches at my wrist.

"Call me if she seems like she's waking up. I don't know how long this will last. It seems to be less and less . . . effective." She shakes her head at something unseen and releases me.

"Can you do it again?" I ask nervously. "Like, just to be safe?"

Lydia stares at me and then I realize she seems to be staring at something beyond me. I almost look behind me. I wouldn't put it past Uncle Morris to be eavesdropping in the hallway while invisible.

"It's dangerous. If I do it too much."

"Oh," I say softly, and the image of a man lying so still on a floor slams through my head. Lydia continues down the hallway to the top of the stairs, and I watch as she and Gabriel dance awkwardly around each other. I have a few seconds to consider the irony that all my life I've felt like an outcast in my family for *not* being Talented while all his life Gabriel must have felt just the opposite. I wonder just how much Lydia must have loved Uncle Phil. Then I wonder why.

Squaring my shoulders, I step into Rowena's room.

A small bedside lamp casts a faint glow across my sister's skin, but even with the extra light I can see just how pale she really is now. Her breathing is shallow and fast, unlike the deep coma breaths she was taking a few hours earlier, and I pause inside the doorway, wanting to call Lydia back. But then Rowena seems to settle deeper and a smile crosses her face. Her hair is spread out across the pillow, glints of gold shining here and there. Three strands are caught in the comb on her night table and I touch them lightly, trying to imagine Aunt Lydia combing my sister's hair. I spin the comb on the tabletop. It must have been James. After settling Rowena in her room, my mother had taken him by the shoulders, turned him in the direction of a spare bedroom, and told him to sleep. It seems he hadn't slept for two days. I had caught my mother's eye then, but she'd shaken her head and sidled away from me and into the library with a mouthed "later."

My sister stirs and I turn back, swallowing hard. If I have to, I can stop her. Then I think about this for a minute. I may be able to stop her from using her Talent on me, but I can't physically stop her from running over me to the door. To get back to Alistair. I need to talk to my mother. I need to talk to . . . I glance at the phone on the table and pick it up quietly, one eye on my sister, who has settled again. I dial the number I know by heart.

"Hello?" Agatha's voice is polite and I realize she doesn't recognize my home number.

"It's me."

"Tam! Where are you? Where have you been? I called your cell, like, five times already and it keeps going to voice mail. What happened to you? I thought we were supposed to—"

"I'm sorry," I rush in. "I . . . there was a home emergency."

"Is everything okay?" Agatha's voice is expectant; I can feel her waiting to be reassured and I bite my lower lip.

"Yeah, it's okay now."

"What's going . . ." She trails off, waiting for me to interrupt her, and when I don't, I can sense her confusion coming in waves over the line. "You didn't even sign out. Hags is going to be *pissed*."

"I know." I rub my forehead. We can get away with a lot at New Hyde Prep, but even Hags has her limits.

"What do I tell her?"

"Look, it's . . . complicated. I mean, everyone's okay," I say, glancing over at Rowena, who twists suddenly and whimpers. "Mostly," I add.

"Tam . . . you're being . . . weird. Are you sure—"

"Yeah. Yeah. I swear. Anyway, I just wanted to let you know I won't be home tonight. And not for the rest of the week. And the weekend, too."

"What about Cynthia's party on Friday? I thought you—"

"I'm sorry," I whisper. "I'll try. But I . . ."

"Okay," Agatha says, but I can tell that everything is not okay.

"Um . . . so how was your day?"

"Good," she says, but now she is too polite, like the

way she answered the phone, and I squeeze my eyes shut until I see needles of light burn and dissolve.

Rowena moves again, her hands scratching across the pillow. The sound of her fingernails on the cotton sheets reminds me of mice in the walls. "I have to go," I whisper. "I'm sorry, Agatha."

"Sorry for what?"

But I shake my head, because what can I say? "Sorry for not calling earlier."

We hang up and I imagine her sitting in our dorm room, staring out the window, more than a little confused. I sit on the edge of Rowena's bed and look down at her. *Wake up! Wake up and tell me what's happening.*

And as if she hears me, her eyes open. "You," she says flatly.

"Hi, Rowena," I say. Her eyes are darker than I've ever seen and glassy. Now that she's awake, I kind of wish she weren't. Nervously, I glance toward the door. How long a break does Lydia need? "Um . . . do you want to go back to sleep?"

"No," she whispers, then closes her eyes as if to make a liar out of herself. We are quiet for a few moments, breathing in ragged concert with each other. Then her face creases with anguish. Still with her eyes closed, she sighs. "You stopped me. All these years I wondered when you'd realize." Her eyes snap open and suddenly all light and air in the room seem to be sucked away.

"What do you mean?" I whisper.

But she is silent. Her eyelids flutter shut and she seems to drift back into sleep. "Rowena," I say sharply. "What are you talking about?" I jab her shoulder.

Keeping her eyes closed, she says in a thistle-thin voice, "All this time they told us not to . . . not to ever . . ."

"Ever what? Ever *what*?" I pinch the skin of her upper arm hard, hard enough for angry pink fingerprints to spring to life. But she doesn't even stir.

"Let her sleep," a low voice comes from behind me, and I whirl to face Lydia, who is standing just inside the doorway. She is looking steadily at me and sympathy flickers in her gaze. Sympathy or something else, I'm not sure.

I swallow. "What did she mean?" I don't even ask if Lydia heard the conversation or not.

Lydia walks toward me, her steps soundless, puts her hands on my shoulders, and turns me toward the door. "Go talk to your mother."

"Who told—"

"She's the one who can answer you, Tamsin." Then her fingers tighten for an instant. "Try not to judge her too harshly."

But when I leave Rowena's room, I don't go find my mother immediately. I mean to. I have every intention of walking through the library door and confronting her and my father and whoever else happens to be in there. Even when I find myself wandering through the now empty hallway and then climbing a short spiral of stairs to my grandmother's wing of the house, I'm still planning in my head what to say to my parents.

My grandmother's sitting room is cold, and glancing at the windows, I see that somebody has left one open. The curtains are snapping and billowing, filling like sails on a ship, and as I cross the room and reach for the window sash, the material winds its way around my arms like a burial shroud. I shake myself free and slam down the window harder than I should. A chip of paint falls from the molding, landing on my shoulder. Brushing it off, I turn and stare at the closed bedroom door. I've never gone into my grandmother's room without being invited. Then I remind myself that I've never done a lot of things before today. With that thought in front of me, I march through the door.

I don't know what I expected. To catch my grandmother muttering some spell or incantation to the new moon glimpsed through her window or maybe consulting some ancient tome. What I do see disturbs me even more than either of those things would have.

She's asleep. Fast asleep. In bed with the covers tucked up to her waist, her hands folded neatly on her chest, and her long white hair in a single braid trailing over the pillow. For one instant the resemblance between her and Rowena is so sharp that I find myself squinting hard into the half-light of the room. But no, it's my grandmother.

The table by her bed holds the customary scattering of fresh flower petals and a small brown bottle with a pale spidery vine of some sort cut into the glass. It looks like one of the bottles that my mother and grandmother hand out to the women who come to the back door in the dead of night.

Trying to make sense of all this only causes a dull throb of pain to echo across my temples. My hand is groping for the doorknob when my mother blinks into view close to my shoulder. A little too close, actually.

"Sorry, Tam," she murmurs.

"It's okay," I mutter. "I wasn't really using that foot anyway."

That should have earned me an exasperated look—one that my mother is pretty happy to dole out to me whenever I speak—but instead she turns and walks toward my grandmother, sinking to her knees by the bed. Her hands travel across the covers until they link with my grandmother's hands and then I have to look away. I don't want to see my mother crying.

"How long has she been like this?"

"Since Rowena . . . Rowena put her under some kind of spell."

My eyes dart again to the little brown bottle on the night table. "She drank that? Wait, how do you know Rowena did it?"

My mother lifts her head slowly to look at me with puffy eyes. "Because she told me. Your sister sat there and told me with a smile on her face and a light in her eyes that—" My mother pauses, smoothes the coverlet over the shape of my grandmother's body. "She told me that *he* wanted her to."

"But . . ." I move closer to the bed and stare down at my grandmother's wax-colored face. "Can't you just wake her up?"

"I've tried. Everything I could. Everything I know. Nothing. Nothing. I can't break a spell of your grandmother's making." My mother's fingers tighten on the coverlet before she goes back to her obsessive smoothing.

"This is *her* spell?"

"Yes," my mother says, and although there is an ocean of bitterness in her voice, she picks up my grandmother's arm very tenderly. "See? She must have drawn her own blood here." I don't want to look, but I do. In the pad of my grandmother's thumb is a bright red pinprick. "And then she mixed it in with valerian root and witchknot and she must have drunk it. All because Rowena sat there and compelled her to." My mother presses her face into the coverlet for a moment and then blots her eyes with the lace edge.

I frown, stare down at the bed, then revise my earlier impression. My grandmother seems stiff, almost as if she's frozen. She doesn't seem asleep in quite the same way that Rowena is now. "That's why Lydia's been using her power on Ro," I say, my eyes skipping away from the blood mark.

"I didn't know what else to try," my mother admits. "If I keep her here, she just tries to leave, and now this. If I let her leave, then she's with that . . . *man*," my mother spits out.

"Alistair Callum," I say, the name dragged from my throat.

"Yes," my mother agrees tiredly. "She told me his name."

A snapshot of his blue handkerchief flashes into my head and the initials stand out clearly, blazing white thread letters against the blue backdrop. *AEK*. And then I remember the nameplate on his office door. "I don't think that's his real name," I say slowly.

"How do you know that?" my mother demands, her hands smoothing the coverlet until long past any hint of a wrinkle is left. "Do you know him?"

I sink down beside her. The room is quiet except for the occasional gasp from my mother, who is crying again. Outside the window a crescent moon glitters in all her sickle-shaped glory.

"He came into the bookstore one night over the summer. He asked for help in finding an old clock. A family heirloom. It had been lost, he said. In 1887."

Now there is no sound in the room at all. It's as if my mother is holding her breath. "Why?" she says finally, anger threading through her voice. "Why didn't you tell us?"

Suddenly, I feel an answering flare of anger. "Why didn't you tell me that I had a Talent? You must have *known!*"

Two dark spots of color have crept across my mother's cheekbones. In one quick moment she gets to her feet. "Your father should know this," she mumbles, not exactly meeting my eyes.

"Wait a minute." And suddenly I know she's about to flick out of the room. Without thinking, I surge toward her in my mind and silently scream, *Stop*. I stumble to my feet and we stare at each other. And once again my grandmother's long-ago words run through my head. *Your daughter will be one of the most powerful we have ever seen in this family.*

"Tamsin," my mother says at last, and one hand goes to her throat. *I'm sorry*, I want to say, and also, *Did it hurt?*

But instead my next words come out like perfect stones to skip across a lake: even and hard.

"Why did you lie to me all these years?"

When my mother and I walk into the library, a small sullen fire is smoking in the fireplace, guarded on either side by the china firedogs. I swallow. Rowena used to make those firedogs sing in rusty yelps and barks and I used to laugh until I cried.

My father is standing by the wall of windows that look out over the fields toward his nursery. As we enter the room, he turns, crosses behind the massive walnut desk that is cluttered with papers and books and pens and the bottles of ink that my mother still loves to use, and meets her halfway across the room. She tilts her head back and looks up at him.

"Tamsin just . . . stopped me from using my Talent."

My father gets this expression on his face that means he's probably wishing that he had something of my mother's gift and could transport himself back to his gardens instantly. "She needs to know," he rumbles at last, speaking directly to my mother. "Althea, whatever she was doing, didn't feel the need to enlighten us, and now I say tell her."

The mention of my grandmother's first name stops me.

My mother presses her hands to her temple, kneads for a minute, then wanders over to a small pink armchair by the fire and sinks into it. Finally, and without looking at me, she says, "Tamsin, you do have a Talent. More than one, it seems."

I lean against the wall because it feels as though my legs have just turned into water.

"No one can use their Talent against you. It simply won't work. You can also stop anyone from using their own power even if they're not trying to use it against you."

"Like I stopped Rowena today. From compelling Gabriel."

"Yes. And from compelling James, too."

"So then . . . whatever's wrong with Rowena, I can stop it." And I can't keep the triumph from spreading through my voice.

But my mother is shaking her head. "That's different. You can stop something *while* it's happening to you or to someone else. And like I said, power won't ever work *against* you. That includes spells. But when it comes to someone else"—and here my mother shakes her head again—"you can't undo what's already been done."

"How?" I breathe. "How do you know this about me already? *When I never even knew this stuff about myself!*"

"When you were four or maybe five," my mother begins, "I found you in the stillroom. Somehow you had climbed up the shelves and found a whole basket of strawberry leaves that I was drying, and then you found your way into the strawberry juice that I was brewing."

I have no memory of this whatsoever.

"It wasn't just strawberry juice, though. It was a very powerful sleeping spell. Designed to knock a grown man out for days. Which is what Cathy Monroe had paid for."

"Who's Cathy Monroe?"

My mother waves her hand. "She used to live on Hancock Street with her husband. Her extremely violent husband. She wanted a three-day head start when she left him."

"Which you made for her."

My mother nods. "Which you drank."

"And?"

"And nothing. You stayed awake. I made another batch and Cathy Monroe had her three-day head start."

"Did you see me drink it?"

My mother permits herself a small smile. "No. Not the first batch. The second and the third and the fourth, yes. Your father drank the second batch with you and slept through the third and the fourth."

I gaze at my father, who is now adjusting the logs in the fireplace with a poker.

"Okay, but how did you know that I could also—"

"Your grandmother has never been able to read your mind."

"Never?" I think back on all the times I prepared empty-headed thoughts in case she was attempting anything. "What about the time when Jerom broke his ankle? I felt her do it then."

"You felt her *try*," my mother corrects me. "Did you also feel dizzy right after that?"

I think back to the day I flew on my cousin's back and recall the sweeping head rush that came over me after I fell. I had always assumed it was a late reflex to the shock of plummeting through the air or from landing so hard. I nod.

"When we first start to use our Talents, it often takes us by surprise. Some of us get dizzy; others get tremendous headaches."

"So glad I'm suddenly part of the 'we' and 'us' club now," I say.

"The more you use your Talent, the more that effect lessens and finally disappears," my mother says, ignoring my comment. She presses her fingers into her forehead so hard that it looks as if she's trying to rub holes in her skin. "There's more," my mother adds, as if wondering how much to reveal. "Your grandmother thinks you can mimic other people's Talents."

"*What?*"

"If someone uses their Talent against you, as in to harm you, it won't work. But if they continue to do it, you can acquire it."

"How does she know this?"

My mother shakes her head. "That I don't know. She said she saw it, that she saw you do it."

I stare at my mother. "When? I can't have . . . I never did that." I touch my locket necklace, twisting the chain in my fingers. "Why . . . why did you keep it secret from me all these years? Why did you let me think I was . . . this big fat disappointment to you all? And why did Rowena get to know and not me?"

"Rowena will succeed your grandmother one day and needs to know certain things," my mother answers.

But I'm hardly listening, because that same tingling wave passes over me, like a chill across my neck, and I whirl and stare into the farthest corner of the room, where even the fire-lit shadows fail to reach. Unthinkingly, I reach out with my mind and *bam*, Uncle Morris pops into view. His eyes shift away from me and he shrugs a little.

"Morris!" my mother cries.

"Forgot my spectacles," he says jauntily as he strides across the room, making a show of searching on a small side table. "Nope, guess they're not here." His edges start to shimmer, but he remains very much in place. His eyebrows skip upward, but I don't relent.

"Tamsin," my father says, but I ignore the quiet rumble of warning in his voice.

"If you want to leave, then leave the normal way," I say, even though part of me flinches along with Uncle Morris. It's not his fault. He gives his goatee a little tug and then, moving faster than I've seen him move in a long time, he hurries toward the door. Pausing, he looks at me, opens his mouth as if to say something, then seems to think better of it. Opening the door, he slips out, and I am left with the look in his eyes. Hurt and bewildered.

"Is this why you didn't tell me? You thought I'd be stopping people all the time from being . . . themselves."

"No," my mother says quietly. "No, we didn't tell you because your grandmother asked us not to. Because she said that although she didn't exactly know why, one day you would need what we could give you."

"And what is that?"

"She . . . she never could say. All she knew was that one day you would need to make a choice and that to raise you the way we did would help you when the time came."

"Who else?" I demand. "Who else knows about me?"

"No one. Just your grandmother, your father, and I."
My mother tucks a piece of hair behind her ear. "And, of
course, Rowena."

"Rowena," I echo. Of course. *Perfect* Rowena, who
will take over the family one day. Even though I've always
known this, I still can't stop this bitter spill of thoughts. In
one small corner of my mind, all day I had been harboring
this crazy, silly hope that now that I did really have a power,
maybe I would be the damn beacon that my grandmother
had foretold—whatever that meant. That for once Rowena wouldn't have the lock on being so Talented, so special.
That maybe I would be the one to guide my family in . . .
I shake my head to scatter those thoughts. "I can't believe
you went along with this," I accuse my mother now.

A low growl of thunder rattles past the windowpanes,
and my father's expression, usually so mild and benign,
much like a warm spring rain, has now shifted into something sharper.

"If that's you doing that, then stop," I snap at him. "Or
I'll stop it for you."

Both of my parents stare at me as if I'm a changeling,
but I'm past caring.

My father opens his mouth, but I rush in. "Who is this
person? Alistair Callum?"

My mother sighs. "Long ago," she begins, overriding
whatever my father was going to say, "long ago there was
a war."

Somehow I have a feeling I'm not about to hear a lecture on the American Revolution.

"A struggle, really, between our family and another much more powerful family. This other family believed in things that . . . our family did not." She pauses as if contemplating those things, then continues hurriedly. "We captured their power and managed to isolate it into one object—it's not clear exactly how," she says, obviously anticipating my next question. "Our history tells us that four members of our family acted together to work a powerful spell and that they made a great sacrifice to do this."

She stops, clasps her hands, and recites, "One stood for North, and one stood for South; one stood for East, and one stood for West. North summoned Air, and South carried Water; East called Fire, and West bore Earth. And all were bound together."

I stare at her. "Um . . . that tells me nothing," I say at last and am rewarded with a reproving frown from my mother before she continues.

"Anyway, that's what we call the Domani—where all this other family's power remains. Anyone who was and is linked to this family through their bloodlines was and is affected by this spell. And of course we hid the Domani very carefully."

"Why didn't you just destroy it?"

My father clears his throat. "Don't you go to school?"

This seems like a particularly odd question to ask right

now. But he continues. "Science class?" Now this is beginning to make more sense. My father loves science. Einstein, Newton, Mendel—they're all his heroes. Whenever possible, he interjects science into the conversation. Never mind if no one's in the mood for it. "Remember the rule that matter can neither be created nor destroyed? Well, that applies here."

"Just changed," my mother adds softly.

"Can it change back?"

My mother takes a breath. "You mean, can they recapture it and reawaken it?"

I nod and the fire pops and hisses just as she answers, "Yes," so the word is lost in the shadowy recesses of the room. "We think it already has reawakened. Somehow."

That *somehow* goes ringing through me like a cold clanging bell. And then I hear the man in the frock coat's words again.

You really don't know what you've done, do you?

SIXTEEN

"THE CLOCK. The clock that he wanted me to find. That was the Domani, wasn't it?"

My mother puts her hand on my father's arm as he stares at me and explains urgently, "Tamsin's met him before. He came into the store over the summer and asked her to help him. He's a professor. Or so he claims," she finishes.

"At your school?" my father says, startled.

"No, Rowena's school," I say sarcastically. Then I bite my lip. "Sorry. At NYU, actually."

"But I don't . . . why did he ask *you* for help?" my father asks.

"Thanks," I say.

"Tamsin," my father says sharply. "That is not at all what I meant. What I meant was, why would he come into the bookstore if he knows anything about this family at all and expect you to help him?"

"What you don't know is that there's a spell of protection cast over this family. It doesn't extend very far," my mother adds weakly. "Not far beyond the borders of this town." I think on this for a second. That explains my mother's deep dislike of anywhere that's not Hedgerow. "And of course, the spell wouldn't work on you anyway. Which is why he was able to approach you in the bookstore."

I scrunch my toes together. "I pretended to be Rowena."

"You *what?*" my mother and father say at the same time, both of them staring at me.

"He thought I was Rowena and I . . . just went along with it. Later he found out that I wasn't." I decide not to mention how *much* later.

"How did you find it for him?" my mother asks. "The clock? How?"

"I saw it. In a painting. At Uncle Chester and Aunt Rennie's house. And then I . . . went there and got it."

"You can *Travel?*" my mother gasps.

The fire bites into a log with a particularly loud snap.

"What's that?" I ask blankly.

"Nobody's been able to Travel in this family for generations. Not to mention that it's not allowed," my mother says, even though this doesn't answer my question at all.

I shrug. I'm not about to give up Gabriel. "How would I know that? It's not like anyone tells me anything around here." Thunder snarls again and I stare at my father before adding, "I mean, maybe if you explained what Traveling is . . ."

"Traveling," my father begins in a ponderous voice, "is an old Talent that seems to have been lost over the years. No one has been Gifted with it for generations." Then he swivels his shaggy head and stares at me. "No one that we know of."

I try not to squirm. "And it's bad?"

My mother sighs. "Let's just say it's not good. Time is—"

"Delicate," my father supplies, and she nods.

"Yes. To put it mildly. Time is fragile, really. If you touch even one thing, disturb the past, then it could have consequences for the future that are—"

"Bleak." My father seems to reconsider and adds, "Disastrous."

"Oh," I say in a small voice.

"When did this happen?" my mother finally asks. "Before Rowena . . . got sick?"

I nod and this minor movement seems to confirm my mother's worst fears, because her hands fly to her face.

"What's going on?" I plead into the silence.

"We think some of the power of the Domani escaped when you Traveled back to it. Did you . . . did you touch it at all?"

My father begins to pace by the windows, his arms swinging loosely, his hands twitching a little, as if he wants nothing more than to pull up this situation by its roots. "Of course she touched it. She's the only one who could have. Was there someone guarding it? A man or a woman?"

"A man." I decide to omit the part about him throwing fireballs at me. "Who was he?"

"The Keeper," my mother says. "The Domani changes every so often, as does its Keeper. No one knows who the Keeper is. It's a way of protecting the Domani."

"He said that! The man in the coat. He was the Keeper. He said the power had passed," I say excitedly.

My father is nodding as if this now confirms his greatest hypothesis. "It must have. Fortunately, whatever you gave this . . . professor wasn't the Domani any longer."

"So then it's okay?" I ask hopefully, even though I know it can't possibly be. Not with both of my parents looking as ashen as they do.

"Just the fact that you touched it means some of its power escaped. Enough to—"

"Enough to give Alistair what he needed to get Rowena," I finish numbly. Somehow, thankfully, there is a chair near enough for me to sink into, because I don't know if my legs can hold out much longer. *Rowena*, I think, and my mind rolls back to the night when Alistair stepped into the cab after her and they drove off. That was the last time my sister was . . . my sister.

My mother rises slowly, walks over to the desk, and opens a heavy brown leather book lying on the green blotter. "Have you ever seen this book before?"

I feel as if I'm moving through dense, brackish water as I get to my feet and walk over to stand beside her. With one finger I trace the worked leather scrolls and leaves that cover the spine. My mother seems to be holding her breath. I shake my head.

"This book is very valuable. It contains the history of our family and also a glimpse of the future as it might happen."

The heat from the fireplace begins to flicker across my ankles and bare feet like some obscure kind of warning: *turn back, turn back*. I hesitate. For so long I have told myself that I don't want anything to do with my family's Talents and all its complications that I seem to have almost convinced myself. Another wavering second and then I step closer, stare down at the page.

Lines and lines of dense dark writing cover what looks like very old vellum. But every time I try to read anything, the words skitter away from me. Without thinking I lower my fingers to the page as if to pin the words in place. But they all slide into the spine of the book like water seeping through a crack.

My mother flicks the pages until she comes to a blank one. In a trembling voice she asks, "Can you see anything? Anything at all?"

The page remains a clean sweep of empty space. "There's nothing to see," I say.

My father sighs. "It was worth a try, Camilla."

My mother's eyes look suspiciously wet and a second later she dabs them against her sleeve.

"I thought you said . . . I was immune to spells."

"There isn't a spell on this. Well, yes," my mother corrects herself. "There is a simple locking spell on the book itself to keep prying eyes away. It's something of a rite of passage for everyone to try to unlock this book and—" Her voice falters as she encounters my stony look.

"I wouldn't know," I say dryly.

"This is a Talent. To read the future."

"Like the way you read the future in all those women's teacups and all those—"

"Not their future. Nothing like that. Our future. The future of this family. I thought maybe since you have other Talents like Traveling . . ." Here she gives me a hard, searching look, but I refuse to let my face shift one iota, not one particle, until she looks back at the book. "I thought you might have this one."

"So who can read this?" But I know the answer.

"Your grandmother," my mother confirms. "It takes a tremendous amount of Talent to be able to decipher the future. And then it's often frustrating, as the future can change like *that*." My mother snaps her fingers together, making me jump a little. "Still, whoever can read this book is the one who guides our family. It's always been this way."

"So, whatever Grandmother reads in here influences her decisions?" When my mother nods, I can't help adding, "So she read something that made her want to lie to me all these years?" I stare at the book again until the page billows into a white shimmer.

"Your grandmother doesn't lie," my mother says severely.

"Spare me, Mom," I mutter. "You all lied. It doesn't matter if it wasn't exactly in words." There is a small, nasty swell of silence among us all and then a clap of thunder so loud that it makes both my mother and me jump.

My father paces toward me. "You. Lied. Too," he exclaims, his finger pointing straight at me. "If you had told us what you did for this man sooner, then maybe your sister wouldn't be—"

"I did!" I shout. The flames in the fireplace flare silently in response and I stare at them, distracted for a moment by the pulsing feeling in my palms. Then I force myself to continue. "I told Grandmother that he came into the store one night and asked me to find something and that I did. I did find it."

Both of my parents are staring at me, but it's my mother who recovers first. "You told her?" my mother whispers. "When?" Then her face seems to lengthen and grow pale in the shadows of the room. "When you called home."

I nod. "I didn't tell her everything. But I told her that I found something that I didn't think I should have found." I pause, thinking back on my grandmother's words. "And she told me that since I started this, I had to see it through.

That she didn't see any other way for me. Or for any of us."
I shake my head. "I didn't know what she meant. I thought
it was just . . ." I shrug and let my words trail off.

"But if she knew who he was, why would she tell
Tamsin to 'see it through'?" my mother asks. Her question
doesn't seem to be aimed at me, so I look at my father, but
he seems equally lost.

Finally, he says, "Because Althea must have foreseen
something worse if Tamsin didn't help him."

"Who is he?" I whisper.

"He's one of the Knights. That was their family name.
The Knights," my father says heavily because my mother
seems unable to answer. She's staring down at the book,
squinting occasionally as if something lingers just outside
the boundaries of her vision.

"Oh." Knights conjure images of shining armor and
bright shields embossed with gold and green. Jousting
and—

"They were never content with what we had."

"'We'?"

"Oh, yes. At one point there was no division between
us. Between any of us. We were all Talented. We came to
this new country seeking a place to start over. We had been
persecuted in other countries. You learned about witch
hunts in school?" my father continues, his hands clasped
behind his back. He really should have been a professor in
a college somewhere.

I nod. "That was us?"

"Well, some of us. History doesn't always have it right. But yes, we were persecuted until we came here."

"But there were witch hunts here, too. I remember we studied the Salem witch trials and . . ." And then Leah Connelly and Melanie Nightingale cornered me in the girls' bathroom during recess, turned on the taps, and tried to force my head under the sink to see if I wouldn't drown like a true witch. They were planning to do the prick test, too, until I split Melanie's lip open.

"Yes," my mother agrees, lifting her head finally and rubbing at her eyes. "But by then we had learned how to mingle, how to disappear into society."

"Really?" I ask. "Um . . . did we forget how to do that now? Because we're not so great at mingling and disappearing."

My father makes another rumbling sound, but this time it sounds more like laughter. My mother shrugs. "Oh, that. Times are different now. Anyway, back then some of us chose to use our Talents to heal and others chose to use our Talents to farm. Peaceful choices. Except for the Knights. Over time they began what they had started doing back in the old countries. Always they had to explore the deeper and darker realms of their Talents, pushing them past their limits until their Talents turned. Warped." My mother's voice falls away on the last word and she presses her hands to her eyes again for an instant. "Some of their . . .

explorations involved other humans. They found ways to extend their natural life span by draining away the life force in humans."

"How?" I whispered, but my mother shakes her head.

"We've never known. They used spells, the origins of which we never could understand. Spells that involved their victims' blood."

All at once Rowena's black umbrella blooms in my mind and I see again the long red scratch on her hand. And Alistair dabbing away her blood with his handkerchief.

My father clears his throat and says, "At first they were content with using Talentless people. But then once they had mastered that, they began to move on to Talented people. Now instead of extending only their life span, they extend their powers as well." He begins pacing again, pauses. "You studied parasites in school?"

A brief lesson on whales and their various barnacle guests comes swimming back to me. "Um . . . yeah?"

"Well," my father says, leaping back into lecture mode, "think of a parasite and how it leeches everything away from its host. Sometimes without the host knowing."

"Or knowing after it's too late," my mother interjects.

"Rowena," I whisper. "Her wrist," I blurt out. "He's . . . taking her blood?"

"Yes. Being part of the Knight family, this man would know the spell. He may not have been able to use it all these years, but he would have been ready and waiting for just the right time, when enough of the power of the Domani had escaped." My mother turns the pages of the book again with shaking hands, as if hoping the answers will suddenly appear. "He's in her blood now, like a fever. Or like an addiction. One that's very, very hard to break."

"Can't you just . . . kill him?"

My father regards me gravely. "We've thought of that. I would take another person's life gladly in this case." My mother puts her hand on his arm.

"Even though life is sacred, as you know," she says. "But there's another aspect to this spell. There's a mirror effect. Whatever you do to the spell caster reflects back onto the enspelled," my mother whispers as if quoting a text by heart. "Three times over."

"What if I . . . Traveled, then?" I whisper. "Back to the time when . . . when . . ."

"No," my mother says sharply. She comes around the desk and seizes my upper arms. "You cannot Travel again. Do you understand?"

"No," I say, trying to shift out of her grasp, but her fingers dig into me too deeply.

"There have been horrible consequences already from your Traveling—don't you see?" my mother hisses.

"But why can't I just go back and fix it?"

My mother gives me a little shake. Enough to make my back teeth rattle. "Ow, Mom—"

"You cannot just 'fix it' as you so blithely call it, because

Time, as we have been telling you, is extremely delicate. Once you pull one thread, you warp something else in the pattern."

"Okay, but—"

"Promise me you will not do this. *Promise*." My mother's eyes are narrowed points of light boring into my skull.

"Okay, okay." Finally, she releases me and takes a step back and the blood starts returning to my arms.

"Tell her," my father says softly behind her, and the color seems to drain out of her face. "Tell her why."

"Rowena can . . . can read the future, too."

"Of course she can," I mutter. And really I'm not surprised. Rowena is the most powerful one in our family, next to my grandmother. I've always known this, accepted this. Until today.

But abruptly I tune back in to my mother, who is adding, "And she's . . . she's read some of it. Before I caught her. Before I stopped her."

I feel myself grow very still. "And she told you what she read?" I whisper.

"She read . . . she read where you Traveled and you didn't come back. You couldn't, for some reason."

I press my lips flat as if that can contain the trembling. It doesn't work.

"Please, Tamsin," my mother says, and then her voice cracks. "I don't need to lose you and your sister both."

SEVENTEEN

I FIND GABRIEL in the downstairs parlor, playing cards with my cousins Jerom and Silda and Aunt Beatrice, of all people. I let myself in quietly and shrug at Gabriel in response to his raised eyebrows. His hands flick cards around the small walnut table, and they are either exchanged by the players or folded away in what seems to be a discard pile. Occasionally, Gabriel allots a few more from the deck that rests in the center of the table next to three beer bottles and a tiny crystal glass of what looks like sherry. No doubt who that one belongs to. In one swift movement Aunt Beatrice knocks back the contents, then bangs the glass staccato style on the table until, rolling her eyes, Silda gets up to retrieve a decanter from the sideboard. "Here, Aunt Beatrice," she says and dribbles a little more amber liquid into the glass. "But that's it, now. No more."

Somehow, I think she's said this before.

Apparently, Aunt Beatrice doesn't seem too fazed,

either, because she salutes Silda with "Mud in your eye," cackles, and slaps her cards face-up on the table.

Everyone groans as Beatrice flings out her hands and scoops up a pair of earrings, a pair of cuff links, and several crumpled bills.

"No poker chips," Gabriel explains as I walk over to stand behind him. I pick up what I hope is his beer and take a healthy slug. "Everything okay?"

I shrug. "Not really. But keep playing," I urge in a whisper as Jerom deals out the cards this time, his fingers an impossible blur. Gabriel sinks back in his seat.

"Want to play, Tam?" Silda asks, already inching her chair over to make room.

I shake my head and remain standing. "No, thanks." Then with a grin I add, "But you should probably know that Jerom just made a couple of cards disappear. My guess is that they're aces."

"What?" my cousin says, his hands frozen over the table in the act of dealing a card to Aunt Beatrice. "That's such a lie," he insists, his blue eyes widening dramatically.

Silda looks at him, her mouth pursed in a small button shape. "Did you cheat *again*, Jerom?"

"I've never cheated," her brother persists, rolling his eyes up to the ceiling as if seeking verification there.

"Oh, yeah? Well, what's this?" Gabriel says, reaching down around Jerom's foot and pulling up a thin rectangle of a card. The queen of spades seems to wink at us all.

"Jerom!" Silda cries.

"Oh, dear!" Aunt Beatrice says. She peers at the card closely. "Is that the one . . . no, that's not what I lost." She sighs, slurps down most of her sherry, then begins waving her glass in a swooping arc above everyone's head. Drops of liquid rain down across the table and cards, and everyone starts speaking at once.

"Aunt Beatrice!"

"Someone deal. Someone besides Jerom!"

"Well, isn't it amazingly convenient how Gabriel's been *finding* all of his cards just in the nick of time!"

"Hey! I just got lucky."

I reach over Gabriel's shoulder, snap up the pack, and riffle through it. "Who changed all these to aces?" I ask as I flip over four aces and then five more staggered throughout the deck. "I'm no poker champion, but I'm pretty sure there are only four aces in each deck."

"Silda," Jerom says, his voice heavy with disapproval. "You? I can't believe you," he finishes, shaking his head.

"Oh, shut up, Jerom. Like you weren't cheating the whole time."

"I could use another drop or two," Aunt Beatrice says, coughing delicately. "And then perhaps Tamsin could deal. She can stop all this nonsense anyway. Don't you know what she can do?"

A small freeze settles over the table.

"Is it true, Tam?" Silda asks finally, her voice hard to

read. She slides a look at me while spinning a beer cap between her fingers. For one instant it flashes into a diamond, then a sapphire, then a ruby, before she abruptly plunks it back onto the table as a thin disc of aluminum once more. "Is it true that you can stop us from . . . using our Talents?"

I open my mouth. Silda and I have always gotten along on a peripheral level. Maybe because she's Gwyneth's sister, so we naturally bonded over the fact that we were both cursed with perfect older sisters who could apparently do no wrong. Some of my fondest memories are of stealing Gwyneth's and Rowena's things—a pair of crystal earrings or high heels—and then watching Silda quickly change them to marbles or muddy sneakers while our sisters howled the house down and called us thieves. But then when my own Talent didn't appear, Silda and I drifted far enough apart for me to avoid her like everyone else at family gatherings.

Now I take a breath and wait until she looks at me again, then nod. "Apparently." I glance around the silent table. Aunt Beatrice meets my gaze, and I am startled by the sudden droop of her mouth, the tears filming over her dark eyes. I gulp and say swiftly, "So . . . no more cheating, everyone. Because I'll know. That goes for you, too, Gabriel." I knock the deck of cards lightly on the back of his head and he smiles at me before taking the deck out of my hands. But he's the only one who does. I notice that Jerom and Silda suddenly hunch their chairs closer together.

"Right," Jerom says. "What about gin, then? Thirteen cards? I'm sick of poker." His words are bright and cheerful, but I can't help feeling this awful sense of dread sinking through me. *What did you expect, anyway?* Gabriel's hand closes around my wrist in a warm squeeze, but I shake myself free as unobtrusively as possible.

"Oh, I love gin," Aunt Beatrice cackles, her cheery mood seemingly restored by the word association of fresh alcohol. "And sherry," she says pointedly to Silda, who ignores her. Grateful for the distraction, I pull the glass from Aunt Beatrice's unresisting fingers and cross to the sideboard, tipping out a small amount of sherry. Tears are pricking along the edges of my eyelids and I take a deep breath.

As I give the glass back to Aunt Beatrice, she looks up, her eyes bright and beady on me. "I know you, dear," she says, her hand frozen in midmotion. "You can stop people, can't you? You stopped me," she whispers. She takes the glass from me, downs the contents in a single swallow, and presses her tongue to the corner of her mouth. "And then I lost it. I lost everything." Her voice sharpens into its usual keen. "I lost it and I wasn't able to find it again. Ever."

"Aunt Beatrice," Silda says, making a motion for me to take away the old woman's glass, "I really think you've had enough."

"No!" I say sharply. "Have some more." I dash over to the sideboard, snatch the bottle, and slosh a full amount into Aunt Beatrice's glass.

"Tamsin!" Silda says, her voice filled with shock.

"Seriously, Tam. It's not pretty when she gets drunk," Jerom mutters.

But Aunt Beatrice swallows without evident pleasure, her eyes mournful again.

"When was this, Aunt Beatrice?" I ask, leaning down so that she has to look at me. Her mouth trembles, seems to slacken for a few seconds, and then she sits up straight, her head nearly smashing into my face in the process.

"In 1939. Oh, the parties we used to have." She claps her hands together once, then again, as if delighted with the tinkle of her crystal bracelets.

"Here?" I exchange a look with Gabriel, who has put down the cards and is listening intently.

"No. Not here, of course. I didn't come here until later. Much later. After my Roberto died." Her mouth softens.

"At Uncle Chester and Aunt Rennie's," I say slowly.

"*My* house," Aunt Beatrice says grandly. "It was *my* house then. Still is," she adds with a quaver in her voice, and I'm afraid the melancholy will take hold. But then she aims a radiant smile at us and says, "New York City. It was beautiful. And I was so young then. So strong," she whispers. She holds up her thin bird-claw hands and looks at them. "One move and I could freeze you. But not you, dear. I couldn't. You, yes," she says, swinging her head toward Gabriel.

Gabriel's eyebrows slant up and he points one finger toward his chest as if to ask, *Me?*

"Well, that's just silly, Aunt Beatrice," Silda snaps, then says to me, "She's wandering. She thinks you're someone else."

"I *know* her," Aunt Beatrice insists. "I know who she is. Why did you do it, Tamsin?" she asks me softly, and her voice is filled with such sadness that I swallow, shake my head.

"I'm sorry," I whisper, and Silda juts back her chair and stands.

"That's enough, now," she says briskly, but her hands are gentle as she pulls Aunt Beatrice from the chair. "Let's get you to bed. Jerom? A little help here?"

Jerom throws down his hand, giving Gabriel a look. "Next time you're not going to be so '*lucky,*'" he says before moving around to Aunt Beatrice's other side.

"Whatever," Gabriel replies cheerfully as he begins to stack the cards again into one neat pile.

"I'm fine," Aunt Beatrice says, batting at Jerom, but he ducks, lifts her into his arms, and moves toward the door with Silda trailing them.

For an instant, Silda looks back at me. "Tam, don't take anything that she says to heart, okay? She's . . . well, you know how she is." And with a shrug she closes the door behind them.

It's only then that I notice just how cold the room is. The earlier rain seems to have seeped into the walls and left a damp, musty air behind. Shivering, I move toward the fireplace, stack wood from the basket onto the hearth, and sprinkle a fair amount of kindling on it before lighting a long taper match. The flame smokes and hisses before it licks the wood and begins to grow. I sit back on my heels as a chair scrapes behind me and then Gabriel hunkers down next to me. He is still holding the deck of cards, face-up this time, and he automatically shuffles it over and over. The snap of the cards is punctuated by the slide of logs as they settle deeper into the fire. Half-light plays across Gabriel's hands, softening the flat features of the jack of spades, the king of hearts, the queen of diamonds, as they spin in an endless jumble before my eyes.

"Did you know?" I whisper at last. "That I had a Talent?"

"How could I know?" Gabriel says. "You didn't even know yourself until today."

"My parents knew," I say darkly. "And my grand-mother. And Rowena! This whole time. But somehow they —oh, and they told me that I could pick up other people's Talents. If they try to use them against me enough times."

"How many times?"

"I don't know."

"Tam," Gabriel says slowly. "That man in 1899. Didn't he try to throw fire at you three times? Do you think . . ."

We stare at each other. I take in a ragged breath, examine my palms. They still look ordinary to me. Slowly I raise one hand and aim it at the fireplace. A gust of blood flares brightly under my skin and then a sphere of flame shoots from my palm, exploding with a soft *whoosh* into the fireplace. The actual fire that I built a few minutes ago blazes in response before dying back down to its feeble light.

Trembling, I gaze at my palm. The skin is unbroken and cool to the touch, but my whole hand is ringing like a bell that's been struck.

"That's why they told us . . ." Gabriel says softly, his voice trailing away.

I whip my head toward him. "Told you? Told you *what?*"

He meets my eyes directly and this comforts me. But his next words turn me cold. "Right before I left, I remember your mother gathering a bunch of us—kids, mostly—and telling us that you were . . . probably not going to have a Talent at all. So we should be extra careful when using our Talent in front of you. And that we were never, ever supposed to use a Talent *against* you. I didn't think anyone would pay attention to that. But then your grandmother came in and gave us all that look. You know that look? And it was as if Rowena took it as her personal mission to make sure we all followed this law."

"I bet." Fire gushes from my palm again, slams into the fireplace. A log cracks in the sudden onslaught of heat and a shower of sparks flies up the chimney. I want to burn something else, but I hold back. "But why would they do that?"

Gabriel flips through the deck of cards. "Maybe they were afraid you'd get to be . . . too powerful."

I blink, blink again, but not fast enough to stop the tears leaking from my eyes.

"Hey," Gabriel says softly. He tucks long fingers under my chin and turns my face until we are inches apart.

"Why didn't you tell me this before?"

"I—"

I dab at my cheeks with my fingers. "I mean, wouldn't you have wanted to know? If it were you?"

"Yeah." He looks down at the pack of cards, then sets it aside. "I probably would have told you. If I'd stayed. Or if we'd stayed friends earlier. I'm sorry, Tam," he whispers. He reaches out and skims one finger over my cheekbone, brushing away my tears. His hand slips down to trace the outline of my mouth and he leans forward. I close my eyes.

"What the hell?" Gabriel exclaims.

Opening my eyes, I see him leap up. I turn. A flutter of white flies past the window, then bumps up against the glass with a gentle *thunk*. I stumble to my feet, yank the sash up, and lean out. The wind is gusting fiercely now and something long and knotted slaps at my face. I draw back, then look up. A twisted rope of sheets hangs from the upstairs window.

"Shit," I say, and Gabriel elbows me out of the way, catching at the rope. We turn to each other. "Rowena," I cry.

"My mom," he says at the same time. We turn and peer out the window again. The crescent moon sheds enough light for us to see that the long driveway is empty except for potholes and gravel and gloomy shadows.

She's gone.

EIGHTEEN

"NO," MY MOTHER says for the third time, her face very white under the glare of the kitchen lights. "You will not go near this man. Ever again."

"But he wants—"

"I don't care what he wants, Tamsin. He is extremely dangerous. Extremely dangerous," my mother repeats, as if making sure I really hear her. She knots a dishtowel until the cheerful print of roses and tulips mangles under her hands, then wrings it out, hanging it on a wooden peg by the stove. "Your father and I will deal with him."

"What are you going to do?" I say.

"We will talk to him."

I snort. "Yeah, that's going to work."

"I'm so sorry, Camilla," Aunt Lydia says for the third time from her chair at the kitchen table. A mug of tea sits before her, but I don't think she's taken even one sip. Her eyes are red rimmed and swollen.

"It's not your fault," my mother replies automatically, also for the third time, her eyes skipping restlessly over the kitchen walls. "It couldn't be helped."

Apparently, Rowena woke up an hour ago, feigned sleep until Lydia's head was turned, and then began compelling her. She persuaded Lydia to keep silent and still, except for when she required her help to knot the sheets.

"I couldn't even do anything but watch as I tied the sheets together. And all the time I just thought it was the most natural thing in the world to do what she said. Whatever she said. I would have jumped out the window myself if she had asked me to." Lydia holds out her hands in front of her as if silently asking them how they could have betrayed her. "I didn't know she could be so . . . powerful." Her voice breaks a little, and Gabriel, who is sitting next to his mother, nudges the cup of tea closer to her.

"She is," my mother says grimly.

"Which is why you need my help!" I insist, pushing back my chair. Its legs jerk across the tile floor, and my mother closes her eyes briefly.

"No."

"Seriously, Aunt Camilla," Gabriel says. "Tamsin can really stop—"

"I don't want her near this man!"

"What happens?" I ask finally. "What are you afraid of? What did Ro tell you she read?"

My mother shakes her head. "Not enough that's clear. But all I know is that somehow with that . . . creature . . . you—" And then she makes this strangled kind of noise. After a minute I realize my mother is trying not to cry.

"I die?" I say blankly, and Gabriel lifts his head, staring first at my mother and then at me.

She makes a stiff motion with her head that could be a nod.

"Well," I say, because I'm not sure exactly what I'm supposed to do when just told such good news. "But you said nothing's written in stone, right?"

"Yes," my mother says on an exhale. "Yes, that's right. The future's written in water," she says firmly, as if reminding herself of an important truth. "Which is why you are staying far, far, *far* away from that man. Is that clear?"

Uncle Morris materializes in the kitchen and we all jump, except for my mother, who seems to have regained her composure. She stands swiftly and tucks her hair behind her ears, a useless motion as it just springs out again in all its corkscrew-curled glory.

"Wait here for me," she says. "Whatever happens . . . if we don't come back . . . I want you to burn the book."

"What?"

"If we don't come—"

"You're coming back!"

"Burn it if we don't. I'd rather it burn than fall into the wrong hands."

"Has Rowena read it?"

"Not since . . . not since that time that I stopped her. So I don't know how much she knows. There are some things she doesn't know. There's that at least," my mother adds, almost speaking to herself. "But she will have told him about you. He knows . . . what you can do." Then she presses her lips to my forehead and blurs out of existence. Running to the window, I am just in time to see her materialize in the driveway next to our brown station wagon that rarely leaves the barn.

My father is already at the wheel and he lifts a hand through the driver's side window, waving in the general direction of the house as if he knows we're all watching from various viewpoints. I press my hand against the window, my fingertips coming to rest on the fine crack in the glass that's been there for years. I swallow the urge to call out after them, knowing they won't listen anyway. My father eases the car into a three-point turn, the tires dipping into potholes here and there, and then the station wagon chugs away, its taillights winking red in the dark.

"Now what?" Gabriel says, sprawled on my bed, watching me smoke another cigarette down to the filter. I flick the butt through a hole in the screen, imagining too late my father's horrified face if he could see it land on his precious flower beds below. Then I wonder if I'll ever see him again, horrified or not.

This is the kind of thinking that has led me to chain-smoke for the past half hour.

"I don't know," I say, beginning to pace. Pacing and chain smoking together is making me dizzy so I'm trying to do each in turn. "How long have they been gone?"

"Since you last asked me? Two hours and now six minutes." He takes a swig from the glass of water he's holding and the cords in his throat flicker briefly. "So let me get this straight." Gabriel has been saying that a lot tonight since I told him everything that I learned in the library with my parents. "Supposedly, we messed everything up by Traveling back to 1899 to get the clock."

"Maybe not everything, but enough. I guess enough of the power leaked out to allow Alistair to use whatever he needed to on Rowena." A small trickle of flame twirls from my fingers. The edge of my bed sheet begins to burn.

"Shit," Gabriel says and dumps the remainder of his water onto the flame. With a hiss the water extinguishes the fire, but the smell of scorched fabric fills the air. "Pyro, can you stop doing that? *Please?*"

"Sorry. But it's not like I've had nine years to learn how to control this."

Gabriel doesn't comment on that. Instead, he sets the empty glass back onto my dresser, then asks, "So why can't we just Travel back to the time right before that and not go for the clock?"

I shake my head but keep pacing. "Because from the very little that they explained to me about Traveling, every time we do it, we unravel some sort of thread in the whole . . . freaking pattern. Whatever that means. And plus we can't go back to a time when we could encounter ourselves again. It seems it's not possible to return to a time where we already exist—the theory being that matter is neither created nor destroyed but only changed. So we can't add to us by having a double us. Apparently, that would be very, very bad."

"I don't know," Gabriel says contemplatively. "Two of you? Could be kind of kinky."

"Please!" I stop my pacing, glare at him. "Is that all you can think about at a time like this?"

Gabriel rolls up on one elbow and smiles at me. "I'm a guy. It's what I think about *all* the time. But uh . . . some thoughts I should just keep to myself, right?"

"Yes!"

I resume pacing and Gabriel resumes being silent, thinking whatever he's thinking until he says, "But what about Aunt Beatrice? I mean, clearly you Traveled then. *We* did, since she apparently knows me, too. Why did we do that?"

"I've been thinking about that," I say slowly. "Because she was a Keeper. She must have been, Gabriel." Abruptly, I sit down on the bed.

"And we tried to take the clock from her?"

"I don't think it's a clock anymore," I muse. "It changes every time the Keeper changes. That's what my parents told me. And no one gets to know the identity of the Keeper. That's what makes it safe. So we must have tried to take it from her."

Gabriel flexes his hand ruefully. "We tried that again? Why were we so stupid?"

"We must have thought it was a good idea at the time. I don't know what made us think that."

"Or what *will* make us think that," Gabriel says softly after a moment.

"Who knows. Maybe we won't now. According to my mother, the future is written in water."

"I doubt it," Gabriel interjects. "Not about the future being written in water. Everyone knows that."

"I didn't—"

"Tamsin . . . you're not that ignorant. I mean, you must have attended some rituals around here. Enough to know the corresponding elements."

I wave my hand as if to swat away his words. "Fine, but—"

"Anyway, I meant that I doubt that we're not going to still do it. Because she already remembers it."

"Ahh! This is making my head spin," I say, slumping against the headboard. I trace the carving on the bedpost knob that I did when I was ten. *Rowena sucks.* Gouged out in thin, defiant letters. Suddenly, I think I might start crying.

"Come on," Gabriel says, standing up and holding out his hand. "Let's go for a walk. You can smoke another cigarette in the fresh air at least."

I let him pull me to my feet.

And then my cell phone hums on my night table like an overgrown bee. I snatch it up and sigh. "It's only Agatha." I press the talk button, then hold the phone away from my head. Noise spills out, loud raucous voices and a heavy bass guitar. Gabriel flexes his hand again, begins moving his fingers in what I can only assume are air chords. Guys are so strange sometimes. "Hello? Agatha? I can barely hear you," I shout back at the tiny buzz in my ear.

"Tam? Is that better?"

"Yeah, a little." I roll my eyes at Gabriel, who sticks his hands into his pockets and begins examining the items scattered on my dresser.

"Tam, I'm at the Lion's Head Tavern. You know, the one on Mercer Street? The one we never go into?"

"Uh-huh. Let me guess—you met a guy?" Well, at least someone's night is going well. And if she called to tell me about it, then she's probably not experiencing any residual weirdness from our earlier conversation.

"No. It was so funny." Agatha's voice is looping in and out.

"Are you drunk?"

She giggles a little, her Agatha giggle—two high-pitched huffs and a gurgle. I have to smile just hearing it. "A tad. Can you tell?" Then she rushes on without waiting for my answer. "Anyway, I wasn't going to go out tonight at all and then it was so funny. Your sister called our room and I answered and she told me she was in the city and asked if I'd like to meet her for a drink."

All of a sudden it feels as though there's not enough air in the room.

"No!" I gasp, and Gabriel turns, giving me a *what's up* look.

"She's so *nice*, Tam. I know you guys don't always get along, but she's really, really sweet. I mean, at first I felt kind of weird and I was like, 'I've got all this studying to do,' but then she was, like, so sweet and she just, I guess she just—"

"Persuaded you?" I supply grimly.

"Yeah! Anyway, I just decided to go for a little bit and then we've been talking and—"

"What did you drink? What did you *drink*, Agatha?"

Agatha giggles again. "Beer. And your sister bought all the rounds. I drank, like, three beers and she wouldn't let me pay or anything. She went and got them every time, too. It was so sweet of her."

"Oh, Agatha." My voice breaks.

Gabriel crosses the room, says in a low voice, "What's happening?"

I shake my head, too numb. There is a burst of static on the line and then Agatha's voice returns. "Really sweet and—"

"Is Rowena there now?" I interrupt.

There's a pause in which I hear someone shout something unintelligible and then the music seems to grow even louder. "Um . . . no. She went to the bathroom, I think. I don't know. That was a while ago." Mild confusion enters her voice. "I cut my arm," she says on an entirely different tack.

"Is it bad? Maybe you should go to the hospital?"

"No, it's okay, s'okay," she says. "I needed to cut my arm—I remember now. Your sister—"

Agatha's voice saws in and out of my brain as she babbles on and on about how my sister helped her to cut her arm in the bathroom and how the blood had slipped through the fine slash in her skin into this little vial that Rowena just happened to have. I close my eyes, trying in vain to drive away the picture of earnest Agatha, red-faced and probably still giggling, leaning against my sister or against some scummed-over bathroom wall while Rowena extracted her blood drop by drop like plucking a chicken's feathers.

"Agatha," I blurt out, "you should go home right now. And lock the door, okay?"

But she doesn't seem to hear my last words. "Wait . . .

shit, I really am kind of drunk. She said to tell you that he's waiting for you. Who's 'he'? Your boyfriend?" she asks and giggles again.

"Go home, Ag, seriously. I'll be there soon, okay?"

"Okay, Tam. You're the best. And hey, maybe we can all have lunch tomorrow. You and me and Rowena."

"Yeah," I say brightly. "That'd be swell."

Luckily, Agatha is too far gone to register the sarcasm. She says something else and then the line goes dead.

"Let me guess," Gabriel says. "More bad news?"

NINETEEN

ONE LIGHT IS SHINING from a small window in Lerner Hall as Gabriel pulls the car to the curb, wedging it between a truck parked in a no-parking zone and a dumpster. "How are we planning on getting in, exactly?" Gabriel asks as a woman clothed in rags and plastic trash bags pushes an overloaded shopping cart past the passenger side of the car. One plastic bag swishes away down the street and the woman stops, staring after it forlornly as though she's watching one of her beloved children depart forever. Then she moves on slowly, shaking her head in time with the *squeak, squeak, squeak* of a broken cart wheel.

"We're not."

"A stakeout?" Gabriel says, moving his fingers restlessly across the steering wheel.

"No." I take a breath, turn a little in my seat to face him. "I'm going in. You've got to wait here."

"No. No way," he says, and his voice is so even and emphatic that I blink. I had been prepared for shouting.

"Please, Gabriel, it's the only—"

"No, Tam." He twists in the seat, his knee jutting into mine. "You heard your mother. I shouldn't have even brought us back here tonight, but . . . no . . . you're not facing him alone. What if you die?" The words are stark and plain and they do have this sort of heart-stopping effect, which I try my best to ignore.

"I'm not going to die."

"Oh, really? The last time I checked, despite all your other Talents, you can't read the future. Or was I misinformed?"

"Shut up. No, you weren't. But think about it. No, listen to me," I say, pressing my fingers over his open mouth. After a second he leans away from my hand but remains quiet. "He wants me alive. He wants me to find that . . . thing for him. The clock that's not the clock anymore. The Domani. He needs that, for some reason."

"So he can get his family's power back," Gabriel offers in a flat voice, as if he thinks I'm being idiotic. "Why you're going to help him, I'm not exactly sure—"

"I'm not going to *help* help him," I say, frustrated now because I don't understand why he's not immediately grasping my hastily thought-out plan that has more holes than a slice of Swiss cheese. I stare out the windshield. A small shadow, almost indiscernible from the dark cobblestones, scurries across the street and disappears into the sewer.

"Okay, so what *is* your plan, then?"

"I'm going in there and I'm going to talk to him."

"You're going to talk to him? That's it? That's the big plan?"

My hand goes to my locket and I press the tiny catch. It opens with a soft *snick*. I close it, open it, close it again. I'm a little too aware that I threw pretty much the same question at my mother earlier this evening just before she left. And that she hasn't come back yet as far as I know—

The sound of the car engine hacking to life smashes my reverie to pieces. "What are you doing?"

Gabriel flips on his blinker.

"Stop," I say, clamping my hand over his wrist.

"You can stop me from using my Talent. I'm pretty sure you can't stop me from driving your ass back home."

"Gabriel! Just hold on a minute, will you?"

He leaves the blinker on but otherwise allows the car to idle at the curb. A quiet ticking, too reminiscent of the sound of a clock, fills the interior of the car.

"He's . . . dangerous."

"All the more reason you're not going in there alone and—"

"He seems to be aiming at everyone in my life. First Rowena, now Agatha. I can't let you be the third casualty."

Gabriel snorts. "I'm pretty sure I can take him."

I punch his shoulder, probably harder than I should. "Would you not be such a guy about this? You can't 'take' him because he's not . . . normal, really. He's evil. I shouldn't have to explain this to you, of all people." I take a breath. "Please. I don't want him to know that you're . . . important to me. He can't know that."

The engine mutters and skips beneath us and I stare at the green blinker light flashing on the dashboard. And then without warning Gabriel turns to me, grips the back of my neck with one hand, and pulls me to him. He kisses me hard, briefly, on my mouth. "Ten minutes," he says, and his voice is husky. "You've got ten minutes and then I'm coming after you. And I'm walking you into the lobby at least."

Coming to a standstill before the huge darkened doors, I peer through the smudged glass. A security guard is slumped over the front desk, his head lolling on his folded arms. "She's in there, right?" I ask for the fifth time, and to his credit Gabriel doesn't point that out.

"She hasn't left," he says quietly.

As if his words conjure her up, Rowena comes skipping into sight. She is alone. I rap on the glass and she smiles, waves at me as if we're playing a game. She crosses the floor and leans over the security guard, her lips curving close to his ear. He turns his head in his sleep, and although his eyes never open, he fumbles at his belt, holds up a shining ring of keys, selects one, and hands it to her. My sister smiles again and says something else to him, at which point he buries his head in his arms and seems to pass out again.

She looms brightly toward us, unlocks the heavy doors, and swings them open.

"You made it," she says, as if she were the hostess of some spectacular party. "Alistair will be so pleased to see you. Not you, though," Rowena adds with a frown that is still somehow charming. "He said only her," she says cajolingly to Gabriel, flexing one finger at me.

"Stop it," I say briefly. "He's not coming in with me so don't waste your time."

"Well!" Rowena huffs in an entirely different voice. I lean closer and examine my sister. Despite her relatively good spirits, she looks even paler than before and the whites of her eyes have taken on a yellowish tinge. She's still wearing the black dress, only now it's sporting a long muddy streak down the right side and a ragged chunk of the hem is missing.

"You look like shit, Ro," I say matter-of-factly. "And that's saying a lot."

"I'm in love," she replies haughtily, her fingers flying to her cheeks.

"What about James?" If he's lucky, he's still comatose to this nightmare, tucked away somewhere in one of the house's many bedrooms. I look around the foyer of Lerner Hall. One fluorescent light buzzes and drones above the sleeping security guard's head. Other than that the building is dark and quiet.

Rowena hesitates, her lips parted. Then something

within her seems to stiffen and she pirouettes, moving away in bobbing steps like a balloon being pulled on a string. "He's waiting," is all she says. I put my hand on Gabriel's arm—he looks distinctly unhappy.

"Ten minutes," he reminds me pointedly, and I nod.

"Ten minutes," I repeat, and for a second I wonder if he's going to kiss me again. Or if I should kiss him. But he doesn't and I don't. Instead, I follow my sister, the back of my neck prickling.

It seems like years since I walked down this hallway during that first week of school, so determined to show my family that I wasn't useless after all, so hopeful that I would find whatever Alistair wanted. Or what he said he wanted.

All too soon we approach his office. My sister raises one white knot of a fist and gives the door more of a caress than a knock. I roll my eyes—only for my own benefit, I know, but being snide gives me something like courage. Which I need now more than ever.

The door opens under Rowena's hand and we proceed into the room. Alistair is seated behind his desk. In contrast to my sister, his skin glows with health and his glasses gleam as if he's just polished them. A simple brass tray holding two crystal glasses and a cut crystal decanter of some murky brownish-red liquid waits in the vicinity of one pointed black-suited elbow. My eyes skip over the tray quickly, scan the walls, then return to his face, which holds a politely patient expression.

"Tamsin," he says softly, and I try not to visibly shudder at the quiet exultation in his voice. I think back to the last time I was here and how well he played the part of the anxious professor.

"Dr. Callum," I reply, my voice calm. "Or should I say Dr. Knight?"

He bares his teeth in a silent laugh. Then he turns to my sister, who has been hovering lovingly by his side, and says, "Wait outside," his voice low and expressionless.

Her face goes slack as if all her features are sliding off her skin. But she doesn't protest, only runs her hand across Alistair's arm, touching his fingers lightly with her own before moving toward the door. Alistair acknowledges neither her parting gesture nor her departure.

"Sit?" he asks.

"No, thanks," I say as breezily as possible. "And don't offer me any more tea or whatever that is to drink, either," I say, pointing to the decanter. "I'm not in the mood for your hospitality."

I'm not really into sports, but I figure a good offense is the best defense.

"This?" Alistair says with a little chuckle, pointing toward the decanter. "I doubt very much you'd want to drink this. You're too . . . *ethically minded*. But then again, that's always been the problem with your family." He folds his hands together on the desk and looks at me. "Seriously, do you know how foolish your family is . . . and has been throughout the years? Do you know how *small* they've made their lives and their Talents? What a waste. A sheer waste."

"Where are my parents?" I ask through numb lips. Not that I expect him to really tell me the truth, but at least maybe I can tell if he's lying.

But he waves his hand dismissively and says, "I wasn't interested in what they had to offer."

I can't imagine what that would have been, but I'm not going to give him the satisfaction of asking. He leans across the desk, fixing me with his icy eyes, and I'm reminded of a large black crane. "I am interested in what you can do for me."

"And what is that?"

Alistair smiles. "You can bring me what I want."

"I think I already did that. I brought you the clock," I say, "and now my obligation is done."

He touches the rim of a crystal glass lightly. A hollow ringing sound fills the space between us. "Perhaps you can be persuaded to try again."

"And if I won't?"

Sharp lines stamp themselves onto his forehead. "'Won't'?" he repeats softly. Then he lifts his voice just a notch and says, "Rowena, come in here please."

The door opens at once and my sister glides back into the room. I wonder if she had her ear pressed to the wood the whole time. And then I wonder if she even understands what she has heard. She brushes past me and goes to his side, and I can't help but notice the joyful expression on her face.

"I need your help," Alistair says to her with an awful gentleness, and then he pulls open his desk drawer and clatters around for a few seconds before offering my sister a bone-handled knife.

"Don't!" I say, but neither of them even looks at me. Instead, Rowena extends her arm, the white underside of it flashing to the ceiling, and without even a fraction of hesitation she sinks the curve of the blade into her skin, as if slicing through a piece of meat.

"Stop!" I shriek and leap forward, snatching the blade from my sister's fingers. My hand tightens over the smooth handle and for one paralyzing second as I stare into Alistair's eyes I picture myself plunging the knife straight into his heart.

"Do it and you won't like what happens to your sister," he hisses. Suddenly, I remember my mother's warning about the spell's mirror effect on Rowena and I throw the knife into the corner of the room, where it skitters across the floor and then comes to rest. Turning back to Rowena, I almost throw up when I see that she is squeezing her arm calmly, watching the blood thicken and dribble from the fresh marks on her skin into a little white china cup that Alistair has so thoughtfully provided.

"Ro," I whisper, and wadding up my shirt I try to stanch the bleeding.

"No, Tamsin," she says gently, far more gently than the real Rowena would have if I ever got in her way. "I need to give him this," she explains earnestly. "It's so he can live."

"Thank you, my dear. That will be enough for now," Alistair says and reaches for the cup. My hand darts down and I snatch up the cup, flinging it at the wall behind me. The cup crashes directly into a framed print of a medieval hunting scene and shatters. Its contents ooze down the picture in a sticky red smear. I'm delighted to see that I've also managed to crack the glass of the frame. I turn back to Alistair, smile pleasantly.

"Oops. I always seem to be breaking cups in your office."

Alistair's lips thin into a needle-flat line, but it is my sister who speaks first.

"Tamsin," Rowena cries. "Why did you do that?" She crouches in the corner of the room and begins to pick up shattered bits of china, her fingers instantly stained crimson.

"Leave it," Alistair says, and his voice is almost as sharp as the knife and seems to cut as deeply, because my sister looks up, the expression of dismay on her face almost too much to bear. "You may go," he says, still in that cold tone, and my sister bows her head, rises to her feet, and, still cradling the pieces of the cup tenderly, slips out.

"You and I are more alike than you think," Alistair says at last, his voice thoughtful, his eyes quietly fixed on mine.

I snort. I can't help it. "I don't see that at all," I say, kicking aside a shard of china. It bounces off the baseboard. "Besides the fact that we both lied about our names," I add.

But he ignores that. "We would both do anything for our families."

I lift my gaze, stare at him, then open my mouth. No words. I have no words to deny this.

"And we've both been deprived of what is naturally ours. By the doing of your family."

"That's not true," I say instantly.

One eyebrow twists up. "Isn't it? Hasn't your family kept the truth about your Talents from you?" He leans across the desk, eyes pinning me to the wall. "All these years?"

I force myself to say, "They had their reasons."

"Amazing. That you would defend the very people who have denied you your birthright." He shakes his head as if I am a particularly difficult specimen to classify. "I have no such compunctions."

"What is this?" I manage finally. "The explanation of a madman before you kill me?"

"A madman?" And now he looks amused. "Oh, no, Tamsin. Not a madman. I take objection to that. I am nothing if not methodical. I had to be. When all you have is a single name to go on all these years, you learn to be . . . precise."

There is a ringing in my ears. "A name?" I say stupidly, and then it dawns on me. "Rowena's name. That's why you came into the bookstore that night. You were looking for Rowena. *Why?*"

Alistair smiles. "Yes, Rowena Greene. It's the name that's been promised as our salvation. When your family murdered mine, our only hope was one glimpse into the future, one glimpse at the book that your grandmother, your whole family, sets such store by."

"And you saw Rowena's name?" I breathe.

Alistair shrugs. "Of course *I* didn't. This was more than one hundred years ago. My relative did and that's the name we've held on to for centuries. We knew that she was to be the key."

"What do you mean my family *murdered* yours? We didn't kill anybody!"

"Are you so sure about that?"

"You were the ones murdering people. That's why we stopped you. That's what my—" I swallow the rest of my words. *That's what my mother told me* sounds incredibly childish here.

"Is that what you think? That we were murdering people and therefore the Greene family swooped in and saved the day? Lies," he says crisply. "Your family cared nothing, *nothing* about who we took for ourselves as long as it wasn't one of their own. But be that as it may," he says, his voice rising, "make no mistake about the word *murder*."

I stare at him, at the way his mouth splits and curls into a snarl.

"Do you know what it's like to grow up knowing that you were meant to be something else, something so very different from all the ordinary filth you see in the streets around you, something beyond this ordinary mortal life? To walk around and know that you should have a Talent, know that with all your heart, and yet you don't because of something that happened more than a hundred years ago?" He stares at me, his hands curling and uncurling on his desk blotter. Then he takes a breath and says softly, "When you deprive someone of their Talent, of their right to have a Talent, you kill a part of that person. From what your sister has told me, I think you just might be able to understand that. Think, Tamsin. Think how different your life could have been."

I shut my eyes, my brain rushing and tumbling with scenes like a river swollen with rain: Rowena and Gwyneth laughing, their mouths wide and red; Gabriel and his unanswered letters; Silda pulling gradually away from me; and the early years of school, when people looked at me as if I was weird when I was really no different from them. What if all that had never happened? What if I had known from my eighth birthday just exactly what I could do? There's no part of my life that would be the same.

Then I open my eyes. Alistair is watching me, satisfaction smeared across his long face. We stare at each other for the length of a heartbeat before I look toward the door, wondering if my sister is still bleeding. "What do I get in return? If I help you?"

"Your sister's life," he says, leaning back in his chair and touching his finger to the rim of the goblet again.

"And Agatha's," I say, trying to keep the cold, trembling sickness that's welling up inside me out of my voice.

His eyes flick to the decanter again, and now there is such a possessive hunger on his face that I almost look away. "Perhaps."

"'Perhaps'?" I echo. "What does that mean?"

"Perhaps it depends on you. If you can find what I want and bring it to me soon enough, perhaps it won't be too late for the lovely, *lively* Agatha."

My mouth feels as if it's full of cotton, but I force the words out. "What do you want with Agatha? She doesn't have a Talent—she's . . . normal . . ."

"Agatha is useful in helping me . . . sustain myself."

"Like Rowena is?" I ask.

He inclines his head thoughtfully in an awful parody of a professor considering a question from a student. "In a different way."

"And what will happen to them? If I bring you what you want? Will you free them?"

"Whatever there is left to free," he adds softly, and this time I can't keep the shudder from traveling across my face. "Time is running out for them, Tamsin. And when time runs out for them, be sure that there are others on the list." He steeples his hands, eyes the clock pointedly, and smiles at me. "I think your young man out there is perhaps becoming a tad anxious."

"How long do I have to bring you what you want? And why can't you just get it yourself if you're so powerful?"

The edge of a frown crosses his face and I feel that even though I haven't accomplished much during this interview, there's that at least. "It appears that someone of your special Talents is required." And in the little silence that follows, I almost laugh at the sad fact that I once wanted so badly to be Talented and now I would trade anything not to be.

But all laughter, hysterical or otherwise, vanishes at the sound of a clock chiming the hour. Turning, I locate the source of the sound: the clock that was once the Domani, in the corner of the office.

"A keepsake," Alistair murmurs. "And it does prove useful," he adds, and I jerk my head back toward him just in time to see him unstop the decanter and pour out some of the murky liquid into a glass. He holds the glass aloft, letting it catch the light so that it sparkles brightly. "To your . . . success," he says with a horrible politeness and drains the contents in one long swallow. I watch the muscles of his throat twitch and then he smiles at me, his lips shining wet.

Agatha!

I turn and flee the room, knocking past my sister, who is curled up outside the door, her eyes closed. Alistair's laugh follows me all the way down the hall.

TWENTY

"ARE YOU SURE you want to do this?" Gabriel asks me again through the partially open door that connects Aunt Rennie's and Uncle Chester's dressing rooms.

"What choice do I have?" I mutter miserably, sliding into the dress that I snatched from my closet back in my dorm room. Gabriel and I drove there after I'd managed to explain in between mostly incoherent gasps what Alistair had said. Agatha was asleep, and maybe it was my imagination, but it seemed unlike her usual deep coma. As I moved around the room, gathering up everything I thought I needed, she tossed and turned and murmured. Once she had cried out, "No, please!" I debated waking her and then decided not to. Instead, I stood over her for a minute while Gabriel waited outside, and I pressed my hand against her forehead. But she twisted away from me and turned toward the wall, and that's when I saw the cuts on her arm that were barely crusted over. I had to run away then before I started hyperventilating again.

Now I try to take comfort in the silky fabric of the dress, but even that reminds me too much of Agatha and her squealing excitement when I had come out of the dressing room of that East Village thrift shop. She convinced me to buy the dress even though I couldn't afford it and even though I didn't have one single place to wear a full-length rose-colored evening gown from the 1930s. Last month I thought stupidly that I would wear it to Rowena's wedding. "Maybe I still will," I whisper to myself now as I twist the dress into place.

"How's it going in there?"

"Okay," I gasp. "I can't really breathe, but other than that, okay."

"Breathing's overrated," Gabriel advises me. "I'm discovering that right about now with this damn tie."

I trip across the room to stand in front of Aunt Rennie's huge mirror. The dress says 1930s, but my hair gives it away. I search through my stack of hairpins, settle on a few crystal bobby pins. So what that they're from the chain store Claire's? How many people are going to be peering that closely at my hairpins? How long are we going to be stuck in 1939, anyway? Just long enough to apparently wreck Aunt Beatrice's life and get out. And before I can confront that uncomfortable thought, Gabriel walks through the adjoining door. I catch sight of his reflection in the mirror as I attempt to twist my dark curls into something resembling a 1930s hairstyle.

"You look great," I exclaim just as half my hair falls out of the knot I'm attempting to pin it in. I sigh. "I give up."

Gabriel, wearing one of Uncle Chester's charcoal suits, advances toward me. "You give up? You give up your foolish resistance to my undeniable charms? I knew you'd cave eventually. They always do."

I stick out my tongue at his mirrored reflection. Holding up my collection of hairpins, I say, "I give up on my hair, idiot."

He holds out his hand. "Give them to me," he says and sets to work.

"Ow," I say as he jabs my head with a pin. But it didn't really hurt. I just said that because he's standing so close.

"Sorry," he murmurs, his breath whispering across the bare nape of my neck.

"It's okay," I say through gritted teeth, hoping my goose bumps aren't visible.

"There. What do you think?" He takes half a step back and I look at myself in the mirror again. Somehow, he has managed where I failed to roll my hair and pin it low on my neck. The curl that keeps escaping has now been positioned behind my ear.

"Not bad," I say. "You know, if the musician thing doesn't work out, you could always be a—"

Behind me Gabriel makes a stabbing motion over his heart and I grin at him in the mirror. "Lipstick," I say in a rush.

"Nah, you don't need it. Why do girls wear that shit anyway?"

"It's 1939. I can't not wear lipstick," I say and search through what I've brought before settling on Agatha's tube of Rev Me Up Red by L'Oréal. But my hands are shaking, and as a result I end up scrubbing lipstick off my front teeth. "Okay," I say at last. "Ready, I think."

Gabriel pulls a picture from inside his voluminous jacket pocket and studies it. In the attic I found an old photo album covered with a layer of musty grime. Thank the elements that Aunt Rennie never seems to throw anything away. "Do you always need something like that?" I ask now. "Like the painting or this photo here? You know, to help you . . . Travel?"

Gabriel studies the photo for a minute longer. "I think it helps. I've never been able to do it without some sort of . . . guide like this or the painting. Concentrating?"

I nod, staring at the photo of the girl in a swooping hat. Her face is tilted up and she is smiling widely. In one hand she's holding a cigarette encased in a long holder, and in her other hand she's cradling what looks like an old-fashioned champagne glass. She's looking at something outside the borders of the picture. *Beatrice, 1939* is written in spidery letters across the bottom of the photo. Gabriel's fingers tighten around mine and suddenly we're whirling through space and I feel the dress slipping and swaying against my legs. I have time to wonder distractedly if my hair will stay put and then music is blaring in my ear and what feels like hard stone is wedged up against my shoulder.

"Ow!" I say, peeling myself away from a brick wall. I blink and let go of Gabriel's hand.

"Sorry," he says sheepishly. "I did tell you that this isn't an exact science."

"Where are we?" My eyes adjust to the dimness until I can make out rows and rows of bottles and jars all containing what looks like dried herbs or oils. Sniffing the air experimentally, I encounter a familiar earthy scent. "The stillroom," I say, taking a step forward, and as if to reward me for my guess, something cool and feathery splays across my face. I reach up to bat away a hanging bouquet of lavender, the flowers silky against my fingers. A crack of light shines along the far end of the room and I think back to the configurations of Aunt Rennie's house. The stillroom opens onto the garden, and judging from the music on the other side of the door, that's where the party is.

"I think—"

"Quiet," Gabriel hisses. "Someone's coming."

I whirl toward where I know the second door should be, the one that leads into the kitchen, and sure enough, right outside it are heavy, dragging footsteps. We sidle into the farthest corner of the room as this door is flung open. I can just make out the outline of a large woman, her hair skinned tightly in a bun that is cemented to the back of her head. She rattles along the shelves, muttering, "More honey syrup, Bertha. More hyssops for the punch, Bertha. The guests are thirsty. Don't dawdle, Bertha, Bertha, Bertha! And all the while my bones are aching for a sit-down." She stomps into the center of the room and reaches up toward the ceiling. The second before she snaps the light on, I realize what she intends to do.

Careening into Gabriel, I pull his face down onto mine, my hands artfully splayed across his cheeks to hide as much as I can. Just as his lips crash into mine, bright spangles of light burst against my closed eyelids.

"Oh!" I hear Bertha gasp. "Beg your pardon," she stammers. A wheel of heavy boots, a slam of the door, and she's gone.

"Sorry," I mutter, pulling back out of Gabriel's arms. "That was kind of sloppy. Not my best."

"I don't mind," he says, and his voice is this side of unsteady. Then he straightens his tie and smoothes the front of his suit jacket. "You're blushing."

"Yeah . . . well, you're wearing lipstick now." I reach up to smudge it off him as best I can, trying not to let my fingers linger on the curve of his lower lip.

"Thanks. Ready?"

"No," I say, but he squeezes my hand and opens the door to the garden anyway. We spill out into a crowd of people. All of them seem to be drinking and smoking; the women are holding slim gold and ivory cigarette holders while the men puff on thick toffee-colored cigars or pipes. A swirl of color catches my eye. A woman wearing a feathery bronze headdress is holding court, her long eyes painted with purple eye shadow, her mouth a slash of scarlet. Torches staked into the ground provide a soft flickering light, and the cheerful sweep of a jazz quartet occasionally breaks through the swells and billows of conversation. An enormous white tent in the middle of the garden has been set up for dancing, and various couples move in and out of the twilight.

"See her?" Gabriel says to me in a low voice just as a waiter glides to a stop before us, holding out a tray. The man's eyes are steady on a spot between my shoulder and Gabriel's, and after we take two bell-shaped champagne glasses he moves off without even looking at us once. I begin to breathe a little.

"Not yet," I say, swigging my champagne.

"Easy on that," Gabriel warns, his eyes shifting past me. I turn to find a trio of girls, each dressed in pink, looking at us—or rather, at Gabriel—with what seems like admiration. Just in time I catch a smile flit across his face as he gazes back at them.

"Easy on *that*," I say, and after linking arms, we move into the crowd as casually as possible. I take my cue from the waiter and don't make eye contact with anyone in particular.

But we're discovered anyway.

"Darling," a woman's voice purrs into my ear, and I nearly spill my glass of champagne. "I have been looking for you everywhere. When did you get here?"

"Um . . . a few minutes ago." I nod at her and try to move on, but her hand is wrapped around my arm. She is small and sharp featured, and her red hair breaks in glossy waves all around her head.

"Of course you did. How like you!" she exclaims, as if praising me for doing something very clever. Her black feather boa draped across her shoulder seems to be a living, breathing creature. I am staring at it, fascinated, when she leans into me and says in a loud stage whisper, "And just who is this *beautiful* man with you?" Without waiting for my answer, she winks at Gabriel and nudges between us. Her boa arcs through the air and wraps itself tightly around their hips.

I open my mouth, but just then a hearty voice booms out to my right. "Melora. Every time I turn around, you've disappeared. What is the meaning of this, really?" A massively florid man wobbles into view and slaps one meaty paw down onto the woman's shoulder in what is supposed to be a caress but looks more like a death grip. Melora's boa seems to wilt under his onslaught.

"Oh! Charles!" Melora says, and even though she's smiling, I can tell she's really trying not to shriek. "I just had to greet Cousin—" And here she shoots me a look.

"Agatha," I say blithely.

The man peers at me for a second, then blinks, shakes his head. "So many cousins," he roars jovially. "Cousin Agatha," he says and kisses me on each cheek. Ignoring

Gabriel completely, he turns back to Melora and says, "Now, you really must come with me. There's something I want to discuss with you."

Distaste flutters across Melora's features, but she allows the man to begin leading her away, his hand still clamped on her shoulder. But in the next second the boa floats up again as if stirred by an errant breeze and winds itself briefly around the man's arm. With a surprisingly high-pitched yelp, he snatches his hand back and wrings it out once, twice. "Damn thing bit me!" he exclaims.

"No, lambkins," Melora coos, cradling his hand. "It absolutely did not." Then she looks sidelong at me and winks before they both disappear into the darkness.

"Did she just call him lambskin?" Gabriel asks, and we move back into the crowd. "This way," he adds, and we veer to the left and duck under the white tent, skirting the dance floor of polished wooden squares that seems to have been laid just for this evening. "Are you related to them?"

"I wouldn't be surprised if that turns out to be Gwyneth's grandmother. She had that nasty viper look."

Snips and snatches of conversation swirl toward me as we weave our way around clumps of people. "I tell you, they were right to finally start pulling in Roosevelt. Ever since the New Deal—"

"Darling, you promised. You know Cousin Lindel is a Roosevelt man. Why must you always bait him?"

"But I—"

Gabriel pulls me sideways. A figure with a white painted face undulates past us, turning silk scarves into birds and then back again. I blink, trying to figure out if he's Talented or merely hired entertainment for the evening, when Gabriel says softly, "There." We stop beside the garden wall in the shadow of a large magnolia tree. A young woman dressed in a mermaid-cut black dress and a silver fur stole is tipping back her dark head, laughing with wide white teeth. On her wrists diamonds glitter and flash like fallen stars.

"That's her," Gabriel says, but I find that I am staring at a girl who looks about my age, dressed all in white. She's standing close to Aunt Beatrice, and at first glance they appear to be deep in conversation, but then her eyes shift across the crowd, probing like two searchlights across dark water. Suddenly, she swings her head toward me and meets my gaze for one second—as if in acknowledgment—before turning back to Aunt Beatrice.

I feel a thump deep in my chest as if my heart has stopped and has just started again with a bang, and then the moment is gone. A light breeze stirs through the garden, rippling dresses and shawls. A pink curtain of magnolia petals veils my vision. When I look again, a tall, robust man is lighting Aunt Beatrice's cigarette.

"Can you . . . sense the Domani?" I ask hopefully.

Gabriel shakes his head, saying nothing right away. His brows draw together, his fingers twitch, and then he looks down at me before saying with some frustration, "I don't know what I'm looking for. Needle? Haystack? Not the clock, obviously. What? What is it?" he says softly, more to himself than me. Absently, he reaches over, pulls a flower from my hair, and holds it to his nose. "Time," he says after a minute. "There's a ticking in my head."

I must look alarmed, because he smiles. "Not like a bomb."

"This is worse than a needle in *three* haystacks," I say glumly after a minute when nothing seems to be happening. "Why did I think we could do this?"

"Because we *did* do it. We just don't know how yet," Gabriel answers, and I smile at him, squeezing his hand. At that moment the band strikes up a slow, stately tune. "Let's dance. Dancing always makes me think better."

I give him a dubious look. "It does? And is that really a good idea?"

"Killjoy," Gabriel explains patiently, "I'm wearing a suit. You're wearing the prettiest dress ever. It's 1939, and who knows what's going to happen next. Come on, Tamsin. It's the best idea I can come up with right now." And with that he leads me from the shadow of the tree onto the torch-lit dance floor, where we join the throng of other entwined couples.

"I can't dance," I mutter.

"This is a waltz," Gabriel says in the exact same way you'd say, *This is an orange.*

"I still can't dance."

"I can," Gabriel says and pulls me toward him. With one arm wrapped around my waist, he begins to whirl me around the floor so fast that I don't have time to think about how I have no idea what to do next. Faces flicker in and out of the shadows over Gabriel's shoulder as we fly through the flower-scented air. The music swells softly until it becomes a part of my feet and suddenly we're moving in perfect step with each other. Just when I feel this could and should go on forever, the music stops and my dress swirls against my legs. I'm gasping lightly and my hair is coming undone.

"Ah, young love," a baritone croons to my left, and I see the tall, robust man who lit Aunt Beatrice's cigarette standing next to us. He beams at us, turns back to his partner, who I realize is Aunt Beatrice, and whispers something in her ear. She tilts her head toward his, one bejeweled hand reaching up to caress his face, her mouth budding into a tiny smile. *Uncle Roberto*, I think suddenly.

I arch on my toes. *Beatrice's husband*, I mouth to Gabriel. As we watch, Uncle Roberto reaches into his gray vest pocket and pulls out a shining gold pocket watch. The chain dangling from the watch gleams briefly.

Gabriel's hand tightens on mine. All of a sudden, I think back to that first night that Gabriel came home when we stood in the living room with Aunt Beatrice. *She hasn't lost anything that I can find. I tried earlier. It was something about a pocket watch.*

"Very well, my dear," the man says, "but I must tell the cooks to hold off for another fifteen minutes, then. They will doubtlessly be unhappy with me." He kisses her hand. "Of course, I'll take a thousand of their frowns for one smile of yours." As he moves off the floor, Aunt Beatrice touches three fingers to her lips and blows a kiss to the man's retreating figure before she sways through the crowd in the opposite direction.

"Do you think that's—"

"One way to find out," Gabriel says, and we follow Uncle Roberto.

TWENTY-ONE

"EXCUSE ME, sir," Gabriel calls to Uncle Roberto as he reaches the relatively deserted gravel path leading to the kitchen.

Uncle Roberto turns, smiles beatifically upon us. "Ah, young people. Are you enjoying yourselves this evening?"

"Oh, yes." I nod feverishly. "You and Aunt Beatrice always throw the best parties." This may be putting it on a little too thick, but as we step closer to Uncle Roberto, I realize with relief that he is more than a little drunk. His face has a moist all-over sheen to it and his eyes are benevolently glassy.

"So you're a relative of Beatrice's, then. I certainly would remember if you were related to me," he adds with a chuckle and a wink at Gabriel that's obviously meant to convey something in male language. I jab Gabriel in the side and he belts out a late laugh.

"Sir, we were wondering if we could see—" I start when Gabriel cuts me off.

"We were wondering if you'd like to see a card trick that you won't believe." From seemingly out of nowhere, a deck of cards has appeared in Gabriel's hand. I stare at him. This was not what we had planned. Truthfully, we hadn't planned much. We were just going to ask Uncle Roberto about his watch and hope that something vaguely providential occurred. Apparently, Gabriel hadn't thought much of this plan.

"Oh, now." Uncle Roberto gives us another gentle chuckle accompanied by a shake of his head. "I'm afraid the guests will be wondering when their supper is going to arrive and I must speak with the cooks. But my wife is fond of card tricks. Perhaps you should—"

"We did try it on several of your guests already. And Aunt Beatrice," Gabriel says smoothly. Then a note of pride enters his voice. "None of them, including your wife, could get it. But she said that you might. She said that no one can get a card trick past you."

Inwardly I groan. This is definitely laying it on too thick. Uncle Roberto is eyeing us with what I am sure is suspicion.

"How did you say you're related to my wife, again?" he asks softly.

My mouth goes dry, but Gabriel says with a careless laugh, "Oh, you know how this family works. People coming out of the woodwork all the time. Especially at parties. My father, may he rest in peace, was like you." And here he gives a subtle weight to the word *you*. "He was a great friend of Uncle Charles's, too. 'So many cousins' was their little joke between them." Gabriel riffles the deck with a casually confiding air. With his eyes on the cascade of cards, he adds, "It's anyone's guess how you guys really manage to put up with this family."

Uncle Roberto gives a bellow of a laugh that nearly jolts me out of my skin. "That's for damn sure. Your father, he was . . ."

"A self-made man," Gabriel fills in. "God rest his soul."

"Eh, now." Uncle Roberto steps closer. "I didn't know you folks believed in God. I mean, Beatrice's explained it all to me. How you practice white magic, so to speak."

I swallow my smile to hear it broken down in these terms. My grandmother and mother would have howled with laughter.

"Well, my father had a few things to say about that when it came time for my first Communion," Gabriel says, altar-boy earnest now. I try not to stare at him. Religious devotion does not figure into what little I remember about Gabriel's father, Uncle Phil. Unless he was a member of the Church of Boring Sports. In that case, I do remember a lot of *Goddamn*s and *thank you, Jesus*es being shouted at the football and baseball games that flickered in and out of reception on the rickety television set my mother had placed in a small side room. That was where you could always find Uncle Phil ensconced—if you wanted to do such a thing. Most of us didn't.

"Good man," Uncle Roberto grunts. "I might have a few things to say about that, too, if Beatrice and I ever . . . well . . . that's not talk for a party, now is it?" Then he shakes away whatever he was thinking, steps forward, and claps a hand on Gabriel's shoulder. "Let's see this trick. But this is a real trick, right? None of your . . ." He swallows and I suddenly feel a pang of sympathy for Uncle Roberto. Apparently, there is some truth to what Gabriel said about not knowing how he tolerates the family.

"None of it at all. Not my Talent, anyway," Gabriel says, honest at last, and the cards snap in his hands and suddenly the movement of his fingers is too fast to follow. After a few seconds of complicated shuffling and rearranging, he fans the cards and holds them out to Uncle Roberto. "First pick one card, any card." Uncle Roberto does so and holds it in his hands expectantly. "And you can look at it, but please do not show it to me or my assistant."

Uncle Roberto nods, his face going carefully blank as he takes a quick peek at the card. "Now place it in your left pocket," Gabriel instructs. "Good, excellent. Now pick another, whichever one you'd like. And look at it, please, but again don't show it to anyone . . . Perfect. Now hand it to my assistant face-down so I can't see it. Perfect. She's going to place it in your right vest pocket." I step forward, my heart suddenly thwacking my rib cage. Hoping that

Uncle Roberto won't notice that my fingers are trembling, I reach for the second card. The slick plastic feels cool to my fingers, and as I step closer to Uncle Roberto, I can smell the sweet perfume of alcohol and after-shave coming off him.

"Sorry, sir," I mumble as my fingers slip against his chest.

"You did this trick on ladies, too?" Uncle Roberto says with another bellow of laughter.

"That's why I have my lovely assistant. So no one can complain," Gabriel says, his voice magnanimous and light, betraying no hint of the nerves I know he must be feeling. "Okay, Ta—er, Agatha. Place the card in his front right pocket now. *Now,*" Gabriel coaxes me, and suddenly, just as I realize that he has nowhere to go with this trick, Uncle Roberto takes the card from me and places it in his own pocket, smiling kindly at me.

"I think your assistant needs a little practice," he says gently and then turns with an expectant look on his face. "And now what, my young man?"

"And now . . ." Gabriel says and pauses for what must seem like a dramatic flourish, but really I know it's his way of buying time. "And now, please take the first card out of your pocket and look at it again." As Uncle Roberto fumbles for the first card, Gabriel sends me a look that clearly reads as *what the hell is wrong with you* and I send him a look back that I hope conveys *I'm sorry!*

"Now what?" Uncle Roberto says, holding the card aloft, looking at each of us in turn. He rocks back on his heels a little, smiling happily.

"It's still the same card?" Gabriel asks.

"That it is."

"Are you sure?" Gabriel says, stepping closer.

"I am," Uncle Roberto replies with the first hint of impatience. "Look—"

"But what about your second card? Please, allow me," Gabriel says, and before Uncle Roberto can react, Gabriel steps in smoothly, inserts his hand into Uncle Roberto's pocket, and flicks the card free. It tumbles to the ground, landing face-up. The queen of hearts winks at me.

"That's not your first card?" Gabriel says with a swagger.

"No, it certainly isn't," Uncle Roberto says with a grin. He thinks he's beaten the trick. "I think it's not just your assistant who needs a little practice."

"Maybe so," Gabriel concedes with a disarming smile and then adds, "But I'm not so sure. Let me see what other cards are in here."

"Oh, ho!" Uncle Roberto says, clearly willing to give us one more second.

"Gabriel, don't," I say with a catch in my throat as he leans forward and draws out the pocket watch from Uncle Roberto's pocket. He is holding it by the chain, his fingers not quite touching the watch face.

For one second, one minute, one eon, nothing happens,

and then Uncle Roberto steps back, a frown creasing his face. "See here, what's this about?"

It's not it, I think with a sinking heart, and then Gabriel gives a short, sharp twist and the pocket watch comes free of the chain and spins through the air, its face gleaming and glittering. With a flash Gabriel puts out his right hand and catches it just before Uncle Roberto does.

"Tamsin," Gabriel gasps. "This is—"

"Idiot," I moan. Silvery ribbons are snaking up from the watch, entwining themselves with a sinuous fluidity all around Gabriel's hand before shooting up his forearm.

"Cold," he murmurs. "So cold."

"What's . . . I . . . why did you—do something," Uncle Roberto blusters, and with a shock I realize he isn't talking to me. I turn and Aunt Beatrice glides forward from the shadows, cocking her head to the side and examining Gabriel dispassionately.

"Do something," Uncle Roberto says again to his wife, and she smiles at him, a gentle smile, one that a teacher would give to a pupil who wasn't maybe her best and brightest but who held her heart just the same.

"I *am* doing something, dear. What I'm supposed to be doing. But this isn't something you should have to see." And with a light brush of her fingers she touches her husband's forehead tenderly. All at once Uncle Roberto stops moving. His eyes remain wide open but unblinking.

I lurch toward Gabriel, but somehow Aunt Beatrice

blocks my path, anchors me to her by grabbing both of my wrists in one hand. She is holding me so tightly that my palms and fingers tingle unpleasantly.

"Gabriel!" I shriek. "Drop it. Drop it now."

With what seems like great effort, Gabriel turns his hand over, but the pocket watch has adhered to his fingers.

"Good thing it wasn't his left hand," Aunt Beatrice says musingly as she turns her attention back to Gabriel. "Otherwise, he'd have died by now. But then again it'll just take another minute or two to reach his heart this way."

"What?" I cry, tearing my eyes away from Gabriel's stone-colored face. "Stop this!" I say fiercely to Aunt Beatrice, trying to pry her fingers from my wrist. "Now or you'll regret it."

She smiles at me, a very different smile from the one she just gave her husband, and my skin crawls trying to equate this sword blade of a woman with my dotty great-aunt. With her free hand, she reaches up and flicks her fingers against my forehead with what seems like considerably more strength than when she touched Uncle Roberto. Her eyes gleam with a cold and righteous anger. Inwardly, I feel the familiar dizzy wave roll over me and then it's gone.

Twisting my wrists in her grasp, I finally manage to angle my palms away from each other. Flames erupt from my right hand and sizzle into the grass near her feet.

"Oh!" she shrieks, beating frantically at the hem of her dress. Taking advantage of her distraction, I wrench myself free of her, step forward, and snatch the watch from Gabriel's hand.

Instantly, the silver ribbons engraved in his skin begin to shimmer and fade, but he remains motionless. All at once I remember how Gabriel, the fire, and even time itself seemed to have stopped when I touched the clock in 1899.

"What have you done?" Aunt Beatrice whispers, staring at me now. Her lips are trembling and her eyes dart from me to Gabriel, then back to me again. I stare at the watch in my hand, then flick it open. Faint writing has appeared on the lid, but try as I might I can't read it. Just as I seem to catch a word here and there, it squiggles away from me. With a start I realize these letters are behaving in the same way as the ones on the clock in 1899. And in my family's book.

Ten seconds have passed. "What does this writing say?" I whisper hoarsely.

"I don't know," Aunt Beatrice answers immediately.

Even though I know somehow that she's not lying, I say anyway, "What do you mean you don't know? You're the Keeper, aren't you?"

She flinches, nods once. "But I still can't read it. I don't have that Talent."

"How long have you been the Keeper?"

Twenty-five seconds have passed.

"Three years." She closes her eyes briefly. "And now I will lose it."

"Why?"

"Once the power's breached, it goes to someone else."

"Who?"

"I don't know. Keepers never know who the next Keeper will be. The Domani chooses them."

Thirty, thirty-five seconds have passed.

"Why was Uncle Roberto able to touch the watch without . . . without those snaky things attacking him?"

"Because my husband has no Talent. He's an ordinary man." And the way she says *ordinary* sounds like *wonderful*. I swallow. "Since he has no Talent, the Domani doesn't recognize him."

"So this writing would never appear if . . . when . . . he touches it?"

Aunt Beatrice shakes her head.

"But if I read this writing, what would happen?"

Aunt Beatrice blanches, shakes her head again.

"*What would happen?* If I read this aloud? Would I be able to destroy it? Would I be able to destroy the Domani?"

"No," Aunt Beatrice whispers. "You would be able to return to the time when it didn't exist."

"To the time it didn't . . . to the war between the families? Is that what you mean?"

Aunt Beatrice nods stiffly, looks at me fearfully. The clock's second hand reaches the roman numeral XII. One long shudder rips through her, her eyelids fluttering wildly. Then she opens her eyes and looks at me through the liquid dark. "Who *are* you?" she whispers. "Do I know you?"

I shake my head, hand her the pocket watch mutely. She clicks it open, shuts it again.

"I've lost it," she says, and there is such a flatness and finality in her voice that I can't speak even if I had known what to say. For one heartbeat we are silent as a breeze tosses through the trees above us, and then she says more fiercely, "Why were you able to touch the Domani? Without harm? No one but the Keeper can touch it without harm." Her voice dips suddenly and she raises one shaking hand, saying, "Are you the next—"

"I don't think so," I say. "Wouldn't I know?"

"Oh, yes," she says reverently. "You would know." She seems to be looking at something beyond me. "With every shred of your soul you would feel the tie. It is the highest honor." Her hand falls back to her side and she steps closer to me. "And why didn't my Talent work on you? Why didn't you freeze?" And quick as a snake she reaches up, taps my forehead again, and stares at me expectantly.

I blink, step back. This time I felt only the barest push inside me. "Try it again," I say wonderingly, and though I'm not exactly sure why, Aunt Beatrice obeys me and touches my forehead again, this time gazing into my eyes. Nothing. Not even a ripple.

Experimentally I reach out and touch her forehead. Even though I know what's going to happen, I'm still shocked when it actually does. It's as though she turns into a living column of stone, her eyes caught wide and unblinking, her mouth held half open in an expression of surprise or fear. "Aunt Beatrice," I whisper. "Stop now. That's enough." Somewhere a door creaks open and I jerk toward the house. Several white-capped figures move back and forth inside the great windows, carrying silver trays and platters. Sooner or later someone is going to come down this path and know something is terribly wrong.

Desperately, I look at Gabriel, Uncle Roberto, and Aunt Beatrice, all motionless as if we're playing a game of freeze tag. "Okay, um . . ." I say, my voice rising a little in panic. "Enough, now."

Footsteps crunch lightly across the gravel pathway and I spin to find only the shadows gathering beyond the small circles of torch light. Just as I'm wondering if I imagined the sound, a girl steps into view. It is the girl in white who was standing next to Aunt Beatrice in the garden earlier.

"I don't know what to do," I say to her miserably, one high-heeled shoe digging into the moist earth of the garden. "I don't know what's happening."

The girl glances around the garden, her eyes lingering on Uncle Roberto, then Gabriel, and finally Aunt Beatrice. "You froze her," she states, and there is just the faintest hint of admiration in her voice. She studies me for a minute, then closes her right eye completely while the other remains wide open, pinning me in place. "Ah," she adds softly.

TWENTY-TWO

I STARE AT MY GRANDMOTHER, stunned. *Of course, of course*, my brain sings. *She's Aunt Beatrice's sister, so why wouldn't she be here?* My eyes skip over her appearance, trying to find my grandmother's prune of a face in this girl's clear, smooth skin and large eyes.

"Grandmother," I say softly to her and then backtrack. "Well, technically, I suppose you're not my grandmother yet, are you? It's me . . . it's Tamsin. I know it doesn't make much sense right now, but . . ."

The moon breaks away from a barrier of clouds, and its soft silver light coats the trees surrounding us. My grandmother walks toward me, the skirt of her filmy white dress skimming the shadowy grass. Coming to a stop before me, she reaches out with one hand, traces the curve of my cheek. "Tamsin," she murmurs. "I've been watching for you." Her voice is deep and clear, the exact same as I remember, and just hearing it unlocks something in me. I want to sink to my knees, bury my face in her dress, and cry.

But I need to ask something first. "Why did you . . . why did you let me live for so many years thinking I had nothing? Nothing at all. Why did you—"

My grandmother holds up her hand and I fall silent. When she speaks, her voice is softer than I've ever heard it. "Believe me, what I did . . ." She pauses, shakes her head. "What I *will* do will never be done lightly. If you've gotten here it confirms what I've always suspected."

"And what's that?"

"That the Knight family is rising again."

Her confirmation of my parents' fears spirals into me and I shudder, letting my eyes rove across the garden, half expecting Alistair to step from the shadows. "I thought we already defeated them. When you . . . whoever it was . . . formed the Domani. Wasn't that enough?"

Tilting her head back, my grandmother studies the sky for a moment as if reading the stars before she recites, "One stood for North, and one stood for South; one stood for East, and one stood for West. And one stood Center. North summoned Air, and South carried Water; East called Fire, and West bore Earth. And the Center offered blood. And all were bound together."

"Wait a minute," I interject. "Mom mumbled that same spiel, but she didn't mention anything about a Center. And she certainly didn't mention anything about *blood*. Air, water, fire, earth, yes, but not blood." I swallow queasily. Maybe that's what she meant by sacrifice.

My grandmother's face seems to shrink in on itself, as if she is suddenly weary, and for one instant she appears as the grandmother I know, not the young girl in front of me. "She doesn't know," she whispers at last. "Very few of us now know what our family did. We took a life. A terrible solution to solve a terrible problem." She pauses, then adds, "But it didn't solve it. In fact, I think that was part of its undoing."

I feel a sinking, shifting feeling as Alistair's voice comes snarling back at me. *Make no mistake about the word murder.*

I stare at the ground, stir the pebbles with the edge of one glittering shoe. "I started all of this, you know. By pretending to be Rowena. He thought I was Rowena and I let him think that. It was . . . sort of an accident."

"Nothing is an accident, Tamsin. Even if it seems like one at the time." She sighs and steps closer. "Will you let me show you what I've seen? Will you allow me?"

I nod, swallowing hard as she raises her hands and presses them to my temples. "Close your eyes," she says, and I do.

All at once I am standing in a vast green field, and it takes me a second to realize that it's the field behind our house. My right hand is fused with Rowena's, my left with Gabriel's. Gwyneth and Jerom and Silda are standing opposite me and we're all swinging in a loose circle. The edges of the field keep blurring and flickering and the light seems to dance with us, shining down on our faces, warm and golden.

Catch me, my sister calls, her voice ringing pure and sweet through the soft air, and then we're all running and running through tall grass. Wild daises and purple aster brush at my splayed fingers as I stretch my arms out to my sister, who is always flying just a step ahead of me. We come to the edge of the woods, and all of a sudden Rowena is gone and the light is fading, fading, falling to darkness. *Rowena,* I cry, hovering at the edge of the forest. Massive twisted tree trunks soar into a colorless sky, and I freeze in the act of taking a step, unable to move. The others have disappeared. I am alone.

Rowena, I call again and am rewarded by a flash of her golden hair as she moves through the trees ahead of me, the shadows swallowing up her slender form. Suddenly, I'm walking again, then running, but my heart is pounding—*too late, too late, too late,* an insistent staccato rhythm that begins to thrum faster and faster through my brain. Up ahead of me Rowena stops in midflight, her hands falling to her sides. Just beyond her a tall, dark figure stands quietly waiting.

Rowena! I scream, and with an agonizing dream-speed slowness she turns. The color is slowly seeping out of her hair, and then strands begin to fall out in ribbons of ash that float on the breeze and disappear. Her face grows paler and paler, sharpening to a knife-blade thinness, while her eyes, fixed on me, darken. She stretches out one wisp-thin hand, the tips of her fingers blurring into nothingness. *Tamsin.* Her mouth shapes my name before her features slacken and lose all definitive form. Her body fades like a gust of smoke and she is gone.

Then I'm standing in the backyard staring at my family's house—or what's left of it. A desolate silence seems to grip the worn wooden beams and a cold wind is whistling through the gaping mouths of the windows. At my feet withered and graying stalks of lilacs are scattered across the black earth. The altar lies in two jagged pieces as if struck by lightning. Everyone is gone.

The cool pressure of my grandmother's hands vanishes suddenly and I open my mouth, gasping as if I have just surfaced from a dark lake. The sound of my ragged breathing fills the garden. "What do I have to do?"

"I don't know," my grandmother says, and for the first time in my life and maybe in hers, she sounds afraid.

I stare at her for a second. *"What?"* The word bursts from me before I can check myself. "What do you mean you don't know? You're supposed to know everything."

"Even if I could read the future completely and accurately, something no one in our family has ever been able to do, I couldn't tell you what to do. It changes so easily, so swiftly, depending on everything that we do now. Every second you stay here, something changes in the future. Something small, inconsequential, perhaps . . . or perhaps not so inconsequential. You must know that by now."

My grandmother turns away, begins pacing through the garden, wending her way among the statue forms of Uncle Roberto, Gabriel, and Aunt Beatrice. She pauses by my aunt and touches the pocket watch that dangles from her curved fingers. "All I know is that you have a terrible choice ahead of you. That's what I can see."

In the distance the quartet begins another waltz, the music rising slow and sweet. *A terrible choice?* "He's got Agatha, too," I say at last.

My grandmother frowns at me. "Who is Agatha? Is she one of our family?"

"No." *Thankfully.* "She's my friend from school. My roommate. She's—"

"A Talentless one?"

"Yeah, but—"

But she speaks over me. "When you go back, you will find the Domani again."

"But how—I mean, Aunt Beatrice is . . . was . . ." I glance at my aunt wildly, as if she's going to confirm this information. But her eyes remain unblinking, her mouth still shaped in that bubble of surprise.

"Assuming I'm still alive," my grandmother says slowly, "I am the Keeper."

"You?" I gasp.

She nods once. "From this moment on, I have become the Keeper."

"Then . . . where is the Domani now?"

"In Grand Central Station."

I close my eyes and call up the hustle and hum of that busy hub. So many times I've rushed through it, always late to catch a train upstate with the clock ticking away the last few seconds I have. *Late.* My eyes snap open. "The *clock?*"

"How did you know that?" my grandmother asks.

"It's always something to do with time, isn't it?" I think back. "It was a wall clock in 1899 and it is—I mean, *was*—a pocket watch here in 1939. So it has to be a clock in my time." But now something else is niggling at me. "What do you mean, assuming you're still alive?" I demand.

At this she smiles. "Tamsin. Hard as it may be for me to imagine right now, I will grow old." She glances at her hands curiously as if trying to picture the protruding bulbs of veins and age spots that will sprout on her currently smooth, tight skin.

"When?" I ask miserably. "When will you—"

She laughs, her face lighting up all at once, and I'm suddenly struck by how beautiful my grandmother really is. "Are you asking me to predict the exact time of my own death?"

"No . . . I'm sorry," I whisper, but she's still smiling at me.

Her fingers come up again and press into my cheekbone for an instant. "You have to save your sister. If you don't, if he takes her back with him, back to where this all started, then he'll be unstoppable. Everything ends then if he takes her."

"So," I begin, and the lump in my throat feels more like a boulder. I try again. "So, what you said about me being one of the most powerful, that's all true? But still, next to Rowena I'm not . . . I'll never be like her . . . I'll never be . . ." I trail off, realizing that for once I really do wish that my grandmother could read my mind.

We contemplate each other in the softly falling darkness, and somewhere above us a night bird warbles three trilling notes. I blink, then blink double time, trying to stop my eyes from filling with tears.

"You have your own role to play. You are a beacon for us all," my grandmother says at last, her voice unexpectedly gentle.

I roll my eyes. "By the way, you mention that, the beacon thing, when I'm born. Maybe you shouldn't, because it kind of puts a lot of pressure on me." Inwardly, I marvel that I can talk to my grandmother like this, in a way that I never could back in my real life. Maybe it's because of everything that's happened. Maybe it's because she doesn't look so much like my grandmother at the moment.

A door slams somewhere in the vicinity of the house and my grandmother takes a step back. "Time is moving in your world, too. You have to go now."

I nod, then suddenly turn back to the three motionless figures behind us. "But what about Aunt Beatrice?

What did I do to her? Gabriel . . . will he . . . be okay? How do I . . ."

"You know how to," my grandmother says calmly, and at this I start to lose it a little.

"Actually, I *don't* know what to do. I mean, it's nice that you suddenly have so much faith in me and all, especially after all these years . . . um . . . before all these years that are about to come." I shake my head irritably, then continue. "But I don't know what I did to Aunt Beatrice. I mean, I tapped her on the head, just like this, see?" I take two steps toward Aunt Beatrice, touch her forehead again.

"Oh!" Aunt Beatrice says, blinking at me and stepping back stiffly as if awaking from a long sleep. "You!"

She raises one hand—either to hit me again or to shield herself from me, I'm not sure which—when my grandmother says, "Don't, Beatrice. She's not one of them."

Aunt Beatrice stares at her sister, then back at me. "But she tried to . . ."

"I know," my grandmother agrees. She folds her hands and closes one eye briefly.

"None of that, Althea!" Beatrice's mouth twists into a tight pouch of annoyance, and then she bursts out with "I want to know what's—"

I divide a look between my furious aunt and my serene grandmother before running to Gabriel. I touch him lightly on the head and wait for him to blink. "I've got a lot to tell you," I whisper.

But his face remains frozen.

"It's not working," I cry. "Why?"

"It seems you can't undo what someone else has already done," my grandmother says at last, looking thoughtful. "Which means only Beatrice can release him."

"Well, I won't release him," Aunt Beatrice says, vindication pricking through her voice. "Not until someone tells me exactly what is going on. Right now." She folds her arms across her chest and glares at both of us. "Or he'll stay this way forever!"

"Actually," my grandmother interjects in a dry voice, "it does wear off after a week or two. As I have been so fortunate to discover."

"You can't still be mad about that," Aunt Beatrice insists.

"She doesn't have much time," my grandmother adds.

"Well, I do," Aunt Beatrice says. She swings the pocket watch from her fingers like a pendulum.

I glare at my aunt. "I used to like you," I mutter.

"What was that?"

"Nothing!" Then I clench my back teeth while advancing on my aunt. "If you don't release him, Aunt Beatrice, I swear you'll spend the next week of your life as a statue in your own stupid garden!"

My aunt draws herself up, which would be impressive if she weren't considerably shorter than I am. "Well!" she huffs before stomping over and knocking Gabriel on the head.

With a long shiver Gabriel comes to life, looking around wildly before he sees me. I run across the grass, tripping in my heels, and thud straight into him. "Umph!" he says into my hair. "Warn me before you're going to do that again, okay?" But his arms fold me into him and I breathe in his warm skin.

"I'm glad you're okay," I whisper.

"Me, too. Um . . . what just happened?"

"I'll explain later," I whisper back. "And why did you touch that stupid thing again? Didn't you learn anything from the last century?"

"Well, you weren't exactly doing *anything*, Tam. We were standing there like idiots and that guy was about to—"

"Oh, shush!" I say, putting my fingers over his mouth. He falls silent, but I get the impression that he's smiling at me. "We can fight about this later. Now we've got to get out of here." Reluctantly, I disentangle myself and move back. Over my head Gabriel stares at Aunt Beatrice, who is delivering what looks like one hiss of a monologue into my grandmother's ear.

I spare a glance for poor Uncle Roberto, still caught motionless with one hand over his heart, as if to stop the pocket watch from traveling out of his grasp.

"Wait for one second," I say to Gabriel, then walk back to the two women.

"Thank you," I say softly to my grandmother, who smiles. Aunt Beatrice is gaping at me, but I ignore her as I turn away. Then one last thought tugs at me, so I turn back.

"So why did you name me Tamsin?" I ask. "You always promised to tell me later. Even though, technically, it's earlier."

My grandmother's smile flickers, deepens. "It's how you introduced yourself to me tonight. I just assumed that's what you wanted to be named."

TWENTY-THREE

PALE LIGHT sifts through the curtains, filters across the flat gold carpet. My rose dress is tangled in the arms of Gabriel's suit jacket, and for one second I imagine our clothing rising up and waltzing together like we did last night.

Last night, which happened seventy-something years ago.

We stumbled back to the present just before midnight, found a guest room where the sheets appeared to be relatively fresh, and fell onto the bed. After I had filled him in on what had happened while he was frozen, we both stared at the ceiling for a while.

Finally, Gabriel pulled the white blankets up over our knees, releasing a cloud of dust in the process. After I had finished sneezing and hacking, I turned, curled into his arms, and we slept. Well, he did. I stayed awake most of the night, staring into a blackness that was occasionally punctured by light from the passing cars.

"Tamsin," Gabriel says to me as we're sitting at Aunt Rennie's table, eating the pizza that he picked up. Or at least he's eating it. I'm too busy shredding my pizza crust into shards and then pulverizing the shards into crumbs. "You're not going to do anything stupid, are you?"

"You mean intentionally?" With my fingertips I begin sweeping the crumbs into a pile in the center of my plate.

But he doesn't even smile, just reaches across the table, his hand forcing my chin up until I meet his eyes.

"I don't know," I whisper. All last night I had watched him sleep, my fingers laced together so I wouldn't be tempted to touch his face and possibly wake him. "I'll try not to," I say, attempting to lighten my tone.

My cell phone rings, the word HELLCRATER flashing onto the screen in stark black letters. I swallow against the sudden stab of pain in my throat. This morning, when I'd asked Gabriel to locate my parents, he had closed his eyes for barely a second and then said, "They're home." Relief had swept through me. But right now I don't have the energy to lie to my mother about why I'm back in the city. When at last the phone goes silent, Gabriel says, "Whatever you're thinking, you—"

The house phone shatters the rest of what he was going to say. I jump, my elbow jarring my plate across the table. I glance at the yellow phone shrilling imperiously on the kitchen wall. It seems my mother won't be denied. On stiff legs I walk into the kitchen. "Hello?"

"Tamsin." Clear as ice water, his voice pours into my head.

"Mr. Knight," I say.

There's a low chuckle. "I assume you have something for me?"

"Maybe," I hedge as Gabriel pushes back his chair with what I feel is an unnecessarily loud scrape.

A measured pause, and then Alistair says, "Don't play games, Tamsin. You won't like the results."

I swallow. "How's my sister?"

He ignores this. "When?"

"Tonight," I say slowly, my eyes fixated on the ridiculously cheerful kitchen wallpaper. Red cherries and round pink strawberries dance in loose columns. "Eleven forty-five."

"Where?"

"Let's meet at Grand Central Station. By the information kiosk." I reach one hand out to touch a cherry. It blurs and runs through my fingers.

A small, sharp silence pokes at the connection between us and then I hear Alistair draw in a breath. "Very well," he says, satisfaction brimming in his voice.

"Put my sister on," I say softly.

"Would it really do you any good?" he asks almost gently, and then the dial tone is buzzing in my ear.

I slam down the receiver and then I slam it down a few more times. I start bashing it against the cherries and strawberries, vaguely aware that Gabriel is trying to wrench it from my fingers. Finally, he squeezes my wrist until my hand opens and I drop the receiver for good, letting it crash against the tile floor.

"I'm okay," I say into Gabriel's shoulder, my words muffled in his shirt.

His hand cradles the back of my head. "Yeah," he says, sounding entirely unconvinced.

At a quarter to midnight, Grand Central is a very different place than in the daytime. Only a few people rush through the great marble hall, heading toward train platforms or following the signs marked SUBWAY. All the ticket booths are closed except for one, behind which a sleepy-looking woman eyes us briefly before going back to her magazine.

My eyes wander upward and I let them rest for an instant on the beauty of the gold-worked constellations hanging in the blue domed ceiling. Then I look back down at the four-sided bronze clock that presides over the Main Concourse, its stately faces like unblinking eyes that keep watch in each direction.

As expected, the information kiosk is closed for the night. But still a girl waits there, wearing a torn and tattered black dress, her hair falling across her shoulders like a whisper. As I near her, I can't help but wince. "Ro," I say softly, my hands reaching out for her. Purplish-yellow shadows cluster under her eyes and her lips are dry and cracked, even as they spread into a smile.

"Tamsin," she sighs, and at that Alistair steps out from behind the other side of the kiosk. Unlike my sister's, his skin is flushed and plump with health, his dark raincoat fitting crisply across his shoulders. In one hand he holds a small black traveling case.

His eyes skip coldly over Gabriel before settling on me. "Well?" he says, and my sister turns, reaching out one fluttering hand toward him. He brushes her off, as though she's no more than an insect who has blundered onto his sleeve.

"How do I know that you'll release her?"

He smiles. "Once I have the Domani, I won't need her anymore." I stare at my sister, willing her to acknowledge this, but she only hums a little, plays with a loose thread on her sleeve. It's then that I notice her feet are bare, streaked with dirt. I swallow a surge of anger.

"Or Agatha?"

A smile slithers across his face. "Your delicious little friend?"

I consider throwing up right then and there, but Gabriel presses my fingers with his own. "Easy," he murmurs.

"She was useful," Alistair says, giving a flick of his fingers. "But she'll live." Then his gaze sharpens on me. "If you give me what I want. Now."

"Fine," I say, taking a breath to steady my voice. "But you should know one thing. You and I are *nothing* alike. Talent or no Talent. You're not doing this for your family, whatever you might think. You're doing this for yourself. And that's the difference between you and me."

Alistair stares at me for a second, his face blank, unreadable. "How very touching," he says at last, biting the words off. "Now, shall we proceed?"

I nod. I don't have much bargaining power. "Behind you," I say.

Slowly, Alistair turns, studies the clock above our heads. "Of course," he says softly. "So many times I passed by this. And it was here all along." Then he pivots neatly and in a sickeningly cheerful voice says, "Are you ready, my dear?"

Rowena looks up from the thread on her sleeve, gives him a vacant smile.

"Open it," he says to me as he wraps one hand around my sister's arm, his knuckles suddenly bulging into hard white knobs. My sister looks up at him, then gives a shrill little laugh.

"We're playing a game?" she asks.

I swallow hard, turn back to the clock. "Help me up," I whisper to Gabriel.

"Are you sure this is—"

"Yes," I say, although my teeth are chattering. He cups his palms, and before he can change his mind, I step into them and hoist myself up onto the counter. The clock looms directly above my hand. "Step back," I say to Gabriel, having no idea what might happen otherwise. "You don't want to freeze again."

"Hey!" There's a startled shout from the ticket seller. "Get down from there."

"Hurry," Alistair hisses.

There is no time to rethink this. I arch upward, brush the clock with my fingertips. A shaft of light bursts forth from its domed center. Fixing firmly in my head the image of my grandmother young and healthy in 1939, I let her power sweep over me.

Images scroll across the backs of my eyelids, almost too fast for me to follow. Four people standing in a square, their arms raised. A roiling mass of darkness hovers over their bowed heads and then a fist of fire stabs down toward a fifth person bound in chains. And then the images move at warp speed and blur into white, the white of my family's book's pages that are emptier than a field of freshly fallen snow. *Tamsin,* my grandmother's voice rings through my head. *Don't let him take her. If he takes your sister, he will be unstoppable.*

How, though? I cry silently to her.

Time. Only time and a great distance can break this spell.

I open my eyes.

A quick glance behind me shows that Gabriel is still

alive. He meets my eyes and mouths, *Okay?* I nod, turning back to my sister.

"Ro?" I say, and she lifts her head slowly, her eyes still full of that chilling, unfocused look.

"Well done," Alistair says, and his voice is pure crystal. His mouth is open slightly as if he's panting. "Now, Rowena. Now."

And with horror I watch as my sister turns her still-perfect profile to me and gazes at the clock, which glimmers with a cold, cold light. In scrolling script, letters appear all around the curve of the clock face. Tall, golden letters that wriggle and vanish whenever I stare at them, making it impossible to read them.

But Rowena has no such difficulty.

Her voice rings out as if she is standing by our family's altar, singing thanks to the stars and elements. "Fire in the East and Water for the South; Air for the North and Earth in the West. All of these now Blood does bind. Yet only Time may keep what Blood has wrought."

For one dreaming second nothing happens. And then with a soft whirring noise the clock hands begin to turn *backward*, faster and faster until they are traveling at warp speed.

Lightning rips through the blue domed ceiling, stabs downward, and slams into the clock. *Crack*. Another bolt flares across the gold constellations and then chunks of plaster and stone begin to plummet down. The rain starts a second later, instantly pinning my clothes to my skin. Before my eyes, the clock is growing into monstrous proportions, wreathed in white fire, a fire that seems to be unquenchable despite the rain. "Tamsin," Gabriel hisses into my ear, and then he sprints forward.

The floor beneath my feet pitches and heaves and huge fissures begin to split through the marble tiles, revealing a churning maw of stone underneath. *Fire, water, earth,* I recite to myself. *Air?* As if on cue the wind starts, gusts and gusts of it, screaming through the Main Concourse, like a thousand voices fused together in one unearthly song. Darkness pours through the hallway, a darkness alleviated only by the occasional flash of lightning and by the clock still glowing with that cold white fire. Falling to my knees, I close my eyes, and with all of my might I will this to stop.

Nothing happens. This is not something that I can just stop. This is no one's Talent, I realize suddenly. Instead, this is the power of the four elements, the source of all our Talents, something beyond any one person's control. I open my eyes and stare at the clock.

It's opening.

One face has now become a door that's swinging open. And all the while the hands are still spinning, spinning, unraveling the moments and years.

Ten feet from the door, three figures seem locked in a strange kind of dance, arms and legs distorted by the clock's bright glare. Alistair is pulling my sister toward the door while Gabriel has latched on to her other arm. Rowena twists between them like a rag doll. Alistair's mouth is working and he seems to be saying something to my sister just as Gabriel's hold on her slips slightly.

"No!" I scream, scrambling to my feet just as the floor rumbles again. Leaping across the widening cracks in the marble, I stretch my arms toward my sister. Another slab of ceiling tumbles down, shattering three inches to my left, the spray of debris cutting into my leg.

"Let me go," Rowena is crying, and I think she's talking to Gabriel, but thankfully her voice is lost under the rush of wind. Alistair tugs her again toward the clock door and the complete blackness that waits beyond.

"Rowena!" I scream again. Alistair's eyes—chips of ice—meet mine, and then he yanks hard on my sister's arm, so hard that I think he'll pull it straight from the socket. I hold up my hand, envisioning the comet of fire that will smash into his face. The blood starts to heat under my skin. But then my mother's words come looping back to me. *Whatever you do to the spell caster reflects back onto the enspelled. Three times over.*

The floor pitches me forward again. I roll sideways, raise my palm, and aim as carefully as I can. *I don't want to do this, I don't want to, I don't want to.* "I'm sorry, Ro," I whisper.

A ripple of fire spreads along Rowena's arm, the one that Alistair holds in a death grip. My sister's eyes widen in pain. Screaming, she wrenches her body backward, away from Alistair, and his hold on her breaks. Gabriel releases her hand briefly only to wrap his arms around her waist and tug her backward. As they tumble to the floor, lightning flickers across the ceiling again. A sizable chunk of blue stone spins through the air, smashing into Gabriel's head. He tries to rise, but even from here I can see the dark seep of blood.

Alistair spares me one glittering look, his mouth clamped in fury as the rain runs in rivulets down his face. "Rowena!" he roars to my sister, and she looks up, tears staining her cheeks, her burned arm cradled tenderly in her lap. "Rowena, through the door. Now!" Like a marionette my sister climbs to her feet, stepping across Gabriel's body. He half rolls and makes a feeble swipe for Rowena's hand, but she evades him.

Her eyes are blank and lifeless, her face wax white. I swallow, remembering my grandmother's visions of Rowena's body blurring into nothingness.

I step forward with my fingers outstretched, intending to freeze my sister. If she's frozen then she'll be a dead weight and hopefully Alistair won't be able to carry her through the door. But my arm is seized in midair. Alistair wrenches me backward as my sister runs past me. "You won't get her that easily," he hisses into my ear, his words carrying over the wind and the rain. I twist desperately, watching as my sister reaches the door. With her hands reaching out in front of her, she takes one step, then another.

"Neither will you," I whisper. Then I raise my free hand, palm outward, and shoot a gust of flame to land directly in front of her feet. She shrieks and falls backward as the fire runs along the edge of the clock. Its bright orange glow flares briefly before it's subdued by the cold white light rimming the edges of the door.

The floor shifts again and new fissures begin spreading across the marble like a crazed spider web. My sister slips, her arms flailing, and then falls through a particularly wide crack.

And at the same moment the clock hands stop spinning backward. Slowly the door begins to swing closed.

A terrible choice, my grandmother's voice eddies into my mind like an errant breeze. *You have a terrible choice.*

With a snarl, Alistair throws me to the floor. Darting forward, he pauses at the edge of the precipice, leans down, and holds out one hand. I roll to my knees just as my sister lifts her right hand, tries to catch Alistair's fingers. I throw another gust of flame at them. Just in time she pulls her hand back. My sister's head bobs downward as if she's slipped farther.

"Rowena!" I scream, pulling myself upright. Cracks widen under my feet and I leap away just in time. I stumble forward, pinning my gaze to Rowena's left hand, willing her to hold on just a little longer. The closing clock door casts a shadow across Alistair's face. Twisting, he looks over his shoulder. The door is less than halfway ajar now. Then he looks back at my sister.

It seems I'm not the only one who faces a terrible choice.

With a roar, Alistair comes to his feet, and without a backward glance he throws himself through the narrow opening of the doorway.

Moving forward, I crouch down at the ledge of the precipice. My sister's fingers are clamped to the edge of the floor, her mouth a white line of pain and terror. Her feet are wedged on either side of the chasm, but the gap is widening. Her right foot flails for purchase and kicks through empty air, and her fingers slip down a little farther.

I throw one glance over my shoulder. Another two feet and the door will close. And now the enormity of my own choice comes crashing down on me.

Maybe I could stop all of this before it ever even happens.

Save Rowena or follow Alistair to the time before the war between our families.

Rowena sobs once, a harsh broken noise, and I turn back to her. "Hang on, Ro," I cry, but I don't think she can hear me. Her eyes roll back in her head and I realize that my sister is about to faint. Lying flat on my stomach, I reach down, clamp my hands under her elbows, and pull. But her weight pulls me forward and in horror I realize I am sliding slowly but inexorably across the slick marble floor.

Then Gabriel is crouching by my side, his face still dripping blood. He locks his hands around my sister's arms and with one hard tug we pull her up and over the edge and then free of the chasm altogether.

With a thunderclap the clock door slams shut. I close my eyes in the silence, my ears ringing with the sudden absence of all sound. Just when I think this could go on and on forever, I both hear and feel a steady ticking right above my heart.

Prying open my eyes, I stare at the unbroken blue domed ceiling above me, the constellations whole and shining bright. I jackknife up, glance around. The floor is smooth and unmarred, the marble glinting. Lastly I turn my head and look at the clock. It has shrunk back to its normal size.

Next to me Gabriel groans, pulling himself into a sitting position. The blood has dried on his face and one eye is swollen shut, but he reaches for my hand and gives it a reassuring squeeze. I swallow, turn to my sister, and touch her face gently.

Her eyelids flutter once, and then she is looking at me. "Tamsin," she whispers. Her arm is badly burned and her disheveled hair is matted with dust and plaster and rain. Her face is still pale and long scratches mar one side of her neck and shoulder, but her eyes are suddenly focused and clear. I don't think she's ever looked more beautiful.

"Ro? Are you . . . are you *you?*"

One pale eyebrow flexes upward in a look so effortless and elegant, a look that I used to practice for hours before a mirror when I was younger. I still can't do it the way she can. "Who else would I be?" she asks. Then she tries to sit up, grimaces, and seems to think better of it. "What happened?" she asks. A familiar trace of impatience is entering her tone, and I know her *what happened* is about three seconds away from turning into *what have you done?*

Good question.

And as if in response, the ticking above my heart grows still louder until it is echoing in perfect time with my heartbeat. Fumbling at the collar of my shirt, I tug on the chain of the locket and press the tiny catch. Two things become apparent with a dash of ice-cold clarity.

My clocket is now working.

And I have become the Keeper.

"Hi, Mom," I say as we step through the kitchen door. My mother drops the teakettle she has presumably just filled and screams. The kettle smashes to the floor, the lid spinning off. Water sprays and arcs at our feet.

I kind of wish I had prepared her.

"Rowena," she gasps. "Tamsin. Oh, girls, you're home." And then Rowena and I are smashed together as my mother tries to wrap her arms around us both, all the while still shrieking our names.

Half blinded by my mother's hair, I turn my head to see my father, Lydia, and James burst through the door. My father moves toward me, Rowena manages to struggle free only to fling herself into James's arms, and Lydia approaches Gabriel with a smile that begins to lighten all the tired shadows under her eyes.

"How did you do it?" my mother keeps crying, and I hear Rowena murmuring to James, "Yes, it's really me. It's really, *really* me." Everyone keeps talking over one another. Lydia is dabbing Gabriel's head with a damp dishcloth, her fingers tenderly combing through his hair. My mother keeps grabbing first me and then Rowena, and my father grips my shoulder tightly while blotting his sleeve against his eyes. And then Silda and Jerom and Gwyneth pile through the kitchen door and the tumult only grows louder.

Finally, I manage to free myself from my mother's embrace long enough to ask, "Is Grandmother . . ."

My mother gives a firm shake of her head, pushes her hair away from her face. "Still . . . sleeping." She glances at Rowena. "I can't—"

"What?" Rowena asks sharply. She glances at James as if for an answer, and then when he bites his lip, she asks, "What's wrong with Grandmother?" One hand goes to her throat.

But before anyone can speak, the kitchen door swings open for a third time and Aunt Beatrice totters uncertainly into the center of the room, followed by my grandmother. "Look who's awake," Aunt Beatrice crows and then skids on the spilled water from the teakettle, wobbles, and rights herself.

My mother finally lets go of me and, stepping forward, says, "Mother? What happened? How . . . ?" She stares in bewilderment at Aunt Beatrice, then holds out her hands to my grandmother as if to check that she's really there.

"I unfroze her!" Aunt Beatrice says happily, looking from face to shocked face.

"Apparently," my grandmother begins, her voice deep and smooth although she has been sleeping for a week, "Beatrice froze me." She gives Aunt Beatrice a look of half-irritated amusement.

"But we all thought you weren't able to use your power anymore," my mother cries, staring at Aunt Beatrice.

"I never said that! Did I?" Aunt Beatrice muses, scratching her chin. "I thought I lost it," she murmurs, gazing intently at the window, her eyes unfocused. "I haven't . . . used it for so long."

"Why did you—?" Silda begins and then gives a little shriek as Uncle Morris pops into view, holding aloft a glass of red wine.

With his free hand, he pats Silda's shoulder briskly.

"Sorry, my dear. Can't always see where I'm headed. Well, that's not going to come out," he mutters, staring at the spreading crimson stain on her sleeve.

"Why did you freeze her?" Rowena asks.

"Well," Beatrice says indignantly, turning her head with a whiplike motion, "that's a fine question for *you* to ask, Miss Rowena. If you had made her drink any more of that potion, you would have killed her. I couldn't stop you, but I could stop her." Beatrice takes a few steps forward, her bracelets clacking merrily. "Oh, you were so angry with me!" She gives a gleeful hoot even as Rowena lowers her head onto James's shoulder. "But before you could say anything, make me do anything, I ran away and hid. I hid all afternoon in my closet!"

Before anyone can react to her words, Aunt Beatrice cocks her wispy white head. "Hmm . . . if I could have frozen you while I was at it, why didn't I try that?" A small frown pushes the corners of her mouth in. "I suppose I lost it again," she murmurs, her steps slowing to a shuffle. "Oh, well!" she adds, all gaiety returning as she spies the glass of wine in Uncle Morris's hand. And she claps her hands together, executes a little twirl. The hem of her long skirt trails through the water that is still spreading across the floor from the overturned teakettle. I put a steadying hand on her arm and she peers at me.

"Oh! I know you. I remember what you can do!" she says.

"Sorry about that," I murmur.

"What is going on here?" my mother demands, and across the room Gabriel looks at me with his good eye and winks.

I turn back to my grandmother and take one step forward. She touches my face with her gnarled fingers. Then she smiles, and for one second I can see the teenage girl that she was in 1939.

"I told everyone you would be a beacon," she whispers.

A GHOST-WHITE MOON sails through the clear sky and thousands of stars wink and glitter upon the loose circle we have formed. The altar is heaped with apples, their skins the color of wine, and the last of the white and purple asters. Firelight flickers across everyone's face as the smoke from the bonfire twists up through the cold autumn air.

"Greetings," my grandmother calls, her voice ringing out. "Well met tonight as on all nights."

"Well met," I chorus back along with the rest of my family.

"Tonight is Samhain, the most magical night of the year," she continues. "Tonight we guide two members of our family through the Initiation Rites." She stops, gathers her breath, and smiles. "Tamsin and Gabriel, tonight we ask you to light the four candles."

Next to me Rowena disengages her hand from mine and gives me a little push, as my legs seem to have stopped working. I take a step across the grass, then another, as

Gabriel moves from the opposite side of the circle toward me. We meet at the altar and my mother walks forward, handing me the taper that she's lit from the bonfire. But my hand is trembling so much that I can't seem to connect the taper with the first of the eight beeswax candles that represent the four directions and the four elements. And then Gabriel wraps his fingers around mine and I look up into his face, at the new crescent-shaped scar half hidden by his hairline. "Hey," he whispers.

"Hey back." And together we touch the taper to each of the wicks. I gaze at the tiny flames that have bloomed on the candles, aware that Gabriel is still holding my hand.

"We made it," I say.

"I know." He takes a step closer. "So, does this mean you'll finally go out to dinner with me? Or are you still worried that a date would be anticlimactic?"

I smile at him as the lit taper flickers wildly between us. "No."

He raises one eyebrow at me, waits a second. "Are you planning on telling me *which* question you just answered?"

Suddenly, I'm intensely aware of my family locked in a circle all around us. "Can we talk about this later?" I whisper.

"Oh, definitely," he says with a grin.

I give him the sweep-down-of-my-lashes look before stepping back to my place beside Rowena.

After the ceremony I pause for a moment at the edge

of the garden, watching everyone move in and out of the firelight. Uncle Chester is playing a slow song on his violin while Aunt Rennie accompanies him on a slender silver flute. The music unfurls across the garden like a breeze. My mother is smiling up at my father and glancing now and then toward Rowena, who is dancing with James. My sister lifts her hands to James's shoulders. For just an instant she flashes the pale underside of her arms, but her scars are all but invisible in this soft light.

I watch Uncle Morris pop in and out of sight while Silda swats at the empty spaces he just occupied. A small group of children has gathered around Aunt Beatrice, and one by one they lean forward and let her tap their foreheads. They freeze into statues until she taps their foreheads again and, laughing, they're released. Nearby Gwyneth and Lydia are watching this game as if deciding when the best time is to end it.

Finally, my eyes land on Gabriel. He's standing on the far side of the garden, next to Jerom, nodding at whatever Jerom is saying. A deck of cards parachutes from one hand to the other. Just then he looks up and sees me watching him. Pressing the cards into Jerom's hand, he walks toward me. I take a deep breath, resist running a hand over my hair. I know it's a wild, curly mass anyway.

"There you are," he says, coming to stand before me. "Happy birthday."

"Thanks. You know normally I hate my birthday, but this one's not so bad."

Our breath clouds out before us as we regard each other in silence. I study the blue moon tattoo on the side of his neck and experience an overwhelming urge to trace it with my finger.

Just then Uncle Chester begins to play a wild tune, his bow looping on the strings. Aunt Rennie's flute pipes up in response and the music skirls outward, wraps around us. Gabriel seizes my hand. "Come dance with me." Before I can answer he's tugging me forward as all around us people begin to pair off.

"This isn't a waltz," I mutter.

He propels me into the firelight, looks down at me with his quick grin. "Oh, really? Does that mean you *won't* be stepping all over my feet, then?"

I laugh, take his other hand, and let him whirl me into the dance. The music spirals faster and Gabriel spins me around in a circle until I am breathless, until our hands locked together feels like the only tangible thing keeping me on earth.

Later, when the festivities have reached a fever pitch, I slip away back to the house. My head is ringing even though I haven't touched a drop of Uncle Chester's homemade wine this time, ringing with all of the congratulations until

I thought my smile might crack right off my face. The only comfort was exchanging glances with Gabriel across the garden every so often. I massage my temples and think about calling Agatha just to hear her tell me about the Halloween party that I'm missing back at school.

I squeeze my eyes shut, blink, then blink again. There is a light on in the library. Cautiously, I walk forward, press my ear to the solid oak door, then tap it once.

"Come in," my grandmother says, and pushing open the door I find her seated behind the massive desk, looking smaller and more tired than ever.

"Why aren't you outside enjoying—"

"I could ask you the same thing," she says dryly.

We regard each other for a moment and then I look away. "I guess I'm not used to all of this," I answer finally.

"Ah," she says softly and glances back down at the desk. With a chill, I realize she is reading the book that my mother showed me.

I worry my top lip between my teeth for a minute, then ask, "What do you see?"

At first I think she won't answer me and I feel a sudden flash of anger that I *still* won't be allowed to know things. But then she looks up and rubs at the bridge of her nose with splayed and shaking fingers. "Nothing," she says quietly.

"Well, that's good, right? Nothing's going on, all quiet on the western front and all that—" I jump a little as Hector flows through the open window and pauses on the edge of the sill, his tail twitching into a question mark. A tiny brown mouse is clamped between his jaws. Wending his way across a bookshelf, Hector steps onto the desk and deposits the mouse near my grandmother's hand. Then he sits back and watches her with slanted golden eyes.

My grandmother scoops up the mouse with one hand and sets it free on the other side of the desk, seeming not to notice when Hector leaps down to the floor to stalk his prey again.

Instead, she looks directly at me and says, "I can see nothing for our future. Nothing, as in we will no longer exist."

It feels as if my lungs have suddenly stopped working.

"The pages are empty in a way that they never have been before. So," my grandmother continues, "I went back. To our past history, just before the Domani was created." Her fingers skim over the page and I move closer. As usual the words are rearranging themselves into an incomprehensible language and scurrying off the page, but then my grandmother speaks one word of command and the letters line up clearly at last.

In 1887, in the dying days of October, just before Samhain, a stranger arrived in New York City claiming to know more than he possibly could. He was seen calling upon La Spider, the matriarch of the Knight family.

"Alistair," I whisper. I touch the locket around my neck, taking comfort in its steady ticking. "He hasn't succeeded yet," I say insistently.

"No, he hasn't," my grandmother confirms. "And he may never succeed. You certainly crippled his hopes when you prevented him from taking your sister. She would have been an extremely powerful weapon." Then she sighs, closing the book with a quiet *thunk*.

"The power of the Domani has been breached. Badly. The Knight family is not what they once were, true. But the events of last month in Grand Central will have sent out a call, a reverberation, that they will try to answer."

In the corner of the room, a sudden scuffle and a tiny squeaking confirm the mouse's recapture. My grandmother and I lock eyes. "How much time do I have?" I whisper.

She smiles, pushes back her chair, and stands. Reaching out, she clasps my hand and leads me to the window. "You have a little time. Time enough to . . . enjoy this."

Together we stare out at the brightly burning bonfire, at everyone dancing around it. Just then a log bursts and hundreds of sparks fly upward, then blaze like shooting stars across the night sky.